blood lust

blood lust

Gay Erotic Vampire Tales

Edited by

M. CHRISTIAN

and

TODD GREGORY

alyson books
los angeles

Celebrating Twenty-Five Years

Manufactured in the United States of America.

This trade paperback original is published by Alyson Books,
P.O. Box 4371, Los Angeles, California 90078-4371.
Distribution in the United Kingdom by Turnaround Publisher Services Ltd.,
Unit 3, Olympia Trading Estate, Coburg Road, Wood Green,
London N22 6TZ England.

First edition: August 2005

05 06 07 08 09 **a** 10 9 8 7 6 5 4 3 2 1

ISBN 1-55583-843-X
ISBN-13 978-1-55583-843-0

Library of Congress Cataloging-in-Publication Data
   Blood lust : gay erotic vampire tales / edited by M. Christian and Todd Gregory.
      ISBN 1-55583-843-X; ISBN-13 978-1-55583-843-0
      1. Gay men—Fiction. 2. Vampires—Fiction. 3. Erotic stories, American. I. Christian, M. (Muncy). II. Gregory, Todd.
   PS648.H57B59 2005
   813'.010835358'086642—DC22   2005041196

Credits
• "Vampire Joe" by Bob Vickery previously appeared in the November and December 1999 issue of Men magazine. Reprinted with permission of the author.
• "Wet" by M. Christian previously appeared in Sons of Darkness, edited by Michael Rowe & Thomas Roche, © 1996 Cleis Books. Reprinted with permission of the author.
• Cover photography by Juan Silva/Image Bank/Getty Images.
• Cover design by Matt Sams.

To
Paul Willis,
with love

Contents

Introduction

I bid you welcome...

The allure is unquestionable, the evidence overwhelming. Ever since the first Nosferatu creaked open his casket and strolled among the juicy living, there's been something...well, *queer* about vampires. Even though many of these stylish undead seem to have a fondness for blood of the opposite sex, they have always retained a special cultured atmosphere about them that too easily could be considered a gay air. Yet even considering their tastes for the finer things and their dark sensuality, the question remains unanswered: Why exactly are vampires so alluring, so seductive, to gay men?

Todd Gregory and I see this as a problem with no easy solution. What exactly is the down-deep mechanism of that magnetism, the subconscious appeal? After all, if we were going to be selecting stories that effectively melded gay sex with vampires, shouldn't we come to some kind of conclusion as to why bloodsuckers have such a hold over queer boys?

Theories abound. Of course there's the aforementioned style vampires have: Face it: With a few notable exceptions, costume designers have a way of getting vampires to put it on and make it look *good*. It's almost a mystical "those shoes don't work with those pants" and becomes imbued from that initial teeth-meeting-neck.

But style is relative, and knowing how to dress seems like a small reward for ash and smoke at the first touch of daylight.

"Look into my eyes..." Who wouldn't want the power to sway, seduce, and bend the will of others? The world transformed into a buffet of delicious men with no chance of rejection, and who wouldn't want that? You like him? You can have him...or even *them*. Appealing, certainly, but if you could have anyone, wouldn't an eternity of this power quickly make you wonder about your real allure? You could have them, but you'd never know if they wanted you or were merely responding to your masterly stare. Sex would become nothing but masturbating with mannequins.

Ah, eternity: never having to worry about wrinkles, sags, retreating this, expanding that, dropping those, liver spots, arthritis, diabetes, and all those other signs of a looming expiration date. Who wouldn't want that? Time enough for everything—save working on your tan, of course. But it doesn't take a century of pondering to realize that immortality wouldn't be much fun after, say, the first 200 years. Life would go on around you—evolving, changing, and growing—but you wouldn't. You'd remain a velvet-and-lace-Neanderthal clinging to the shadow's edges, unable to catch up, forever left behind.

So what's the fascination? Many are attracted to the teeth. Rather than a denture fetish, I submit that it may be the draw of the predator, the hunter. Hypnotizing prey has its charms, but stalking them is more visceral, more feral. Here the elegant count instead becomes the hissing monster, the beast; and tears into the throats of the innocent, tasting the hot copper of their liquid lives. Sex and death, death and sex: The perfect amalgam of the heads and tails of life. *La Petite Mort* becoming *La Grande Mort*. This vampire attraction is dark and mean but also steaming and ferocious. It's the ultimate S/M scene; the bottom offers his jugular to the top and the top makes the bottom the ultimate submissive, giving up everything, including his blood. Sexy? Absolutely. But despite the high temperature of this aspect, it remains shallow, one-dimensional. Fantasies can certainly last a long time, but there has to be a more complex hook for them to last for centuries; there has to be something else. Ferocious sexuality could be a component of the vampire's queer magic, but I doubt it's the whole attraction.

Being gay, especially in America, is anything but easy. Feeling persecuted, marginalized, demeaned; the constant threat of violence...is it any wonder why so many gay men see the vampire as kin, a fellow outsider? Vampires have secret lives and seductive powers, but their existences are tinged with tragedy. They might like the nightlife, but they can never walk free and easy in the daylight. Gay men can empathize with this life. Yet, does it explain the whole attraction for the undead, the entire affiliation with the vampire? There's a whole pantheon of monsters who would also fit the bill as outsiders, but vampires remain the Count and Master of them all.

So, Todd and I invited the best writers we knew to try and answer this question: to explore, delve into the erotic enticement of the vampire for the gay man. We didn't want the usual clichés of cape and lace, "I never drink...wine," children of the night, eternal rock stars, absinthe sippers, or any form of Count this or that.

What we did get for this project is something truly wonderful: a book of original gay vampire stories that bring a fresh look at an ancient infatuation. In these pages you'll read stories of original creatures and situations, wholly innovative approaches to what a vampire is and what that means to a gay man. Although no single story answers the total mystery of the allure of Dracula's kin, each one is a memorable and powerful statement exploring the attraction: style, seduction, immortality, power, and isolation. Here are humor, horror, love, terror, loneliness, hope, pain, and joy—both for those creatures of the imagination and for all too real gay men.

The answers might never be found, or might never be complete or simple, but one thing that Todd and I know, without any doubt whatsoever, is that this book is more than we could ever have hoped for—these writers have absolutely outdone themselves. We applaud them and thank them for their remarkable work. We can only hope as editors that the stories these authors have given us to enjoy will live on as part of the collective affection we all feel for vampires, and perhaps they will one day help us all see and feel what it means to be gay.

—M. Christian

The Ward
Lukas Scott

He stood in his hospital gown by the window as the sun lay dying. Orange fingers of sunlight caressed him, throwing an enormous shadow against the magnolia walls. When he moved, the sunlight would catch my eyes and I would have to shut them or turn away. Turning away hurt, made me uncomfortable. Blinking made my eyes water. I willed him to stay where he was, my only natural defense against the bright sunset.

"There's these birds," Brian said. Not so much to me, as I hadn't spoken much to him since my arrival. He was a brusque middle-aged man who was a little too willing to share his opinions on everything from Asian doctors to football. Not sharing his points of view, I'd managed to develop a selective deafness to his monologues. Now he was talking half to himself, half to Billy, a bedridden 60-year-old white-haired gent who'd made the mistake of showing interest in Brian's diatribes.

"These birds," Brian continued. "I've been watching them every night. They gather round that tree—see, Billy?" Billy made a half-hearted attempt to shift himself to follow Brian's tubby index finger to a birch tree. I looked at the greasy marks he left on the window every time he stubbed his finger at the glass. "Every night, about now, they swarm around that tree, then fly off like smoke; off into the sky. See, Billy? See?"

"I can't quite..." Billy strained and squinted to no avail. "No, no, I can't—"

"You must see them! Over there! There!" Brian aligned himself with Billy's bed, trying to find a line of vision. "See? Odd. It's odd. Where are they going?"

Billy shrugged his shoulders but continued peering into the distance. The orange lit up his face, then gradually turned it to shadow when the sky became mauve with golden edges.

"Every night they do it. I see them every night," Brian repeated as he got back into bed, throwing the covers over himself in a vain attempt to fight off the drawing-on of night. "Like smoke in the sky."

~

I can't remember the first time I saw him. I can't remember him arriving, or him not being there. He seemed part of it all, with no beginning and no introduction.

Every night, we would do the rounds. Not quite coinciding with the medication, but not long after meals of celery soup and grated cheese salad. I always felt hungry when I saw him. Never quite full enough.

He was a flash of white in the tight-fitting uniform with blue stripes on the shoulders all the male nurses wore. Efficient and friendly, he'd always bring me up to date with the news. Perhaps that's what I choose to remember now. At the time I was just glad to see him.

Of course he's handsome in my memories, although he was not quite as much then: dark eyes and short dark hair cut short in the back and sides. He was always clean-shaven, yet with small dark spots of impending growth on his cheeks as reminders of his masculine hormones coursing through him, fighting to take charge of his sinewy body. He was lithe rather than toned, yet I was always aware of his physique under the amorphous hospital uniform. I was always conscious of every movement he made.

He didn't smell of the hospital like the other staff did: not bleach or antiseptic or vague medications. Instead, he smelled of sandalwood and musk, nightstock and honeysuckle on a balmy summer's evening.

I don't remember when there was the formality of the brief introduction as he prepped my arm with a cotton wool ball before the sudden cold antiseptic. I don't remember the first smell of disposable latex as he put on his gloves, and the snowflakes of talc as he shook out the gloves to fit to his hands. Clean, neatly manicured nails hairless to the wrist, then a dark trail up his forearm. His short sleeves revealed natural biceps, nothing toned but still shapely.

He always smiled. Before the needle, he looked into my eyes and smiled. I swam in his dark stare. Some of the nurses and most of the doctors had trouble finding the vein. Not him. His fingers chased up my arm, hunting the channel: first time, every time. I never felt it. There was no sudden sharp sting, just a warm release as he took the blood. I could feel myself drifting, still looking into his eyes.

I don't know whether he spoke, but I remember always feeling comforted. As if he were wiping my brow, holding me against his warm chest, wrapping his arms around me so that my face was pressed against his crisp white tunic. His heartbeat resounded through me.

And then he'd disappear.

~

I don't remember him visiting Brian or Bill. They never mentioned him, although Brian seemed to have pronouncements about everyone who came onto the ward. He had so much anger in him it was no surprise that he was recovering from a heart attack. Brian carried his anger around with him like a dark cloud. If I squinted my eyes the way Bill used to watch the birds, I could see it over his shoulder. When he fulminated it grew black and large, threatening to crowd out the room. I never saw it calm, the way I saw white clouds in the blue sky in Puerto Rico.

Bill was the opposite. He was always serene, his face like a beatific martyr in a Renaissance painting. But it wasn't a serenity of hope or peace but that of a man who had given up. He seemed to become whiter and whiter the longer he was there. But he wasn't the sickly pallor that besets all invalids but a chalky whiteness that almost glowed. It always seemed he slept with Death.

~

I don't know how I knew his name was Grant. He never had a dark-blue-and-white enamel badge like the other nurses. He knew my history, my diagnosis. He'd told me there was nothing to worry about, that he'd seen plenty of people with heart valve replacements. I remember his looking at the scar with fascination. It embarrassed me, having a wound so much on show. He told me it made me real. "Who wants to read a blank book?" he said. "I like knowing some- one's special. It marks us out."

I never questioned when he talked about us being special. He said it with an undercurrent of pain, as if somehow he hurt too. He wouldn't say what the hurt was, but he wore it around him like barbed cloak. It made it hard to understand him, to get beyond his smile, his professional attitude and detachment.

Yet every time he slipped his silver blade into my veins and looked into my eyes, I could feel us becoming connected. It was like a long kiss from a lost lover, a thirst-quenching drink from a long glass of chilled lemonade on a hot summer afternoon.

I remember the first kiss. I remember the partition with flow- ered curtains, undone from the hooks on the rail in five places and frayed on the right edge, which he always drew closed when he took the blood and his own casual glance to make sure it was in place before he bent down his head and kissed me. I remember the rush of blood to my face, the light-headedness that until then I had only connected with my medication. He put his finger on my lips, vow- ing me to silence as a smile broke his lips like the sudden ripples from a fish breaking the surface of a calm lake.

~

That night I never heard Brian's nightmare-driven murmurs. I didn't hear him pacing between toilet and bed. I didn't notice the lights at the nurses' station, the soft casual chatter as shifts switched.

I didn't hear any of the familiar unfamiliar echoes and shadows of the ward.

I was filled with the smile and the kiss, and a deep, deep peace that I hadn't felt since entering those sanitized corridors and submitting myself to the routine of care and control from a succession of uniformed strangers. I woke and touched the mark his needle had made—a pinprick of half-dried blood that broke and bled. I wet my finger in my mouth and staunched the flow, tasting the bitter iron on my tongue. I smelt honeysuckle and nightstocks, and saw the sun rising over the trees.

~

Brian left some time after that. He came round shaking everybody's hand, and I felt compelled to wish him well. He'd showered at 6:30 that morning, and spent 48 minutes in the bathroom. I'd counted because I needed it for my own purposes, and resented every minute he spent in there. He came out gleaming, like a middle-aged woman who spent half a day at a beauty salon and had nothing to show for it. His gray-flecked hair was swept back, damp, and smelling of lotion. When I made my way to the bathroom, I noticed that he hadn't wiped down the shower basin, so I had to dodge the puddles of soapy water he had left behind.

When he shook my hand it was like he treated me as an old friend. He clasped it with both hands and held it tight. He let go of it like I was a painful memory.

"Keep an eye out for the birds," he said to us both. "In the evening, just over there." He pointed again to his tree, just visible out of the left-hand corner of the window.

Before he left, he playfully tousled Billy's white hair. Billy smiled, but immediately raised his hand to pat his hair back in place.

When Brian had gone, his family bustling him out amid excited but admonishing chatter ("we'll carry that for you, Brian..."), the orderlies came and changed the bedclothes. Two of them removed the sheets and blankets, replacing them with new, clean sheets and blankets. They had a strict routine: strip the bed and place the old bedclothes in a wire basket trolley, then fold down the new under-sheet, position the top sheets, and seal the sheets underneath the mattress at the edges. The operation was completed by an artful turndown of the right-hand top corner, like a floppy ear on a toy rabbit.

Billy stared at the empty bed. Brian had left a small bunch of daffodils in a dried-out vase on the windowsill. They'd started to go brown and crisp at the edges, although the rest of the trumpets were golden but drooping. I remember the simplicity of it, the white sheets and the yellow daffodils.

I was expecting them to fill the bed quickly. There'd been so much on the news about the beds crisis. I thought they'd be backed up in the corridors, groaning to be let into the refuge, like some medieval leper colony.

Nobody came at all. The ward was quiet without Brian. Billy stared out the window at the sunset and smiled.

"I can see them," he said, raising a frail finger and pointing. "The birds, right where he said. Like smoke in the sky."

I went over to the window and sat on the empty bed, squinting into the sunlight. I couldn't see anything, but Billy was insistent.

"Just there," he said. "Rising up from the tree, going up until you can't see them. Up and up."

~

I waited for Grant every night. Ever since that first kiss, I couldn't get enough of him. He made me feel wanted, desired, all over again. He was reliable, appearing with dependable regularity every evening.

"How are the tests?" I asked him the night Brian left.

"Tests?" Grant pulled the partition over. His voice was soft, low.

"For the blood. The hematology."

He put his hand on my shoulder. "You don't have anything to worry about," he reassured me. "Your blood's fine." He laughed in an offhand way. "Trust me, I'm a nurse."

I chuckled as he prepped me. "You'll always be more than a nurse to me, Grant."

He stopped and smiled at me. The ripples broke the lake once again. I blushed and felt the blood rush to my cheeks like sharp pin-pricks in the middle of my face. He kept his warm mouth pressed against mine. His hand held my hand, caressed my hair. I felt his hands wander down my face, the back of his hand resting against my blushing cheeks. I felt hot and awake at his touch. He pulled away to look into my eyes. I tried to look away, but Grant held my head so that he could look into my eyes. He kissed me again, this time longer and deeper than before. I felt the warmth of his tongue entering my mouth, and my own finding him. I felt him drawing the breath from me, knocking the wind from me like a heavyweight prizefighter.

I couldn't believe that so much passion existed in such a sterile environment—on the other side of the curtain everything was in its orderly place, everything pristine and hygienic. Within our cocoon, I felt beautifully soiled. Amid the nightstock and honeysuckle, I could smell Grant's masculine, animal-like sweat and ardor. This was the cologne of a man ready for pleasure, the early warning of sudden lust. That aroma hadn't surrounded me in a long time.

I felt his hands wander under the bedclothes, down my bare chest, and make their way into the soft fabric of my shorts. He kissed me as I gasped, comforted me with his hot lips as I moaned against him. His mouth left mine to kiss his way over my face. He gripped my hardening cock, allowing the blood to rush to the tip until I was erect in his hand. He held the base so that my engorged penis was fully tumescent.

Grant stroked me from tip to base, his warm hand gripping my stiff stem. I could feel his tongue on my neck, lightly running up and down my right-hand side. I closed my eyes but felt the bright haze of the fluorescent strip on the ceiling. It seemed to burst like fireworks above us, burning white dots into my retina.

I felt Grant accelerate his stroking, masturbating me under the covers. I could feel my own milky precome lubricating his motions.

When he bit, I arched my neck into him. It was sudden but not unexpected. I felt my cock twitch in his hand, and he responded by encouraging its growth with quickening strokes. The bite was warm and releasing, and I felt his tongue lapping at the puncture he'd made. It was an easier strike than even the needle he'd used so many times before. I felt myself becoming light-headed with the electric sparks of desire jumping circuits in my mind.

He sensed my impending orgasm and released a low, guttural moan for me as I came. I could feel him feeding on the increased blood flow from my neck, sucking the fluid up with his tongue.

We lay together, and I let him continue to feed until he was satiated. My own orgasm had been the most intense I had experienced, and I could feel myself becoming cold and sticky as he continued his postcoital suckling. He stayed on top of me, his weight immediate and comforting amid the usual hospital noise of trolleys, beeps, chatter, and barked commands. I felt him cooling as he moved his mouth over me and lazily kissed me. The taste of my own blood had dispersed, replaced with a sweet vanilla that hit me with the headiness of rich continental handmade ice cream. I thought of Venice and canals and opera.

I don't remember him leaving. One moment we were locked in an embrace and the next he had gone. I drifted into sleep and dreamed of Christmas and mulled wine, the taste of cloves and cinnamon warm and real.

~

I left the next day. The results of all the blood tests were consistently encouraging, and I was allowed to phone my partner and arrange for my own homecoming. He told me how he'd redecorated our room, how he'd spent the daytime in overalls papering the walls when not visiting me. He described the color as like that of ripe watermelons. I longed to be wrapped in his arms with the smell of fresh paint surrounding us while listening to him boast of all the effort he'd put in. I even longed for the emotional blackmail of having to remind him of how kind and thoughtful he was to do such a thing.

Billy was asleep by the time I was leaving, and I didn't feel like goodbyes. I went to the hospital shop and bought a tub of chocolates to leave for Grant. I mentioned it to the volunteer who was staffing the stall. She frowned and told me she didn't know of any Grant working there. She told me how she prided herself on knowing the names of the staff, ever since they had helped look after her husband during his cancer treatment. "It's good to put something back into the place," she said, as she put the chocolates into a donated plastic bag.

I left the box of chocolates on the bed anyway. Such gifts are never wasted in hospitals anyhow.

I sat on Brian's still-empty bed and watched the sun setting, the purple evening drawing closer. For the first time, I saw the tree and the dark spiral of birds flying upward. I knew, looking closer, that Brian and Bill had both been mistaken. They were not birds, but bats. Hundreds and hundreds, flying up into the darkening sky like smoke rising upward in the sky.

Hemlock Lake
Jeff Mann

The water has returned like the appetite of a warrior whose wounds are slowly healing. Were there starlight tonight, I could see the Pleiades, floating on the black surface like portents in an obsidian mirror, and Orion, with his broad shoulders, sword belt, and glimmering blade.

Hemlock Lake is cyclic, emptying itself every century, slowly refilling its depths over a season or two till it once again laps the dock. It was low when it was first discovered—when, new to America, I followed that band of 18th-century explorers to this mountain, feeding on them abstemiously, taking a dram from a different man each night, then curling in with the timber rattler or the bobcat to sleep by day beneath great stones. Its waters were low at the turn of the 20th century when an academic conference on the Greek god Dionysus convened here. I lost control then, and one handsome classics scholar was found floating facedown in what was left of the lake.

Tonight, renewed by long rains, Hemlock Lake is high and hungry. The red spruce stumps are submerged now, as are the yellow-green grasses of the meadow that grew in years of low water around the dock. Submerged are the finger bones and skull shards the archaeologists haven't found, the sacrifices that a renegade Indian tribe fed to the water, provoking its present thirst.

The thickening fog is heavy with silence and holiness. The power is palpable here, the presence of gods in the greenwood: staghorn and wild grape, the forest's glittering eyes. The lake water laps against sandstone. The night is dense as muscle, blacker within the rhododendron groves.

And now the scent of scotch and smoke: the spice of armpit sweat. I turn toward the massive lodge where it waits, mist-veiled, on the slope above the lake. Music ended at last, lights winking out, the wedding party retiring. He has slipped his mandolin gently into its velvet-lined case with the tenderness he touches his wife or child, and now, boots loud on gravel, he hesitantly descends the foggy path, stopping every fifth stride. He has not chosen this meeting.

I wish I could see Hemlock Lake by day, as he can. We pay a price for power. His heels echo now on the dock's planks. He meets my eyes. Power determines who does the choosing.

~

They have fixed the wedding at dusk for me. Spencer is so grateful to me—after all, my publishing company has helped forge his present reputation as a novelist—and so when I explained that due to my work schedule I could only arrive at nightfall, he and his acquiescent bride-to-be kindly timed the event so as to allow my presence.

What church has a more beautiful view? I stand on the porch and look over the darkening mountains of southwest Virginia— great humps of black still rimmed with red, the tiny lights of distant farmhouses twinkling on—and I again wish for the sunlight I abandoned in 1730 on the Isle of Mull. It was well worth the loss—escaping the mortal death that my enemies thought they ensured by many dagger wounds, to avenge my lover Angus's death with claymore, dirk, and flame. Still, how majestic these hills would look in October sunlight, the first yellow gleaming in tulip trees and the first scarlet in sumac, dawn frost glittering on the grass, frowsy because of fall.

I am a masochist, focusing so often, so perversely, on all that's lost forever. But the wedding music brings me distraction, or rather, the bearded musician brings fascination that dismisses the past and insists on the present.

There's a small crowd in Brandywine Memorial Church, halfway up Hemlock Mountain. Spencer looks aristocratic, flushed, in his tuxedo. Angelique looks both sensuous and elegant in her misty trails of seed pearl satins. As I know, better than most, it is easier to find a mate when you aren't a monster.

This is not the traditional ceremony. Writers so often prefer to do it differently, thus the poetry by Mary Oliver and Kaye Varley and the bluegrass band: guitar, upright bass, and mandolin. The heat suffuses my face, my groin, as I study the mandolin player.

He looks to be a local mountain boy. Thick brown hair falls over his brow, and a trimmed brown beard frames an intelligent face. Dark eyebrows hover over hazel eyes. He's the type that looks best in jeans, flannel shirt, and cowboy boots, though tonight he is dressed semiformally in brown corduroys, tan dress shirt, and dark blue tie. Before the ceremony he'd bent over his instrument with a hand flickering over the strings while the tip of his tongue occasionally showed as he hits the highest notes. Now that the wedding's begun, he stands attentive, cradling his mandolin against his chest. He seems to listen not to the minister's words but to the sound, beyond the church's open door, of autumn wind in the sugar maple boughs outside.

I am listening to the wind too, the vast night encompassing this crowd, church, and mountain. His heartbeat is the center of the night's black sphere. I imagine animal fur covering the mounds of pecs beneath his dress shirt. I imagine his armpits' maddening aroma of salt, leaf meal, and cider press. Inside him, the black blood courses and laps like a lake fed by underground springs and hard rains. I look at the fragmented moon on the water and I cup up in my hands and slowly sip, drinking the sun's reflected light.

~

There was a fine mountaintop reception in one of Hemlock Lake Lodge's conference rooms: dancing with the bride, sipping champagne, watching those partial to solid food as they dine on prime rib, roast potatoes, pasta salad, and pecan pie. The music was always in the background. A beefy bear of a banjo player has joined the church trio, and all evening they rollick through cheerful numbers, interspersed with a few slower songs for more romantic dancing.

Spencer thinks my interest is purely musical, and so I garner from him all the pertinent facts. The band: Hardscrabble Hill. The mandolin player: Tim, 28 years old. Playing weddings and festivals all over southwest Virginia, struggling to make ends meet. Liable to be leaving around midnight, skipping the last set, heading home to help his wife with their new baby.

The band ends the third set with an instrumental version of "Green Grass It Grows Bonny," an excuse for the straight folks to slow-dance. Spencer and Angelique begin, and soon several couples are shuffling together across the dance floor.

It's difficult for me, a man burdened with the double stigmas of a thirst for blood and a lust for men, to conceive of a cosmos where my desire is public, in which my hunger, my aesthetic, meet approving eyes rather than suspicion or hatred. How often an outsider's status propels him into fantasy. This is not the world in which I can take the mandolin from its handsome owner, gently pull him into the dancing throng, wrap my arms around him, feel his thick hair on my cheek, press my lips to his brow, his eyelids, his neck. How wearisome are the limits of possibility and propriety for the ravenous, for those whose hunger makes them exiles.

Instead of dancing with whom I desire, I softly sing the lyrics the band is wisely not singing. These words are far from appropriate for a wedding reception; their song's melody is etched in air by Tim's high strings. It is an old song, one I heard versions of in Scotland, during my human years with Angus.

> *I wonder what's keeping my true love tonight?*
> *I wonder what's keeping you out of my sight?*
> *I wonder if you know all the pain I endure?*
> *And yet you stay from me this night I'm not sure.*

At dawn, I will return to the great heap of boulders at Hemlock Mountain's top and sleep where I slept when this lake was first discovered in 1740. I will sleep alone, curled against cold rock, and I will dream of Angus McCormick, lost to me that Beltane night at Lochbuie, and Mark Carden, lost to me at the Battle of Chickamauga. But tonight, before I return to the stony niche of my self, I will absorb what I can of human warmth.

~

"Scotch?" I offer, holding up my flask.

Tim's a little drunk already. He turns away from the urinal, zipping up, and he stares at the Celtic swirls etched into the pewter flask. Swirls like dark water draining from the lake, a vortex into the subterranean, bones of the drowned slowly swallowed by silt.

Then he looks up at me. I smile. I enter his eyes, and then his brain, like rain seeping through the soil, into thirsty root hairs and down to bedrock. Leaching into the deepest layers, where desire is shaped and will conceived, until I reach those depths. Gently, I find a purchase, and then I gently twist.

Tim closes his eyes, shakes his head. He staggers a little and leans back against the restroom wall. Then he meets my eyes and takes the flask from me.

"Thanks," he says, and swigs.

"Derek Maclaine," I say, proffering my hand.

"Tim Graham," he replies, gripping my hand hard and taking another mouthful.

He stands unsteadily under the florescent light and our stares lock together like stag antlers or sword blades, our palms still skin to skin.

He's afraid. This desire is not natural to him, but it springs up nevertheless, dicotyledons of seedlings pushing up from rich earth, from the seeds I've planted.

"I...I've got to leave now. Got to get home. My wife's expecting me." Confused whisper, heartbeat like the bodhran rhythm of the battlefield.

The hard and proper handshake transforms as I slide my fingers through his fingers and pull him to me. Our brows bump, my goatee brushes his lips. His eyes are fixed on my face like stationary stars. They are satellites losing their freedom, gripped by gravity, hurtling toward the earth. Calluses on his fingertips, sweat filming his palms. "Put your hands behind your back," I whisper, and he does.

I am the monarch butterfly probing milkweed blooms, opening his mouth with my tongue. He sighs against my lips, then sways and falls against me, head on my shoulder.

With my left hand behind his back I grip his wrists together. With my right I find the stiffness of his nipples beneath his shirt's fabric. I stroke them, pressing each between thumb and forefinger. With my thigh I rub the sudden density between his legs, beneath his corduroy pants.

"You will not leave now," I say, lapping his ear. "You'll play until the party's over. After the music ends, you will meet me on the dock."

Against my shoulder, he shakes his head. "No," he grunts, but again I fill his mouth with my tongue, my fingers press deeper into his chest's flesh. I release his wrists now, and his arms wrap around me and hold me close, his head still shaking refusal.

"I can't. I can't," he groans, and I'm about to unzip his pants when a footfall outside the door resounds. Gently I push Tim from me, turn toward the sink, and begin washing my hands.

~

The hemlocks after which this lake is named are dying, another in a long line of extinctions. A foreign parasite, the woolly adelgid, is eating their needles, season by season. I remember the great chestnut trees that used to fill these forests and the graceful droop of the American elm, before the diseases that wiped them out. Tonight, waiting on the dock, watching the fog thicken, the cold fog promising hard frost, I stroke the feathery boughs of the hemlocks, their twigs already crusted with the insects' white fuzz. What good is power if it is not enough to rescue what you love? What good to be a survivor when again and again you are left with nothing but litanies of loss?

Then the scent of him, his heels on the dock. Fear, lust, uncertainty. He fought me for an hour, during the last set, meeting my eyes across the room as he played, then looking nervously away, sweat staining his shirt's armpits. He knew his wife was at home, worrying and wondering why he was late, waiting uneasily for his return. *I wonder what's keeping my true love tonight?* Perhaps, being a solicitous husband, he called her with some excuse.

No matter. Now he is here. I was far from certain that he'd come. It is hard to divert the natural course of a stream. But, young and strong as he is, I am stronger.

He stops three feet from me, summoning up his last resistance. He's wearing no jacket. The cold fog wraps its ropes around him. He hugs himself and shudders.

"What do you want?" he whispers.

I smile, lift one hand, and beckon. A pity to mar Spencer's wedding with a mysterious death. But Tim is so handsome, and I am so hungry. And I've fed this lake before.

He shudders again. He stands still, avoiding my eyes, staring instead at the black water beyond me, as if it offered some escape.

"I've got to go home. Jen's waiting for me." When he speaks, the heat of his words weaves its own mist. He half-turns and makes one step toward the hotel, the distant glimmer of its few lights feathered with fog.

"Tim," I say, and he stops. It's been years since a man put up such a struggle, presented such a delicious challenge.

He turns toward me again. I step forward, clasp his hand, pull him to me. Beneath his clothes I can feel leanness, the hard curves of muscles, the harder angles of bone. Hard and resistant, like his will, like the scattered chips of femurs and phalanges at the bottom of Hemlock Lake. He's shaking violently now, from the chill and the fright, and I hold him in my arms, as if his welfare were all that mattered, as if I had human heat to lend him.

~

The tree's as young as he is, a red maple sapling growing deep in the rhododendron groves. He stands against it as I've ordered.

As I've ordered, he crosses his wrists behind the slender trunk. Slowly I unknot my tie, pull it out of my collar, and with the silken length of it I tightly tie his hands together.

He's shaking still, panting now with a barely stifled panic, beginning to realize what danger he's in. With his belt I cinch his elbows together behind the sapling. I unbutton his shirt, pull the ends of it out of his pants, push the collar back till his chest and shoulders are exposed to the night air.

"Please," he gasps. A plea for release, yes, but neither of us is certain which release he wants the most. The artificial lust I've planted in him still battles with the natural fear. The crotch of his corduroys still bulges.

Now I unknot his tie and push it against his lips. He fights me for half a minute, gritting his teeth and twisting from side to side, and this I allow, for I relish a man's struggle, I savor a man's strength as he's subdued.

Then I speak his name again, and instantly he submits. The cloth slides between his teeth, and in a few deft seconds I have his tie knotted behind his head.

The beauty of sacrifice. I stand back and study him. Broad shoulders, pale in what minimal light the woodland allows, pale as October fog into which his life tonight may well disperse. Thick brown hair matting his muscled chest and lean belly, torso arched forward by the angle of his bound arms. Beneath my gaze, in this silent tabernacle of trees, he hangs his head, ashamed to face, in my smile and the depth of my eyes, the fact of his helplessness made complete.

I step up to him, cup his bearded chin in my hand, and lift his face to mine. Above the dark silk tied between his teeth, his eyes are wide and wet with a growing terror, the terror of a man who suddenly realizes he's met his murderer. No one will find us here, in the middle of the night, in this dense forest, on this mountainside. Neither he nor I know whether he will survive the night.

When I run my tongue around his gagged lips, he starts to pant again, and when I kiss his forehead, he begins to whimper.

"Ssshhh!" I whisper into the thick hair falling over his face, but he's breaking now; the terror has him banishing the last remnants of that desire my mesmerism demanded. When I wrap my arms around him, a seismic tremble runs along his limbs like lightning down the bole of an oak.

Suddenly, Tim jerks himself out of my embrace. He does what any animal scenting its own death would do: He tries to escape. He tugs furiously at the belt around his elbows, the tie about his wrists, growling like a dog into the fabric knotted between his teeth. He twists and curses, twists and tugs some more. The maple tree shakes beneath his frantic efforts. A few red leaves, dislodged, fall about us.

He shouts once—a silk tie looks good in a man's mouth, but it doesn't make an efficient gag—and that's when I slap his face hard, stunning him. I seize his shoulders and slam him back against the tree.

Another red rain of maple leaves. One wet leaf sticks briefly to his bare shoulder like a crimson handprint before continuing its descent.

His struggle's only confirmed his helplessness. He sags in his bonds, in my grip, faces the black earth between his boots, and starts to sob.

The violence of his tears surprises me. Most mountain boys prize their courage, their stoic manhood, and refuse tears in any extremity. It takes great fear to conquer a man's pride. It takes great grief or terror to overcome his shame and permit such unabashed weeping. Tim's crying now with the sort of force with which winter winds tear off tree limbs on this mountain's bleak height. Tears like the steady gray descent that summer thunder leaves in its wake, drumming on the tin roof, waking the sleepers, cutting rivulets into hillsides.

Gently I stroke his temple, but he pulls violently away and keeps sobbing, head down, determined to refuse any comfort from his killer, aiming his muffled sorrow into the leaf meal at his feet, the black rot of centuries.

I step back then, and slowly I unbutton my shirt. No need to ruin another outfit. I've waited long enough. I am hungry, he is beautiful, he is a coward, and that triad of facts has decided his fate. On a mountain laurel bush I hang my blazer and my shirt, listening to his sobs retreat like tides, gather force and breath, and then renew themselves.

Enough. I slam my palm over his mouth and push his head back against the sapling.

"Shut up," I say. "You don't want to die weeping."

Beneath my grasp he shakes his head, and, within seconds, the sobs grade into soft groans against my hand, and then into silence.

His eyes are closed, his chest heaving. He's chewed and fought his tie till it's soaked with spittle. Tears streak his cheeks like sugar sap from a broken maple twig, glimmer in his beard like rain clinging to tamarack needles. Who could resist? I lick the salt, the hot seawater, from his cheeks, from his chin.

"You're going to be brave now? You're going to be quiet?"

He nods. He opens his eyes and stares at me, stares at the fact of his end. Then his glance shifts to the forest behind me, as if acknowledging some invisible witness. His breath slowing, he closes his eyes again, and mumbles something that my hand and his gag render unintelligible.

With a handful of his hair I pull his head to one side. The skin of his neck glimmers as if it were dusted with mica. That bodhran beat again. Soon the drummer will weary, the rhythm will slow and stop. Now my fangs length, and I press one sharp point against the thin skin separating my thirst from his great artery's generous throb. His own thumping fright will pump him halfway dry, will hasten the welling of that underground spring. Only at the end will my mouth need to pull from his body the thickening, dwindling juice, the hot black wine lowering, lowering, till the chalice is empty and his abandoned body gleams against leaf mold like a cold point of quartz.

A wind's worrying the treetops, like the wind that, during the wedding, soothed the maples beyond the church door. He slumps against me, all hope gone, prepared at last to die with courage, a pleasant transformation after those torrents of unseemly tears. I press my fang harder—slowly, slowly, savoring this moment as I savor every entrance, every conquest—and the skin's resistance splits. The first drops of blood wet the corner of my mouth, prelude to the rich flood to follow. I will bury the body beneath boulders on the hill, or I will simply slip the corpse into the lake.

His blood is tinged with pot and scotch, and it wells into my mouth. I press his head against my bare shoulder, gulp the first mouthful, listen to the leaves rustling overhead, listen to his mumbling. He's limp, all struggles over, passing in my arms from passion into peace.

They often mumble when they die, prayers or curses. Few of them go without words of some kind, a soft speech trailing off and disappearing like the wake a ship writes on water.

I lift my hand from his mouth, place it across the muscled mound over his heart, and I take another swallow. I want to feel his heart slow and stop beneath my touch. I run my fingers through his torso's thick fur, over a nipple hard with the autumn chill, hard as a seed. I will leave him here till the hour before dawn. I will leave him gagged and bound, slumped like the Christians' savior against his tree. I will sit on a stone, drink scotch from my flask, and watch his limbs stiffen; study the fog as it thickens about him, painting gray frost across his chest hair. He was not brave enough to deserve life, but he is beautiful enough to deserve a wake.

His blood is surging freely now, so hot and sweet my head swims. Greedily I gulp and gulp. A few more ecstatic mouthfuls, and his life will be over, his future will be entirely consumed.

By my ear Tim's muttering on, and suddenly, without the added obstruction of my hand over his mouth, his muffled words come clear.

"Jenny," he says. "Jenny."

Mouth full of blood, I hesitate. His mutter subsides to a whisper. A name repeated once, twice more, before his head falls against mine and he passes out.

I gulp down the sweetness, the hot honey that makes half-human flesh of my marble. I withdraw my fangs and wipe my beard with the back of my hand. His blood pulses still, trickling down his neck, staining the edge of his shirt.

Beneath my fingers, his heart throbs faintly. Against my neck, his hot breath continues.

~

Tim is so easy to carry, arms and chest hard as a laborer's, but belly flat with youth and poverty. Still stripped to the waist, I stand by the water, this young musician slumped in my arms, and I hum "Green Grass It Grows Bonny," the melancholy tune played only hours ago at the wedding reception.

Hemlock Lake rustles against the dock at my feet, wanting its share, wanting more flesh and bone to join the offerings that came before. It has waited so long. I know how it feels—that ravenous, impatient ache. I remember how eagerly its dark fingers swarmed over the sinking corpse of that classics scholar, just over a century ago.

Tim is sleeping too deeply for the cold water to wake him. How gently I might slide him from my arms and into the lake, and how silently, how painlessly he would drown, facedown in the dark. No chance then that he might resist my mind and remember this night.

~

Local legends say that the lodge is haunted by the old woman who had it built, and I believe it, for tonight there is an interior mistiness that matches the fog outside, a gleaming mist that hovers by the reception desk. Employees have sometimes glimpsed the vague form of a woman, in gray dress and white shawl.

She would approve of mercy, I think. She would approve of life, a lover's last-minute reprieve.

Four A.M., and the foyer is entirely empty. Carefully I lower Tim to the leather couch by the fireplace. Sweet survivor, waylaid wedding guest. Someone left to pluck Scottish melodies from the mandolin; someone to admire, as I can't, the way October sunlight loves Hemlock Lake.

I mistook his tears. Not fear but grief fed them. He wept not for himself but for her.

His shirt is still unbuttoned, and I kiss each of his nipples, warming their hard points with my mouth, giving back the heat I stole, before covering him with a rough Indian blanket I pull off the back of the couch. Someone will find him soon. His memory will be vague, crazy fragments blamed on alcohol and a bad batch of marijuana. His wife will scold him relentlessly. He will be dogged with nightmares for months.

The mist gathers about us, lingering and glimmering. Tim groans and shifts beneath the blanket. I kiss his lips, stroke his soft beard a final time. I slip a wad of bills into his shirt pocket. Then I rise, salute the mist, and stride through the door.

Outside, night fog has left a killing frost on the broad lawn before the lodge. Tomorrow, all about Hemlock Lake, the scarlet leaves of maples will break loose from twigs, ride wind onto water, and float in the sun for hours before joining their forebears' muddy molecules on the lake floor. On the couch, Tim will wake, hold his throbbing head in his hands, and wonder how blood came to be on his shirt, why the tie stuffed in his pants pocket is so moist, as if it had been soaked in dew.

~

The water is bitterly cold. Already it begins to rob me of what little warmth Tim's blood lent me. Naked, I am as pale as he would have been by dawn had I not heard her name.

My body might appease the lake for a while, though it is a morsel the misty water must relinquish before dawn. Soon, from the entrance to my makeshift tomb, I will watch the mountain's edge bleed with the coming day. Soon I will return to the high-water mark of my hunger, sleeping within my stony cave, dreaming of passions mutual, not manipulated. Dreaming of Tim, hairy and naked, his warmth curled against me, grateful and loving, rejoicing in my touch.

Till then, dead silhouette of ivory set in an onyx oval, I float on the surface of Hemlock Lake, listening to the lake water rising, listening to the hemlocks dying. I raise my hand, and above me the prompted fog swirls, thins, and parts, revealing the stars. There is Orion, the brave one brandishing his sword, averting his fate, the rushing width of heaven set between him and the sting of the Scorpion.

Mischief Night
Max Reynolds

The tiny spray of blood on the sheets barely caught Garcia's eye as he dressed in the half-light of a New York twilight in late October. He stopped, one well-muscled leg in mid descent into the soft black wool trousers, staring obliquely at the claret pinpricks on the ocher sheets. It wasn't like him to be messy. He finished dressing.

The room was still, breathless. Foghorns keened their mournful cry out on the Hudson. Past the halogen glow of streetlights coming on like a row of too bright dominoes outside the fifth-floor window, Garcia could see down the narrow strip of street to the river. There sunset had riven the horizon, tearing away the orange-red flesh of the late-afternoon sky, revealing the thick, dark welt of night. Garcia leaned an arm against the window frame, barely glancing at his watch, knowing he must leave. *Nearly 6. Nearly dark.* He ran long, tapered fingers absently through his black hair, smoothed the charcoal cashmere turtleneck against his throat, adjusted his cock within the soft fold of the trousers, and turned away from the bloodied horizon to view what carnage remained in the room.

Jorge still lay on the bed, his lush, silken swimmer's body sprawled with casual grace over the ocher sheets and rust-colored duvet. The line of his burnished bronze body stood in stark relief against the monochromatic palette of the bedclothes. So, too, did that small spray of blood left of his still-swollen cock.

Garcia walked to the bed and bent over the barely warm body of Jorge Vasquez, whom he had killed less than an hour earlier after several hours of sex so intense Garcia's dick stiffened automatically with memory and desire. *Would he have to stand here and masturbate over the body of his dead lover?* He grazed his hand over his swelling cock and pinched the head through his pants, feeling with a rush his body's only warmth. The urge to come again, fast and hard, rose quickly and his fingers played along the zipper, then stopped. Garcia reached over and touched the rough-hewn musculature of Jorge's sculpted back, cupped his hand onto the deltoid simply tattooed VIDA, and ran his index finger down Jorge's side, tapping it like a punctuation point on his hip. Garcia, his cock throbbing, knelt on the bed and turned the body, which seemed only to sleep, over onto the back that was heavily tattooed with a series of stylized crosses. He glanced briefly at the blood once more and then took Jorge's cock in his hand, holding it as one would a lingering handshake in a final farewell. He released it, his other hand pressing hard against his own dick, then bent to kiss his lover's cock, the taste of semen still fresh and salty, like the tequila shots they'd had at lunch before they'd come here, to Jorge's apartment off West End Avenue, pricks thick and stiff from a lunch filled with teasing innuendo and swift touches under the table. Whether the semen that he now licked absently from his lips was his own or Jorge's, he couldn't discern.

Garcia always lunched at Tomatilla when he was in New York— *Nuevo* York, Jorge had called it with something like affection when they had talked over the meal. Jorge who had been in the city for over five years and done so well he missed nothing of home except, sometimes, the food. The food at Tomatilla reminded Garcia of home too, reminded him unpleasantly, like a surprise kick from a burro. No Tex-Mex melange or salsa slackened to match the sensibilities of Anglos. At Tomatilla the unglamorous tables were set with three salsas, two green, one red, thick with blackened peppers, a plate of salt, a small dish of rough-cut limes and a tapered bottle of tabasco, its label *en Español*. There Garcia had sat at a small table by the window. The day was overcast, and though his eyes hurt from the sun seductively hidden behind the thick, rolling clouds of a New York autumn, he took the risk, leaving on his dark glasses and watching the flow of pedestrian traffic along the East Village street, the book he had brought to read during lunch unopened on the table, beside his plate.

Garcia had been stalking the prey throbbing on the sidewalk, feeling a pulse here and there that had sent his own blood racing. He hadn't seen Jorge enter the restaurant. Hadn't noticed him at all until Jorge picked up the copy of Vargas Llosa's strange new novel about Gauguin, seen it was in Spanish, and began talking rapid-fire in a Cuban-tinged patois Garcia hadn't heard in a long time.

Jorge hadn't asked but sat, the book still in his hands; his bright, quick smile flickering in and out between the words that shot out over the table at Garcia. It was a short literary soliloquy about Vargas Llosa, García Marquez, Valenzuela, Perez, Pig (of course Pig, with his intense sexuality, Garcia had thought briefly), even Aslant before she'd gotten overly romantic. Magical realism, spirituality, food, art, politics, sex—all the components of the South Americans were touched upon briefly by Jorge in his impassioned rant. Garcia had said nothing, only listened. Had not removed his glasses (not by the window, not even on a day gray as this). Had not even proffered the bits of food scattered across the small table. And then it was over. The torrent of words ceased and Jorge extended a strong, bronze hand to Garcia and in accented English had said, "Jorge. Jorge Vasquez. I teach swimming at the PS a few blocks over and at the gym over there." He had angled his head toward the direction of the door. His closely shaved head with the finely chiseled Cubano features and the eyes so deeply brown Garcia could not discern their pupils. His lips were rosy and full, and for a moment Garcia could imagine vividly how they would look poised at the head of his dick: barely open, but wet and ready, to take his thick cock down to the hilt.

Was he tall? He seemed the same height as Garcia, just cresting six feet, and similarly built, though Garcia knew his own body to be that of a laborer, a farmhand, the dirt-poor Mexican boy Diego had plucked from the fields when he had seen the 11-year-old drawing in the hot dust with a stick, beginning the long, slow mentioning eventually leading him here. Here, across from Jorge, who could have stepped easily from one of Diego's paintings. Here, across from a young man—still a boy—of what, 25, 26? Who no doubt thought he was dining with a peer—31, 32 at most. Garcia knew well the sinister surprise of youth, which was not youth but the grim disguise he himself now wore.

He looked back across the table, so small the men's knees touched beneath it, and could tell Jorge's body would be broad and muscled in the chest and taper toward the hips; that's what swimming did to a man. He thought he might like to see Jorge lunging from the water and plunging back in, his arms and torso sleek from the water, his cock tight against his body in the minuscule swim trunks.

They had ordered drinks then. Garcia rarely drank in the afternoon, but then he rarely ventured out so early in the day. He usually slept well past noon. As he watched Jorge's animated talk he thought lazily that a siesta might do well, after two tequilas and a thick polenta with tomatilla, *huevos,* and beans. The conversation had ebbed and flowed from literature to food to art to home. The flirting had gone on so long Garcia had begun to wonder if perhaps Jorge was straight, but then the light, quick fingers had reached for his dick under the table, and the immediacy of its stiffening had given Jorge any answer he had needed. They left Tomatilla and headed east toward the river and Jorge's apartment off Horatio.

The building was tall and dark, a tenement remnant of an era Garcia remembered well but which Jorge would only have read about in books. Once inside the cavernous foyer Garcia pushed Jorge hard against the wall near the endless spiral of stairs, knocking his legs apart with a practiced shove of his knee and grabbing his crotch. Above them all was silent, save the susurrations of a radio and the intermittent mewing of a cat. Garcia could feel Jorge's pulse quicken in his throat as he pressed his mouth hard against the vein, feeling the heat, smelling the thick, sweet nectar tantalizingly close.

He ran his tongue wetly along Jorge's neck and heard him gasp as if from far away. He grabbed for Jorge's hand and pushed it roughly against his immense hard-on, rubbing it fast along the ridge in his pants. They kissed each other deeply, Jorge pulling at Garcia's black hair and murmuring in Spanish to be taken, taken now, without waiting, right here.

Each could have come then, their dicks swollen and wet, ready to spurt against the walls, the floor, each other. Jorge pushed Garcia back, even as he slowly unzipped his pants and reached inside for the cock so eager for the swimmer's stroke.

"No." Garcia had to hold himself back, pull Jorge's hand out and slap it lightly, then bring it quickly to his lips. "We must tease it out." His voice was thick with desire, and all through the long, dark foyer he could smell nothing but the maddening invitation of sex and blood.

Vamoose. Jorge's whispered urgency propelled Garcia up the dim-lit stairs, pulling him along like a dog on a leash. *Was this what he wanted?* Garcia knew what lay behind whatever door they entered, and he looked back down the stairs, the foyer receding with each step. He thought about the pulsing here and there on the street outside the restaurant, the staccato beat of blood he had heard, the strong, viscous aroma he had smelled even through the window glass of the restaurant. Bodies empty and anonymous, like carcasses hanging in the butcher shop where he had been sent as a child to retrieve this or that, first for his mother, then later for Diego.

He could leave now, retreat down the stairs, relieve himself of the pent-up desire pulsing in his cock in some bar or alleyway and seek with swift anonymity what else he needed. Garcia looked up at Jorge, sleek-bodied and just short of handsome, in his rough leather jacket and overly faded jeans. Jorge was turning the key in the first of three locks. Once they clicked behind the two men it was Garcia who would leave and Jorge who would never break through a wave again. He stood close to but did not touch Jorge as the door opened. Even in the dim light Garcia could see the little shrine to Guadalupe off to the side of the sofa, its red votives flickering low against the vibrating multihued background of her grotto.

"Amo." Jorge's lips were against Garcia's, his fingers unlashing Garcia's belt and pulling him into the depths of the little apartment that could have been lifted from the streets of the old quarter in Havana decades earlier. Garcia's balls ached, his cock throbbed, his mouth was whetted for a taste of Jorge, for all the tastes of Jorge. He put his hand around the back of Jorge's neck and pulled his mouth to his, biting his lips lightly, tasting enough blood to make his desire surge past any qualm or guilt or tincture of morality he might have felt. This boy was his—this lithe, smooth body peeling off clothes while he watched—rubbing and pulling on his own cock, waiting for Jorge to put those full lips flush against it, licking, sucking, tasting, feeling the most intense desire he would ever feel again before his final release to meet Guadalupe.

They had fucked again and again, come over and over, gotten hard anew almost before their dicks had softened from the shuddering orgasm before. The first time, they had stood against the wall in the apartment's narrow hallway. Garcia hadn't wanted to wait. When Jorge stood naked in front of him—his dick standing straight out, Jorge unabashedly waiting to be taken however Garcia wanted him—Garcia had pushed him against the wall, head turned enough so Garcia could watch the pulse jump and flutter in his neck. Garcia had stripped briskly, efficiently. He had enjoyed watching Jorge take off his clothes, but now he wanted his own, off and fast; wanted to feel Jorge's hot flesh pressed against his too chilled body and too-hot prick. The sunglasses had come off last, but still too soon. Garcia was unprepared for Jorge's tattooed back—the intricate pattern of small crosses emblazoned in purple, magenta and indigo along the base of his spine. It took Garcia's breath away. He looked down at the clothes at his feet and considered leaving, but as he did so, Jorge pulled Garcia's hips against that swimmer's ass, firm and muscled and easily spread. Garcia bent over and grabbed the strip of condoms from his inside jacket pocket, tore one open quickly with his teeth, and rolled it expertly over his stiff dick, jerking himself off a

little as he did so, a gesture that brought a sigh of pleasure from
Jorge.

He kissed the back of Jorge's neck, ran his hands over his shoulders, down his sides, and onto his waiting hips. *"Madre Dios,"* Jorge
breathed, as Garcia's long fingers opened Jorge's ass and guided his
waiting cock into the smooth, dark hole. One hand on Jorge's hip,
the other stroking Jorge's thick cock and ever-tightening balls,
Garcia felt the blood and semen rushing through his body with
exhilarating speed. Jorge breathed hard, his face pressed against
Garcia's, his hands slamming against the wall. Garcia's tongue
flicked over Jorge's lips, pushed against his teeth and tongue, licked
his earlobe. He pulled the small gold ring with his teeth. Jorge
bucked back against Garcia's cock and he knew he would come hard
once he felt the boy begin to spurt in his hand. Suddenly Jorge
gripped Garcia's hand and began to pull it faster and faster, his
breath short gasps, his murmurs in Spanish demanding Garcia over
and over to fuck him hard in the ass, to come with him, shoot deep
into his ass, fuck him, fuck him, fuck him, *Madre Dios...*

The hot come dripping onto Garcia's hand was enough. His
teeth nipped along Jorge's neck as he slammed his dick back and
forth to a stunning orgasm. The taste of blood was in his mouth—
he smelled it stronger than their sweat, or come, or the hot waxy
aroma of the votives nearby. He was weak in the knees from hunger
for Jorge, for all of him, more of him, everything that would come
when he sank his teeth deep into that place that gave him the most
indescribable pleasure he had ever known since that first time in
Mexico, in Juarez, in that border town on that cold desert night
close to Christmas when he was not much older than Jorge was now.
Jorge, who was easing Garcia's still-hard dick from his ass and taking him to the bathroom to wash his cock and hands and start them
up all over again in a flood of hot water in the shower.

They toweled off, utterly spent from jerking each other off
quickly under the surge of water, soapy hands working each other's
dicks and balls, Garcia overwhelmed by Jorge's body flushed with
the heat of the shower, Garcia pulling back as he felt his teeth begin

to lower into the tender space between Jorge's neck and shoulder while they stroked and stroked and stroked each other's cocks.

Afterward, Garcia let Jorge lead him to the bedroom and lay him back on the ocher sheets, a color so purely *Cubano,* so like his Mother's warm tortillas fresh from the hot cast-iron stove, Garcia smiled when he saw them. The men dozed together for a half hour, maybe more, until Garcia was awakened by the warmth of Jorge pressed against him, the heat of Jorge's sleeping body as darkly seductive as that night in Juarez had been for him...how many years ago?

He lay entangled in Jorge's delectable body, feeling the intensity of his heat, and thought about asking Jorge if he wanted it, if he wanted to come with him, cross over, be taken as fully as anyone could ever be. He thought of the passion in the boy's voice and eyes as he had talked about books and Cuba and art over lunch. He thought about the indescribable urgency of the sex downstairs and then again as they had stripped with such frenzied heat. He lifted himself onto an elbow and leaned over the sleeping Jorge, lightly tracing the veins in his neck, his arm. He bent to kiss the pulse in Jorge's wrist, and felt rather than heard the intake of breath from the waking younger man. Garcia reached up, placing his hand behind Jorge's neck, lowering his body onto Jorge's, feeling his cock throbbing against the silken thighs of the swimmer, feeling Jorge stiffen beneath him. He rubbed his cock against Jorge's thighs, took it in his hand, and thrust it tight between Jorge's legs.

Jorge spread his legs, then raised them, opening his ass beneath Garcia, who began to rub his finger around the rim of Jorge's hole, then up and over the base of his balls. Suddenly he stopped touching Jorge between his legs, between his cheeks. He took the boy's face in his hands and looked deep into those eyes that were darker than any he could remember. The sweetness in Jorge crested over him, and he felt himself awash in emotions he had hoped to avoid. He could bring him over, could pull him into the world he had been pulled into without being asked on that chill evening in the windswept desert too far from home. He took Jorge's face in his hands and closed his eyes, kissing him deeply on those full lips, kissing all along his throat, whispering endearments in Spanish, telling Jorge how beautiful, how sexy, how sweet he was. When he opened his eyes, the boy had softened under his gaze, and he wondered suddenly if this was how he himself had looked when Eli had thrust his cock deep into his ass, taken the back of his neck in his teeth until he had felt the blood spurt over his shoulders and then it had all gone dark and incredibly still, until he awoke with a hunger he had never felt before. The hunger he had now for Jorge. Had he gazed at Eli with the simple, blind trust of the unknowing as Jorge now gazed at him? Had his eyes held the kind of mute expectancy Jorge's now shone with?

Garcia looked away and felt the sigh escape Jorge's lips against his face as he lowered himself onto this body he had not planned for. *"Let me do it for you, let me give it to you,"* Jorge breathed, and lightly pushed Garcia onto his back. Jorge ran his tongue down Garcia's hairless chest, tongued his navel and bit lightly at the flesh above his rigid cock. "Let me watch you," Garcia demanded to Jorge as the swimmer took a deep breath and wrapped his lush mouth around Garcia's waiting cock. Garcia leaned back onto the pillows, consumed by the silken heat of Jorge's mouth, the lick and suck and pulse of his tongue and lips, the velvety touch of fingers stroking and squeezing his balls and sliding deep into his ass. Garcia would let Jorge do whatever he wanted to do to him. He could not bring Jorge over—he was too sweet, too giving, too much like he himself had been before Eli took him, unasked, to where he now was. No, Garcia would have to take him, bleed him, then let him move on, forever mortal, but redeemed.

Jorge had Garcia's cock deep in his throat, so deep Garcia could feel the twin pulses of cock and blood-beat meld in Jorge's hot, wet mouth. He wasn't going to let himself come, not yet. *Tease it out,* he told himself, *make this last. Make it more exquisite with the waiting.* Jorge's rigid prick stroked against Garcia's thigh and he reached for it, pulling it lightly, teasingly, feeling Jorge quiver against him, feeling the intake of breath against his cock.

Garcia pulled his dick from Jorge's luscious mouth and kissed him hard, harder, hard enough to take away his breath and push him down onto the bed. Jorge's legs were up and over Garcia's shoulders, the condom slick over Garcia's bulging prick, the shaft disappearing slow, then fast, in and out of Jorge's delicious ass as he breathed and gasped and jerked himself off against Garcia's hard stomach pressing down against it. They were nearly there, ready to come, ready to release all of it. Garcia slowed his thrusts, then pushed Jorge's hand away from his cock. "Don't touch yourself. Just let yourself feel it all," he told Jorge, "feel me deep in you, feel me opening you up as far as you can go, take me into you, take me into you, pull me into you." He was coming, so hard, so deep in Jorge—deep in that hot, silky place that was his human core, his viscera, all those places that his friend Frida used to paint, the places that were as close to the heart as one could get without reaching into a man's chest and pulling the organ out, something he had never done, though he had seen it, once, with Eli, many years ago.

Garcia's orgasm bled him dry. He was spent. He had to give Jorge what he needed, then he had to take what *he* needed. Jorge lay beneath him, breathing hard. Garcia knew his cock ached for release. "What do you want?" Garcia whispered into Jorge's ear, above the madly throbbing vein. "What have you never asked for?"

"Kiss me, again," Jorge breathed back, his voice rough with desire. "Take my cock in your mouth, take my cock in your hand, stroke it till I'm just about to come, then stop and then start again. Do what you said—tease me, then take me over. Take me, all of me."

The words, spilling out in their *Cubano* lilt, stoked Garcia's desire. Jorge wasn't asking for what his words had suggested, Garcia knew that, but it was enticing nevertheless. He took Jorge's prick into his mouth, flicking his tongue over the head, running it along the ridge. He stroked Jorge's balls as he sucked and licked, reached up and pinched his nipples. He could feel Jorge ready to come, he liked the way the boy pulled on his hair and begged him to stop, come up, lay on him, jerk him off while he pressed against him.

Garcia did as he was asked. His teeth bared, he nipped lightly along the vein of Jorge's neck as the boy came hard under him; the hot, wet come slick between them as Garcia continued to pump against Jorge, the flesh of his neck caught between his teeth until Jorge's breath slowed and he seemed to sleep. Garcia released the nerves that had stunned Jorge, brushed his lips lightly over the boy's and inched down again, back to the still-hard cock. Then Jorge moved, took Garcia's head in his hand, murmured something Garcia couldn't hear—an endearment, perhaps?—something low and sweet, and then he seemed to sleep, his hand still tangled in Garcia's hair.

The tender flesh just under Jorge's balls was where Garcia sank his teeth. He licked the spot first, tasting Jorge, imagining everything the boy had ever done before he drank deep, and could feel those experiences coursing through him with the boy's blood. He kissed and sucked and pushed at the flesh from which he drank the blood of Jorge's femoral artery, his cock now unimaginably hard, the desire and need commingling in an almost unbearable orgasmic flood as the hot claret nectar flowed down his throat. For a time he could once again feel his own pulse, the spurt in his own veins mimicking the spurt from his dick onto the sheets and the thigh of the now dead boy.

Garcia lay for some minutes against Jorge until the warmth began to dissipate. Then he rose from the bed, grateful for the expression of just-spent ecstasy on the dead boy's face.

In the shower Garcia continued to see images from Jorge's life flicker behind his eyes. It had been a difficult life. He was lucky to have escaped Cuba, *marrone* that he was. He was less lucky to have come to Tomatilla searching out food from home that afternoon. But dying a pleasurable death could not be overrated, Garcia thought, as he examined the rooms for any remnants of himself.

There was nothing to be done about the blood. Whoever found Jorge would presume a trick gone bad and not be far wrong. They would be confused by the lack of violence, the seeming dearth of evidence of a crime. Perhaps they would find the small marks below the scrotum, perhaps not. Perhaps they would simply assume an unnatural heart attack after sex. Anything was possible.

Garcia was still kneeling over his dead lover, his desire as fresh as it had been when they had entered the building. It had been some time since he had felt such heat and passion, a long time since he had tasted such warmth and sweetness. Jorge had been a gift. Garcia took his implausibly hard cock in his hand and stroked it languorously. He reached into his trousers and touched his balls, caressing them the way Jorge had done, and felt them tighten up against the shaft of his cock. He stroked faster, slapping his dick against his other hand, squeezing the head, pinching along the ridge of his cock until he thought he might pass out from the intensity of pleasure as he began to spurt onto the sheet next to Jorge's beautiful body.

The first orgasm after a kill was exquisitely, deeply satisfying. The blood still fresh within him, he could taste it again in the back of his throat, taste the hot young flesh that had come in his mouth. Garcia lay down on the bed next to the body, now the same temperature as his own. He cradled the young man in his arms, pressed his fingers against the spot where his pulsing life had raged not so long ago, and kissed him one more time. Then he rose, covering Jorge with the sheet and duvet. He walked past the little altar to Guadalupe and nodded in her direction. He picked up his jacket, turned the three locks with the keys from the hall table, and closed the door quietly behind him.

On the bed Jorge slept on as Garcia landed on the night-blackened street. Everywhere the tang of blood wafted in the autumn air, acrid, like the smell of burning leaves. Garcia turned and headed toward the river, and the faceless cruising of the night.

Bicycle Baka
Paul Crumrine

I. Below the City of the Dead

In the late August sunlight the vampires spun down the mountain toward the green hamlet of my birth. Their wheels spun across the timberline and rattled past the houses of the dead. These vampires, young black men with red tresses, had dressed themselves in silver Lycra bicycle shorts with black stripes, matching jerseys, and black shoes. Even from a distance I felt the sensuality radiating from their curvaceous bodies. White goats' hooves clipped into the tree ferns lining the broken asphalt as the silver bicycles clattered past.

Children stood at the edge of the village and hissed at the approaching vampires: *"Mauvais nanm. Mauvais nanm."* They dropped their hand-carved toys in the dust and climbed into the old apple trees that lined the road.

Emmanuel, the lead vampire, stood on his pedals and plucked the oldest boy from a tree. Young Joseph shrieked when he realized that he was being drawn toward the lascivious vampire's face. Then Emmanuel's fangs slid into Joseph's carotids, and the boy tasted shuddering cold and ghastly darkness.

The silver bicycles rattled into our village and people ran screaming before the onslaught. Joel Alexis stood frozen in the invaders' path as though he dared them to slay him. A boy of 15 temporarily escaped capture by throwing himself sideways, tumbling, and leaping to his feet. Emmanuel pointed toward the running boy, and two of the vampire flock pursued him. Meanwhile, Emmanuel descended upon Joel, and my body instinctively responded to protect my lover. I hit Joel like a cannonball, knocking him to safety while stranding my own flesh directly in the vampire's path. Remaining astride his bicycle, Emmanuel grinned lewdly, captured my arm, and sunk his fangs into my hand. I dragged my hand away from the rolling abomination and kicked at the bicycle's wheels. I heard a shriek, felt a blood-chilling sensation, and saw the fallen bicycle twist, shrink, sprout legs, and run toward the city of the dead.

For a second Emmanuel towered over me, and I thought my end had come. But he gave me a terrible smile, a smile like I never hope to see again, and I heard his breathing thoughts uncorrupted by burning words: "Come to me when your hair goes red. Come to seize the pleasure of the bed." Then he rose into the air and flew screeching across the sky. His fellow vampires joined him, and our village was saved.

"Jean frightened the vampires," the children shrieked, but the adults regarded me darkly.

Joel examined my wounded hand and shook his head mournfully. "I will take you to the clinic of the *blancs* in Cap-Haïtien."

I spit on the ground. "What do the *blancs* know? I pointed toward the graveyard, where the *baka* sat perched upon my family's mausoleum and screeched raucously toward the village. "If the *blancs* saw the *baka* with their own eyes, they would not believe."

We buried Joseph and Paul, the 15-year-old boy well away from the waiting *baka*. Old Ernst Nord mixed copious quantities of concrete, and we erected a six-foot monolith over their bodies so they could not crawl out and attack us. Several people argued that I should be buried as well.

"Jean has been bitten," Francine Marcelin said. "He will become like them. He will walk in shadows and feast upon blood."

Joel saved me; my injury seemed to have released him from his overwhelming despair. In addition to being a farmer, Joel was also the village *houngan*, the priest of *vaudou*. He spoke forcefully. "You can't bury a *neg* alive. Jean would become a zombie. I will perform a ceremony of purification." Then he sang softly:

"O kwa, o jibile,
O kwa, o jibile,
O kwa, o jibile,
Ou pa we m inosan?"

People nodded in agreement, and those who spoke against me looked pacified. "The *houngan* will purify him," they repeated.

That night Joel made love to me as he used to do before the *baka* came. I did not know that it would be the last time. In the dark he kissed my mouth and my tongue met his. His tongue entered my mouth and I sucked deep upon it as the love fires kindled within me. I gripped Joel's hard cock, relieved that my heroism had restored his potency. I knew that his essence would soon lie within me.

Soon I knelt before him; on my hands and knees I received him into my burning body. Joel held my ears in the prescribed rite as he deeply thrust from the soft, singing darkness.

The next morning, still wet with love's juices, I opened our shutters and looked toward the city of the dead. The *baka* still perched upon the monument and appeared determined to stay. My nostrils flared as I confronted the source of mischief. I felt only cold hate and implacable resolve, and vowed that I would vanquish this lurking *baka*, just as I had vanquished their vampire riders. Was I not the child of the serpent?

2. papa zaca, spirit of the coumbite

One month before the vampires rode their silver bicycles into the village, I was worrying about Joel. I sat in a small, dusty market on the road to Le Borgne, trying to sell a scrawny, squawking chicken to a buyer from a restaurant. The bitch was a hard sell, and she insisted on my throwing in a dozen plantains. As I halfheartedly bargained the food Joel had raised, I hoped that Joel was hoeing the beans. If he was sitting inside our tiny mud-and-wattle home lamenting his manhood, then weeds would choke our crop and we would go hungry again.

"Three gourdes, *masisi*," the woman said. I took the pittance and watched her drive away with my chicken and plantains.

I looked at the three pitiful notes in my hand and the six tomatoes and green onions I had left to sell. I knew that my lover's depression was not his fault. Our lives had gotten much worse since the *baka* had unmanned him. I looked around the Haïtian open-air market; women were gossiping, bargaining, and struggling for a meager existence. So many people, yet our lives relied upon the whims of unseen powers.

Recently our village had been invaded by *baka*: evil, red-eyed dwarves who uprooted crops, destroyed livestock, and tormented the village folk. Joel had tried to drive them out, even invoking Baron Samedi in a powerful ceremony. But although the Baron himself possessed Joel, the *baka* had overpowered him and given him a terrible darkness of the mind. Joel lost interest in food, work, and sex.

However, soon after the ceremony the *baka* disappeared, and the village generally returned to normal. Still, Joel sat most of the day in our house, not speaking, and holding his head in deep gloom. He no longer assisted in the *coumbite*, so no one came to save our crops. Since that night he had not once made love to me, though I had used all my wiles to awaken his penis to fill me.

I reminded myself that I needed to make a sacrifice to Papa Zaca, the *loa* of agriculture. Our crops depended upon his goodwill, but even Papa Zaca could not lift Joel from his despair.

Soon I traded my onions and tomatoes to a woman from a nearby village for a piece of bright cloth and some lamp oil. A few women would not do business with me because I was an effeminate man. Nevertheless, Joel had told the village that my ass was better than the cunt of any woman in Haïti, and most of the women had accepted that I followed the course of love that Erzulie had chosen for me.

3. The white Darkness

All of the *hounfour* had concluded the feast prior to the cere-mony. Fulfilling his function as our *houngan* for the first time in sev-eral months, Joel had directed the *mambo* priestesses to decorate the peristyle. He stood next to the *poteau-mitan*, where Baron Samedi would enter our world. An altar was elaborately laden with sacred items, candles, vaudou flags, a satin heart, clay figurines of roosters, pigs, dogs, and people, and symbolic items related to the Baron like a bottle of rum, a cigar, a top hat, and a walking stick.

Silently, Joel traced Papa Legba's *vévé* on the ground with corn-meal so Legba could open the doorway between eternity and space and time. Then he traced the *vévé* of Baron Samedi and the purified drums commenced. At last, he drew the *vévé* of Erzulie Freda. When Joel shook his sacred rattle, the *mambo* and the *hounsi* began the *vaudou* dance.

"Jean has been touched by the spirit of Erzulie Freda," said Joel. *"Pi belfl e ce' qui pique 'ou.* In the words of the *blancs*, he is gay. In the eyes of the religions of the *blancs*, not to be tolerated. But in *vaudou*, he is free to be as he wishes. The *vaudou* religion welcomes the homosexual."

The drums beat with increasing intensity as the dance grew more frenzied and the fire next to them grew. Joel filled his mouth with rum and sprayed the dancers.

"There is a great serpent. He is Damballa, and his coils are the cosmos. One day Damballa saw Ayida Wedo, and the beauty of the rainbow so overthrew him that he sprayed his seed across the sky. Look up! See the great Milky Way. You see the semen of Damballa. Look around you. We are the seed of Damballa. We are the children of the serpent and the rainbow."

He again sprayed the people dancing around the fire pit. A mambo leaped barefoot into the flames and danced, but the fire burned her not. The *loa* were coming down the *poteau-mitan*.

"See Jean," droned the houngan. "He is a son of the serpent. And Erzulie Freda has claimed him for her own."

I leaped up and danced with the *hounsi*. The drums rang through northern Haitian mountains, not our drums alone but the answering drums from a thousand other villages, mingled with the shrill of the wind blowing over the denuded hills and the barking of the dogs.

Then reality twisted inside of me; Erzulie Freda possessed me. The goddess mounted me and I entered the white darkness, and thenceforth through the long ceremony I knew not what I did.

4. when one black man hurts another, god laughs

The sound of Joel's voice was making me sick and there was a funny taste in my mouth. "You sat astride every one of the male *hounsi*," he complained. "You dropped your pants and your took them in your ass and rode them before the entire village."

"I don't remember," I said. "Erzulie Freda had my body."

I sat before the sheet of polished tin that we used for a mirror. My hair was turning red. It was also growing fast. I glanced at my fingernails, which were significantly longer than they had been the previous day.

Joel was still running on about my supposed sexual lasciviousness.

"I thought that sexual intercourse was approved when the gods mount you," I protested.

Joel bit his lip. "Yes, but you behaved like a whore." He was jealous. *"Le neg fe neg, Bondye ri."*

"Joel, look at me," I shouted.

He turned, stunned, and looked into my eyes.

"Your eyes are growing gold, Jean," he said with a shaking voice.

"Help me," I pleaded, and held up my fingers before his eyes. "See my nails. I'm turning into a *mauvais nanm*."

Green chameleons scurried backward in color while the corn in our field grew against time.

"Joel, help me."

Joel stood frozen, a cold dew leaking from his forehead. Abruptly he turned and ran out of our house. I sat before the mirror for a half minute and the room changed before my eyes. I could see clearly where the house had always sat in dim light. I saw the lizards crawling in the rafters, the worms beneath our dirt floor, and the chickens pecking at roaches outside. I could hear people breathing around me, and snatches of conversation came to my ears. But most important, I could hear and smell the blood singing in people's veins, their hearts pumping the hot ebb and flow of the life of the flesh.

I ran out of the house and I saw that Joel was alerting the village against me. My hair seemed to grow even longer as I ran. It had turned fiery red, and hung long and straight down my back.

I stopped and pleaded to my lover, "Help me. Help me, Joel."

"The *loa* have failed," Joel shouted. "Hack him to pieces and we'll burn every part."

I couldn't believe that he had turned against me and my own village was preparing for my destruction. People were gathering their machetes and hoes, and several lit torches. I could smell the semen churning in the men's balls, and I caught a whiff of rectum. I raced into the cemetery where the *baka* still perched upon my parents' ornate mausoleum.

The village was after me in earnest by then, and the *baka* seemed to call me. Somehow, I felt safer with the evil spirit than I had with the people I'd known all my life. But the *baka* was nowhere to be seen when I reached the high tomb of my family. Leaning against the blue concrete was a silver bicycle.

I had never ridden a bicycle, but I had seen it done. I touched my bare foot to the pedal and swung my leg over. A shock of evil reverberated into my bowels when my ass touched the seat and I lifted my other foot from the ground and coasted down the mountain toward my own village.

My village stood transfixed as they witnessed my approach. *"Mauvais nanm,"* a child hissed.

"Jean ap monte bisiklèt," Francine screamed.

An eldritch shriek escaped my unbidden mouth as I approached the crowd, and they threw down their implements and scattered. Joel swiped at me with a flaming torch, but I grabbed the burning end and tossed it toward our house. It landed on our frond-thatched roof, and our home, where so many nights Joel had mastered my body with his strong embrace, exploded into flame.

Within seconds I was through the village and madly clattering down the road, my bicycle-*baka*'s wheels swiftly carrying me to my fate.

5. Emmanuel, Devourer of Souls

Silver rainbows rose from the waterfall and hung in the midst. The vampires lay upon the warm earth near the cascade, caught in one another's arms, making love man-to-man. Black men with long red hair stretched naked in the pleasant shade of the mapou trees and drank deeply from one another's bodies. Around them stood pines, ferns, orchids, hibiscus, and bougainvillea, while caimans, flamingos, and egrets fished in the water of the pool beneath the fall. Small tropical birds chattered in the trees.

My bicycle had brought me to this hallowed place. I had only ridden the bicycle-*baka* where it led me. Upon our arrival it shapeshifted to its natural state, a red-eyed dwarf who ran to join his fellows. Emmanuel rose from the arms of another vampire, his penis erect and slick with love's juices. I felt a twitching in my own crotch as he approached me, and I looked down to see my own cock rising to meet that of the *Bocor* of the Vampires.

"Welcome, Jean, to *Le Culte des Morts*," quoth he.

I stood virtually speechless and gazed at him with wonder. I hadn't been able to see him clearly when he first attacked me, but now I saw that he was the most desirable male I'd ever seen. His body was perfectly formed with an almost feminine beauty—albeit belied by his thick black penis that stood so temptingly erect before me.

Without considering the cost, I dropped to my knees before him and tasted his slick wand. It was the first time I'd sucked the manly part, for Joel had not approved of it. I reached for his protrusive derrière: so firm, so rounded, and so enticing beneath my hands. As I caressed his ass, I fed upon him until he filled my mouth with love's juice mingled with vampire blood. I swallowed and fully entered his world.

My senses had already been heightened, but they suddenly became extraordinary. I could see into the deepest heart of things, hear all the inner workings of the human body, smell every individual living thing—be it tree, rabbit, or man—taste the faint traces of semen and blood in my mouth, and feel the wanton lust of my new companions.

I embraced my sensuality for the first time. I realized that I had suppressed my true nature—my entire life had been one of self-repression. Yes, I had been a confirmed homosexual, but only as Joel's object and subject to his dictates, which made me like his woman rather than a true male. As I stood again by Emmanuel and watched the beautiful young men sucking, licking, and fucking in every way imaginable, I felt a powerful bloodlust and sexual aggression coursing through me.

"You feel it now, Jean," Emmanuel said. "You feel the life of the vampire. Debauched. Lascivious. We are lecherous toward the living male, and licentious among ourselves. The Christian priests call us lustful, depraved, and dissolute, but they are blind to the truth that extends far beyond their pathetic imaginations, however lewd. We are wanton in our homosexuality, and profligate with our waste of life. And now you are fully with us, sharing in our lusts."

"I didn't die. Not like young Joseph and Paul."

"We each eat our shroud in our own way," Emmanuel said. "Those children will eventually dig out from beneath that slab your village erected over them. They will join a group of the young, where they will be nurtured until they have matured and can participate in the revelries of our *culte*."

"Vampires age?"

"We can control our aging and stop it altogether when it suits us."

My eyes wandered toward the continuous orgy taking place on the nearby ground. Every fiber of my being urged me to join the happy throng in pursuit of oral and anal bliss. Emmanuel's golden eyes glinted; he could smell my urges.

"Come, Jean," he invited, his breathing words becoming my own burning thoughts. "Join the communion of your race." He took my hand and led me toward the group. "Toss away those peasant rags," he said, pointing at my clothing. "Henceforth, you will dress as we dress, and all men will desire you."

When I threw off my human clothing, all the beautiful young

men rose from their revels and compassed me hard. I saw that my hair had turned fully as red as theirs and my body was changing. I'd always been shapely, but my body hardened and tightened. My muscles had grown in the past few minutes, and when I caught my reflection in a calm pool I saw that I was beautiful.

I heard many names, more than I can recite, and my new companions led me naked into the pool. They bathed my body under the waterfall sacred to so many, but to me no longer. I felt that my soul had separated from the *loa,* Papa Legba, the Baron, Papa Zaca, and the beautiful Erzulie Freda, and I had become like the gods themselves. I had truly tasted the fruit of the tree of knowledge of good and evil and found it delicious.

When the vampires had washed my entire body, and I stood beneath the cool water, refreshed and burning, burning with chill desire and freezing with wondrous strange lust, Emmanuel came to me again. I looked at his firm ebony body, tantalizing with curves and protuberance, and desired him above all others.

"You were the sex object of the *houngan?*" he asked. "His fuck-butt?"

"Yes," I said. "That's all I was to Joel."

His hands caressed my chest, slid over my shoulders, and down my arms. Then he moved to my waist and his hands glided over my buttocks. Abruptly I realized that I was free to touch him as well, and I pushed my face toward his. My mouth met his mouth, and our tongues warred for mastery. We kissed long and deeply, and I found my hands roaming over his body and exploring his cleft.

"You would have me?" he asked.

"Yes," I agreed. I had changed.

He turned his back to me and stuck out his ass. "Then, take it, Jean. Now you are both slave and master, and you give and take as you desire."

I took him then and there, beneath the silver mist of the cascading water, and he opened his body to me gleefully, and the way was hot and slick already, so I joined with him and delivered up the last of my humanity. When I was spent and gasping, a new lust was already kindling within me. I gave myself to him then, and received his vampire's seed within my flesh. At last, filled and drained, we stood in mad embrace, our bodies burning beneath the chill falling water.

When we returned to the shore I saw that vampires were raiding the trees for food. Great banana stalks gave of their sweet crop, and the vampire *negs* plucked breadfruit, avocado, papaya, and mango from trees and threw the heady fruits to their fellows.

"I thought that vampires didn't eat," I said. "Except for blood."

Emmanuel laughed. "They tell many lies about us, and the fantasies of the *blancs* are the worst. Dracula and his ilk! Faugh!" He shook his head in disgust. "Yes, we eat. In fact, vampires can eat anything, but we prefer sweet things. We can live without blood, but we prefer not. Though semen is better than blood. Come, Jean, join your tribe."

I sat down with the vampires and did not feel out of place. Indeed, I sensed an immediate kinship with these fellows, as if we were already privy to one another's innermost secrets, and from them there was nothing I need hide, and shame had flown away.

6. The serpent's son

Then I was wearing the silver bicycle shorts, and mounted upon my bicycle-*baka* to ride with the flock. We pedaled into rural villages far removed from Port-au-Prince. We burst past clumps of palmetto and swaying palm fronds and sampled the blood of their men, young and old. My first kill was an attractive 22-year-old. He had been standing with his back to us in a dirt road, confused about why his friends were running away. He was wearing nothing but thin blue cotton shorts supplied by some American missionary, and I seized him and threw him across my bicycle as I rode.

My own strength amazed me. I held the *neg* as if he were a feather, pulled down his shorts, and sunk my fangs into his right buttock. My fellow vampires urged me on as the delicious blood filled my mouth. When I had drunk deeply, I turned the dying *neg* and drained his cock of its nectar. He died of blood loss in the act of ejaculation, and his corpse bore a smile on its dead face as I tossed it into the tree ferns. I would remember him, and he would be mine to love again when he arose from his grave and joined *Le Culte des Morts*.

We cut a killing swath across southern Haïti from Lake Miragoâne to the Fampadra Mountain near Jérémie, and created a new brood of our race. We lived for a year along the Rivière Glace, consuming the natural resources and enjoying sexual bliss with one another. The *mauvais nanm* has an infinite capacity for pleasure; thus we made love all day and flew during the night.

Emmanuel taught me how to fly, and I'll never forget my first voyage across the sky, streaking like a shooting star until the world news reported mysterious meteor showers raining upon Haïti. We could fly during the daylight hours too, but the night was better.

Emmanuel and I lifted from the damp earth and swiftly rose with the buffeting winds. When I had mastered the basic tricks of flying and alighting my bare feet upon the ground, we arose together into the clouds and sported upon the wind. We kissed atop a cloud bank, and Emmanuel's clawed hand stroked my cock. It was bliss, and I grasped his thick shaft and worried it with my grip. Then like Damballa seeing the rainbow for the first time, our essence sprayed far in the rarefied air until our seed fell upon the earth far below.

Eventually our flock drifted back north, and after raiding the darkling plains of the Artibonite, we skirted the desert lands east of Gonaïves, where the ground was nothing but sand and the cactus grew to twice the height of a *neg*. There, the lightning hit and rolled in balls of fire, so we came to the mountains again. At length, we found ourselves near my village. Time and pleasure had erased my nostalgia, and I felt no sense of home when we rolled down the mountainside.

Again, there were the children hissing *mauvais nanm* from the old apple trees, and the white goats scurrying, and the terrible cemetery where my parents' bones waited for a resurrection that would never come.

I felt the minds of everyone in the village as we passed beneath the apple trees. Old Ernst Nord, the concrete pourer, had died, and Francine Marcelin had thrown out her lazy husband and taken a lover. Joel Alexis had a new lover too—Claude, a young man from a nearby village, happily serving for the *houngan*'s pleasure, a task that I had once relished.

But Joel had rejected me when I needed him. He blamed me when his *vaudou* magic failed. I turned toward Joel, who stood before the drawn shutters of his new house. He seemed to be guarding his door.

"*Ti chen gen fos devan kay met li,*" I jibed and cast Joel aside, bruised but unbitten.

"I am the master of my home," he shrieked.

"No longer, Joel." I rushed into the little house and found Claude stretched facedown and naked upon the sleeping mat.

I sat down beside him and stroked his pretty form, black as jet, sweet with love's juices.

"Aren't you tired of him pinching your ears while he humps you?" I said. "You should enjoy the pleasure as well."

Claude moaned but did not speak. Determined to end his terror, I sunk my fangs into the young man and drank deep—but not too deep. He was beautiful and I saw no reason to make him eat his shroud. Like me, he would pass living into our world. Then I threw Claude across the bar of my bicycle, joined my fellow vampires, and carried my new lover's unconscious form out of Joel's life forever. I eagerly anticipated training this young vampire. I could foresee days of rapture as he learned to cherish the life from which there is no parting.

Haitian Glossary

Ayida Wedo The beautiful spirit of the rainbow, Ayida and Damballa combined portray cosmic sexual totality—the world egg of the serpent and the rainbow.

Baka A dangerous spirit, often represented as a small animal or a dwarf and marked with red eyes that can do the work of sorcery.

Proof exists that these demons can assume the shape and function of bicycles, as evidenced by Murat Brierre's iron sculpture *Modern Vampire* and in Harold Courlander's book *The Drum and the Hoe*.

Blanc A white person; a non-Haïtian.

Bocor A type of *houngan* who practices evil magic.

Coumbite In rural Haïti, families and individuals join together to perform time-consuming tasks. The *coumbite* might work in one farmer's field one day, another farmer's the next, and build a house for a new couple on the next. A *coumbite* consists of not just laborers but also drummers and other musicians.

Le Culte des Morts The dark side of Haïtian spirituality.

Damballa He is the serpent of the sky, though he is often worshipped near earthly springs and rivers. One of the most ancient of the *loa*, he is associated with creativity, dynamic character, peaceful detachment, and quiet wisdom; he is origin of the writhing movement of living things.

Erzulie The *loa* of love and luxury, Erzulie Freda is the patron of homosexual men. However, Erzulie is feminine; she is known to be flirtatious, possessive, an extravagant mistress, fabulously rich, beautiful, divine, and material. She is the great mother who gives "man's myth of life its meaning." According to Maya Deren's film *Divine Horsemen: The Living Gods of Haïti*, Erzulie enjoys "exclusive title to that which distinguishes humans from all other forms." She represents the human "capacity to conceive beyond reality, to desire beyond adequacy, to create beyond need."

Gourde A unit of currency.

Hounfour This word describes the *houngan's* ceremonial location, his parish, if you will, including its paraphernalia and its society—the people who worship there.

Houngan A *vaudou* priest is a shaman initiated by other *houngans*, and he presides over the ceremony and the spiritual—and most material—affairs of his *hounfour*.

Hounsis Students or apprentices of the *houngan* or *mambo*.

Jean ap monte bisiklèt "Jean is riding a bicycle."

Le neg fe neg, Bondye ri "When one black man hurts another, God laughs." An interesting comment on this proverb is provided by Bon Mambo Racine Sans Bout Sa Te La Daginen on her "Vodou Page" (www. members.aol.com/racine125).

Papa Legba The *loa* of the crossroads, the opener of ways.

Loa The gods or spirits or sacred ancestors of the *vaudou* pantheon represent the archetypal attributes of nature and psyche. Believers can contact the *loa* directly through ritual, and the *loa* are a constant and intimate part of the believers' daily lives.

Mambo female *Houngans*, the *mambo* are the high priestesses of the *vaudou* religion.

Mauvais nanm These supernatural blood drinkers of Haïti may also be called *mauvais airs*.

Masisi A derogatory term for a homosexual, equivalent to *faggot*.

Neg A Haïtian male.

O kwa, o jibile, Ou pa we m inosan? "Oh, cross! Oh, jubilee! Don't you see I'm innocent?" An appeal for the reclamation of a soul to Baron Samedi as the divine judge.

Peristyle An open-sided worship space that forms the *vaudou* temple. The peristyle generally has a dirt floor, a thatched roof, and a *poteau-mitan*.

Pi belfl e ce' qui pique 'ou "The most beautiful flowers sting the most." A Haïtian proverb about the nature of women.

Poteau-mitan The center pole in a peristyle represents the navel between the real and the spiritual or central axis of the world. The *loa* enter the physical world by climbing down the *poteau-mitan*.

Baron Samedi This Master of the Cemetery and guardian of ancestral knowledge has a nasal voice, carries a stick, swears frequently, and attires himself in black or purple. He is considered the last resort against deaths caused by magic, and he can restore sexual potency.

Ti chen gen fos devan kay met li "A little dog is brave in front of his master's house." Rural Haïtians speak with rich proverbs that befuddle visitors, even people from Port-au-Prince.

Vévé A design the *houngan* traces around the *poteau-mitan* in cornmeal, flour, coffee, brick dust, or ashes. Each *loa's vévé* is unique, embodying the characteristics of the *loa*. When the *houngan* offers the correct salutations, and the offerings are acceptable, the tracing of a *vévé* compels the *loa* to attend.

Vaudou The popular folk religion of Haïti, often referred to as voodoo, is—unlike pulp-fiction portrayals—a positive, nature-oriented religion occupied with healing the sick, dealing with economic and social problems, and bringing harmony to the community. The word *vaudou* (with its variant spellings *voudon*, *voudoun*, *vodun*, etc.) comes from *vòdû* in the language of the Fon people of

Dahomey, meaning "god," "spirit," or "sacred object."

Papa Zaca Sometimes called Azaka, this *loa* dresses in a wide straw hat and peasant attire. He usually has a sack slung across his shoulder. Zaca is the god in charge of agricultural labor and crops.

Zombie A walking corpse, often used as a manual laborer.

Blade and Burn
Alyn Rosselini

The wretched, smiling people made me want to fade into the wall. Sometimes I wonder what their facial expressions feel like. Smiles and laughter in their mouths and eyes prove to be too much for me to bear. I can't shake the feeling. Emptiness resides in the depths of my soul. The loneliness and despair eats away at the fiber of my existence. Sometimes I wish I were dead just so I know what it felt like to be alive.

I've toyed with death, danced around the edges of it with little things here and there. Once I tried to choke myself, but my body wanted to breathe. Another time I tried to stick my head in the bathtub and force my lungs to fill up with water, but my mother walked in on me and ruined the entire experience. Each time I almost made an attempt at suicide I felt the warm glow fill inside the hollowness of my body as if I had accepted Jesus Christ into my life. However, the feeling only brought me deeper into depression.

I watched the happy people around me drinking their coffee and tea and fished the matchstick out of the box and struck it. The flame ignited and my eyes danced along with the light. This little flame had the power to destroy. I could set it on the counter and let the bright orange living and breathing entity spread to the paper, onto the table, and then eventually throughout this entire café, consuming everything in its path with no regard for anyone or anything; absolutely no remorse.

The smoke danced in the air, forming all sorts of undefined shapes. *Sort of like a metaphor of my life.* The thought was too much for me; I dipped my thumb and finger in my mouth to extinguish the miniature flame. For a short while I was in control of my small universe.

"What are you doing?" The dark-haired man with lips lined in black asked, taking the chair directly in front of me. "What's that on your hands?"

From time to time I had seen him come into the coffee shop, but I never paid attention to him. For that matter, I never paid much attention to anyone. The insignificant people around here addressed the fellow as Riggan. My eyes lowered to graze across the raised violent scars as I recoiled away from him. The stories of why I did what I did were mine and mine alone. They were not for me to share with anyone, especially a complete stranger.

"Nothing."

"They look like burn marks combined with razor cuts. Hardly call that nothing. Are you into self-mutilation or something?" Riggan said, trying to find some way to get the conversation rolling.

Whatever he was doing, he needed to stop. Riggan needed to pick himself up from the chair and take himself to another table, preferably to the one on the other side of this horrendous place.

He did not budge, and he stayed put until I gave him an answer. His dark tongue played with his sharp eyetooth, and soon, right before my eyes, he pierced the fleshy muscle. The richest, most colorful crimson droplets spilled from the self-inflicted wound, and for extra effect, he slid the blood-lined tip of his tongue across his black lips. The exquisite shimmer of the liquid that sustained his life softened me. A sense of exhilaration flowed through me; Riggan had hinted that he understood my burning hunger to walk in the shadow of death.

I wanted to walk that path alongside him. No longer did I view him as one of the "others"; he was of my world. The air about him suggested to me that he too was tired of feeling dead. He too want-ed to feel alive. My mind spun in sheer madness as I thought of the many beautiful ways we could explore the darkest aspects of our minds. The excitement grew between my legs, and I shifted myself to adjust my growing cock.

My erection forced me out of my delirium, and I quickly glanced over at the clock on the wall. Time continued to amaze me. The minutes went by fast some days, while on other days dragged on and each passing second felt like an eternity. Today was fast. Without much thought, I scrambled to gather my things and stuffed them in the depths of my pockets. "I need to get going. I'm late and if I don't get there—"

"Late for what?" His eyes shot to a darker shade of blue.

"What? You want me to tell you that I'm late for my psychia-trist appointment?" I could hardly believe this guy was invading my personal space. Didn't he get the message that I wanted nothing to do with him?

"No. Not at all. If you think you can scare me away with this facade that you're crazy, then you're doing a terrible job of it. Listen, why don't you just come up to my place? I've got something that might interest you. It'll be a hell of a lot better than going to some stuffy clinical doctor's office and spilling out your deepest mental problems."

"He can cure me."

Without paying much attention to his reaction, I pulled back the hangnail from my right thumb. Without flinching, I tore away the skin only to leave behind a small drop of blood. The coppery taste lined the tip of my tongue, only a reminder that I was a living being.

"How long have you been going?" Riggan asked, piling up the burned matches in the center of the table.

"Twelve years." I reached into my pocket to find a box of match-es, but it was futile. I need to stop by Save Mart after my "deep introspective" therapy.

"And...you're still haunted by the same demons? I can cure you in just a few minutes. Besides, you'll like what I have to show you."

The invitation was not the least bit enticing. I felt he would be another disappointment, another guy who thought he could get somewhere with a freak. All of my life, people felt it was their duty to step in the path of my self-misery, like they were going to save me and deliver my soul to God on a platter. All of their actions had agendas. For once, just once, I wanted someone to stop trying to save my fucking soul and just talk to me like a human being. I wanted someone to look past the cuts and the burns and have a decent conversation about the weather or some morbid movie they had just seen.

These wishes were never granted. I straightened myself out as if that would get my point across and prepared to turn down the stranger. Somehow, when I looked into his eyes, there was an air of sincerity that made me relent.

"Is your place far?" I asked as we walked down the street that was still wet from the early-morning rains. I know I should have asked more questions, like "How can you cure me?" or "Are you planning on having sex with me to chase away the burning demons that haunt my soul every second of the day?" Or "What is the source of your torment?" I didn't ask a one.

"Not really," he said.

Riggan led me past the condemned buildings and deep into the bowels of the warehouse district. Our strides felt automatic. I would have never ventured out this way with anyone else. This was a seedier part of town that I'd never felt compelled to visit. The city once had every intention of bringing all of this back to life, but it had shifted focus to another part of town and abandoned the plans for renovation. My psychologist's office was so far from here that there was no way I could leave. As I walked on, I envisioned Dr. Eglin pacing around his office, waiting for me.

I struggled to keep my balance on the railroad tracks. There were many fragments of metal missing because people stole and pawned large chunks of track. The broken railroad led to an abandoned train station. It felt like a fractured *Wizard of Oz*, like I would find a little piece of myself if I continued. Once inside, a dank musky smell enveloped me. A sense of life and death hung in a delicate balance in this place. The ceilings were high, and broken lights dangled from tattered chains. Thick, silky cobwebs formed in the corners and on any untouched object. Dust piled against the wooden benches, and a single black glove hung over the railing. Time was preserved here. Life in here was just as is.

I marveled at the faint etchings along the walls and the dilapidated ticket booth. On the board inside was a train schedule. The writing was barely visible, but I managed to read all of the destinations scribbled on the sign. Some of the places were many miles away from here, while others were right around the bend.

"Is this your place?"

"Yeah," Riggan said, sliding the metal door open. "My father owns this building, and his way of telling me to get out of his life was to give me this place along with a nice check every month."

My hands trailed along the walls to check if I could feel subtle changes in the brick wall. "Must be nice to have Daddy hand you everything."

"Sometimes. You never did tell me why you play with matches the way you do."

There were so many answers I could have given him, but instead of going into detail, I just said, "To see if I could feel something."

"And do you?"

"No."

"Why else do you do it?"

"Power and control. It's about the only thing in my life that I can be God-like over. When it comes to being with other men, I can't control them. No matter what I do, they are still entities onto themselves. But each cut I make and each burn mark I inflict feels like a tiny death. When the wounds heal, I feel reborn."

I heard the lock click, and he walked further into the room. I stayed right where I was in case I needed to bolt. The inside of his place was nothing like the decay outside. He must have refurbished everything before he moved in. Still, along the walls I could see traces of the old train station, fighting to reclaim what it had once been.

"Take your clothes off and come to me." He held two unlit torches in his hands. The tips of the torches were wrapped with white gauze.

No man had ever been so commanding toward me. The fluttering feeling in my stomach intensified as I unfastened my shirt buttons. I wasn't going to let it drop, but a strong sense of curiosity made me let go. The material of my silk shirt slipped past my lanky body, and then I stripped off my socks, pants, and underwear.

Thirteen years of scars decorated my flesh. Each slice had a story. Fear surged through me as I waited for his reaction. In some small, morbid way, I hoped that he would accept everything. Usually one look was all it took before the guy was repulsed. Most of them were too disgusted with my marks that they requested that we make love in absolute darkness. A part of me died each time I did this, and it took a long time for me to resurrect. Now, the draft blew past my skin and I shuddered as I waited for his response. Instead of fear, a light of excitement raged through Riggan's eyes.

"I don't know if I want to do this." I stepped out of my clothes. My heart thumped in anticipation of what was to come. Yet, I wanted Riggan to do this to me.

He dismissed my statement and lit the torches with his green lighter. The small flames spread around the tips until each surface was covered with the enigmatic orange glow. A sudden twinge of excitement surged between my legs. It ached as I struggled to contain the urge to reach out and wave my hand over the fire. Then he asked, "Have you ever mixed the two?"

"What do you mean?" I asked, not taking my eyes off the flaming torches as he placed them in their stands. Then he picked a knife off the velvet stand. In one smooth motion the silver blade glided across his thumb and sunk into his flesh. Not once did he flinch.

How automatic it was for me to place my fingers to relieve the intensifying fire between my legs. Feeling warm and sublime, I caressed my cock until I had a slight twinge of pleasure.

"Flames and blades?" He waited for my answer as he licked the blood from the razor-sharp edge, and then he waved the blade over the torch. The effect he wanted from me was already apparent.

"No," I said. Not wanting him to know that I switched to the heat from flames whenever I grew tired of the dull pain from the cuts. Still, it never occurred to me to combine them.

As he spoke, I continued to rub my cock and hoped that I could end the agonizing escalation of euphoria. Relief would not come, so I stopped.

"Don't stop," he whispered.

"Why not?"

Without any warning he approached me from behind, took the blade and, coincidentally, sliced it over the scar where I made my first cut, the one that bit through me like a quick jolt and sent my body reeling through orgasmic pleasure for days. Since then, I've been chasing the white dragon. Memories of the exhilarating feeling surged through me as I embraced the sweetness. Only this time he made the cut deeper, forcing me to my knees.

Riggan allowed me to slide my tongue over the edge coated with my blood. Electrifying feelings tumbled through my entire body. The demons in my head were being silenced, but I knew that it would be short-lived. This was just the tip of the iceberg, because I needed more.

Sensing that my endorphins had reached their zenith, Riggan brought the knife back to my thigh and shoved his hard cock into my ass. The searing pain of the blade sinking into my thigh along with him wielding his entire cock in my hungry flesh sent me into a world of pure ecstasy. While I was blanketed in the pleasure of him fucking me and smearing my snow-white skin with my crimson blood, he took the flaming torch and held it close to my leg.

Never having that big of a flame against me, I trembled in fear as I felt him pound himself inside of my greedy ass. I teetered upon the two worlds of pleasure and pain. My cock throbbed and it tried to expand past its normal capability. Out of desperation for relief, I stroked my cock to match Riggan's rhythm. As our bodies were united, blood seeped from my cuts and soon I felt the warm feel of the torch against the surface of my bloodied flesh, a feeling I'd never experienced.

I gasped at the sheer pleasure of it all: the burning tongues of flames flickering against my skin, the gaping cuts that hurt so much. I needed Riggan to push me over the edge because I was barely there.

As I relished the flame that danced along the surface of my scarred flesh, I was amazed that he didn't burn me outright like I used to. I leaned forward and he ran the torch down the length of my spine all the way down to my buttocks. Only to work it up my back once more, then he asked, "Are you ready for something new?"

"What could possibly top the torches and the cutting?" I wondered out loud.

The answer did not come right away. This felt like a punishment for not immediately answering Riggan at the coffee shop. He set the torch down and then smoothed his large hand over the fleshy part of my shoulder. Too wrapped up in my own private world of pleasure, I was not prepared for what was to come. In one swift movement Riggan bit on my neck and my essence came barreling forth. Silky, clear come lined my hand, but I could not stop. My body jerked and my hips shuddered, but Riggan clasped his muscular arms around me to still my movements. Still, there was something in the depths of me that longed for more. Before I could access what it was exactly that I hungered for, Riggan came into me fast and hard. Soon I milked every drop of come he had to offer.

After it was all over there was no strength left inside of me to stand. I collapsed to the floor, embracing the continuous pleasure streaming through me. Through heavy eyes I watched him walk over to the grill and grab a long slender stick. When he removed it, I saw a bright orange glow in an arrow design. My eyes widened and I squirmed in anticipation. Never had I ever dreamed of branding. Before I could scream in protest, the smell of burning flesh hit my nose and the searing pain shot through me. Then I screamed; not from pain, but from sheer, unadulterated pleasure.

~

Months went by, and still Riggan never answered me when I inquired about his life and how he managed to effectively combine such a thrill for me. But I knew there was something more about him than he let on. His magnetism was strong, because if he did not have it, then he would have never lured me out of the coffee shop.

"This is going to be a lot of fun," he said one night in a singsong voice. The sinister musical tone sent shivers across the surface of my scarred skin.

The light dancing in Riggan's eyes was a mixture of the flames and razor's-edge excitement. Sheer crimson sheets hung down from the metal canopy frame as he watched me writhe around to try to free myself from the ropes he bound around my wrists. Death whispered in the dark corner that was untouched by the rays of the light from the torch.

"Just free me," I pleaded, knowing that he wanted more from me than I could give. "Don't do anything crazy."

Each passing minute with Riggan became dangerous. I was able to handle the light play, but Riggan always wanted to draw out more blood from me. But in some magical way, he was always able to replenish what he took.

"No," he said, his pale white face framed by deep black hair that fell past his slender neck and cascaded down his shoulders. "You said that you wanted to know all of my experiences, both good and bad. For months you pressured me to disclose the mystery behind the flames in my eyes. Those stories about the souls I have trapped in my body. The only reason why you're tied down is to protect you."

Riggan was so beautiful, he had plush lips that I would graze my dagger across and nick just to taste the rich, coppery blood, but he always drew away from me.

A silver dagger with a blade made of encrusted rubies and glazed carnelian grazed past my bare chest that was covered with the various thin scars from our past union. Riggan slinked his wiry body against mine, slipped my hardness inside of his warm vortex, and skillfully moved his hips to allow me to hit all the right places.

The tip of the blade danced along the surface of his rosy nipples and floated like flowers in the middle of a clear pond during the hot summer months. Each drop of sweat beaded out from his pores and looked like the rare diamonds that were only found in the deep bowels of the African coal mine. Riggan smelled like the sweet scent of the black roses that bloomed around my estate in the springtime.

The temptation to free my hands from the ropes that bound me from touching every inch of his body made me wish I had the strength of the Gods. Those curves, full and muscular, drove me to the point of madness.

As he circulated his hips like that of those gypsy belly dancers that stopped to camp near my estate on the night of the full moon, I threw my head back to fight the small fraction of my soul that wanted to mesh with him.

Like all the nights past, Riggan pushed the blade of the dagger as it caught the light of the flames from the torch into the fleshy part of my nipple. My cock impaled the spot where fractions of my soul were taken each night when he would come and devour me. The invisible tug that connected me to him seized me, seized me every time I wanted to end the madness.

Thin red rivulets streamed down my chest as I expanded my lungs. The pain was so sweet. I wondered how he knew to rub his fingers against the fresh cut, manipulating and intensifying the pleasurable feelings that shot down to the core of my cock.

"Cut me again," I begged, hoping Riggan would aim for the place where he made his first cut on me. A new cut on top of a fresh cut was the best form of his love that he could express to me.

As Riggan decorated my chest with violent cuts, the muscles of his experienced hand milked my cock of every drop I had to offer. Once he finished his task, his voluptuous body moved past the sweat of my flesh intertwined with my blood and he straddled my face. A space no more than six inches stood between his hardened cock and a mouth filled with nothing but pure hunger. Riggan presented a nicely shaved display of his perfect, immortal gems and the delectable musky perfume of our union wafted around my nose.

With his hand he pulled up the sac that rested between his hard organ.

"Bite down on me," Riggan whispered, running his hands through my thick brown hair. "Break past the layer of skin and finally get to know me. Expose all of my secrets that you have been wanting to know."

"You want me to what?"

"Now." Riggan lowered himself down to where I could reach him. The fluids of our union dripped down on me as I opened my mouth to embrace our sweet and salty taste. "Free me from the hell that torments my mind. Cristobal, you're the only one who can do this for me. Each night I go and feast on the flesh of young virgins, draining their souls through their nocturnal emissions. It's far too much for me to bear. Make my experiences yours as well. No longer do I want to do this alone."

"Riggan. As much as I want to relieve you of this torment, you must know that I have my own demons to deal with…"

In one motion, he took the ruby-and-carnelian encrusted dagger and sliced his frenum. Blood combined with my semen as it rushed to form a large liquid mass. Ever so slowly, the drops of blood spilled down onto my lips, and my primal nature won out. Tiny corpuscles popped inside every fiber of my being as I lapped up the droplets of his inner being.

He was warm and open. In gratitude, I raised my head up from the pillow, my lips stained red, and my ivory weapons bit down on the fleshy part where he had made the cut. A scream of release expelled from him as the sound deafened my ears. Each lap I made to soak up the coveted blood with my tongue made my mind reel back with the colorful and vivid images of his experiences.

The bloodbath of St. Augustine during the times of the Crusaders seized my thoughts like a vise as I heard the earth-shattering screams of pain from thousands of men murdered for unknown reasons. Laughter filled the dark realm of dead bodies. Riggan was so saturated inside that the sweet nectar that sustained the lives of those men seeped out of him.

Another droplet of blood fell against the tip of my tongue, only to stream into the vivid consciousness. Young virgin men, pleading to be pardoned as Riggan forbade it. The beautiful image of Riggan swimming around in the blood of innocents forced my cock upright. Now the pain was too much for me to bear, and my skin felt as if would not accommodate the pleasure.

As the river of his life filled the space in my mouth, I experienced all that he had. Every single tear shed, the laughter that filled his belly, and the love that warmed his heart. I felt his disappointment for the first time his captor caught him and changed him into the predatory vampire he was now, and the first time he was forced to steal the soul of a man he had come to love so long ago. Finally he said, "Bite me again. This time do it and don't let go. I want to feel you in me. For you to be a part of me."

Drunk with pleasurable emotion, I zeroed in on the smooth mound of his round sac that hung down next to his erect cock. I knew I would forever be chasing the white dragon if I bit down on that spot. Riggan creeping into my room at night and forcing me to participate in his twisted blood sex was nothing compared to what I was about to unleash. For a second, I hesitated, wondering if it were him that needed to be tied up. Then my ears drummed of the craving I felt for him built up inside of me, egging me on, luring me to the target.

"Hold on." I tried to fight my burning desire to become him and for him to become me, but the call of the other tales that needed to be told lured my mouth over the smooth surface of my target. The dull ridges of the enamel of my ivory teeth hit the surface of his moist flesh. I bit down, finally breaking past the pink layers, which were pried apart by his fingers. Riggan curled his entire body around my head, forcing me against him as if he wanted to drown my body into his. For there to be some magical way that I could climb into the inner sanctuary of his blood-lined semen sac.

With my teeth anchored into him, my tongue swirled around his swollen sacs so that the blood lined the inside of my mouth: sweet and sublime mixed in with a dash of salt. I made gentle flicks against his pulsating vein and then made light motions in a continuous circle. Riggan uncurled his body and straightened himself out. The gentle hum of a melody echoed around us, and Riggan ripped himself away from me.

Trembling with fear, he asked, "Why are you here?"

The question was not addressed to me, but the sound of the intensified humming melody. An anonymous voice broke through the thin air. "Do you think you can get out of this, my sweet?"

I could not see who was speaking because Riggan's muscular figure blocked my view. Out of sincere concern, I asked Riggan if he was OK.

Again he ignored me, and took the dagger to his chest and carved a Saint Andrew's cross across his abdomen. The cut was a quarter of an inch thick, but it did not affect him. "I would rather die than kill for you. Why don't you find someone else to do your dirty work? It was you who took me and forced me into this world. No longer do I want it. Please release me."

"Never!" The sinister laughter caused the hairs all over my body to stand on end. "You've tried that before. All of these centuries you have tried to evade me, but I will always find you. Take the soul of that man and ingest it, for it is yours to take."

"Don't make me end his life. Please don't make me do it." Salty tears flowed from his eyes as he flipped his hair aside. As he spoke, his hips inched back down to my hard cock and forced me inside of him once more. His sorrow dripped down from his face and onto his blood-stained chest that bore the supposed protection of the divine beings from the heavens above.

The power that the dark being had counteracted any intervention from the angels Riggan had wanted to help him escape. I think the disappointment and the shock that he felt now was nothing new, because the divine entities ignored his cries the night he was transformed into this soul-stealing vampire.

A stream of dark howling, like the coyotes do at the forest line, filled the chambers. Despite my heart, which palpitated in fear, Riggan continued to lure the climax out of me. For the first time, I felt the sense of calm wave over me as he managed to draw one orgasm after the other out of me. My wrists turned and tugged at the rope in hope of getting him off me, because the feeling was too much for me to handle. Riggan should've given me some time to recover, but he did not relent.

All that I had to give ran dry and I heard the voice again. "Take his soul now!"

"Please understand. I loved you," Riggan cried, but forces beyond his control bade him to do the will of the man draped in black cloth. The dagger was raised above his head and it plunged down into my beating heart. "Please forgive me for doing this to you. For betraying our love like this."

Intense pain filled my body as my soul separated itself from the entire experience. It floated up toward the lure of his deep blue eyes like a gentle leaf in the warm summer wind. As much as I tried to fight my fate, the pull of the forces inside of me drew into the depths of his cock. No longer did I exist in my body with the deep ruddy scars of the blade play we did for many nights. Now, I remained trapped along with the mosaic of emotions from all the souls before me, only to look out through the windows of his eyes.

Hours after he stilled my heart and left my corpse for dead, I watched him creep into the coffee shop. The way the young boy played with his switchblade suggested to me that he was not expecting him. I closed my eyes; I already knew how it was all going to play out. The rest of the souls and myself coursed through his veins, waiting to be infused with the blood of his next meal.

Bring Me the Disco King
David Salcido

Eartha Kitt. They always seem to come back to Eartha Kitt. The old man smiles in spite of himself. Oblivious to his appreciation, the dusky drag queen expertly lip-synchs "My Discarded Men," strutting seductively in gold lamé and batting abnormally long eyelashes at the young men seated inches away at the small cocktail tables ringing her stage area. She's good. They all are tonight, which perfectly explains His presence here at this innocuous little cabaret in uptown Phoenix. He never could resist a good drag show.

Glancing up at the tilted mirror above his head, the old man once again zeroes in on his prey. Seated as he is at the bar, he can watch every move the other Man makes without drawing attention to himself. The cabaret is crowded tonight, every table and booth filled, which means standing room only. This too works in the old man's favor—remaining hidden until he's ready to make his presence known. The mirror was a good idea, though he doubts the engineers had anything but cruising in mind when they installed it.

"Can I get you anything else, sweetie," the bartender, Craig, asks. The old man looks down at the still-full cup of coffee, now gone stone-cold. Craig smiles, flashing white even teeth. He's practiced in his profession, but his blue eyes can't hide the revulsion he feels for this sad, decrepit old fossil taking up space at his bar. "Maybe something a little stronger?"

The old man ponders, then replies, "Cognac. Remy Martin. VSOP."

Craig seems surprised. "We don't get much call for that, honey. One of the *girls* occasionally asks, so we've got some in the back, but it's pretty expensive..."

The old man reaches into his coat pocket and pulls out a wad of bills. Flipping through them, he extricates a 50 and pushes it across the bar. "That should cover it, I think."

Craig, eyebrows in hairline, nods, snatches up the bill, and rolls pretty blue eyes up to pierce sharp gray ones. "And then some. I'll be right back."

The old man sits back to resume his vigil. Around him the crowd erupts in enthusiastic applause for the statuesque drag queen exiting the stage area. The ensuing chaos makes him momentarily lose his prey, but he knows He is still there. Another performer is introduced, the lights begin to pulse to a familiar beat, and the crowd settles back. There, across the small room, seated in a corner booth and surrounded by beautiful young men, sits the Enemy. Staring at Him again, after so long, the old man can't help but grow hard.

Then the music has him. He blinks. Onstage, the new drag queen is dressed in a hot-pink jumpsuit, complete with flared legs and glittery platform boots. Her wig is a huge blond Afro and her eyelashes are sparkling like the rays of a brilliant pink sun. Blaring through the speakers is the unmistakable voice of Alicia Bridges singing "I Love the Nightlife." Unbidden, the memories flutter back in a techno-sexual disco dance ball swirl, bittersweet like acid on a mint wafer.

He is young again, beautiful and full of hope. The music is new and the energy fresh. It's a steamy summer night in 1978 and the Disco King has singled him out. Apparently bored with the harem of gorgeous young men and women. He normally surrounds himself with, the raven-haired god of the dance floor has sent for him, danced with him, bought him drinks, had eyes for only him. And as Alicia belts out those magic words, the Disco

King leans over and says, with a slight Euro-American accent, "I, too, love the nightlife. Are you game?"

Entranced, the young man nods and the pact is made. The rest of the night is a barely remembered swirl of bars, dance clubs, and limousines: beautiful poseurs vying for His attention, soft lips and desperate promises made to ensure that they are included in whatever it is the Disco King has in mind for this hot new acquisition. In the end, however, it's just the two of them, alone. Dancing, dancing, dancing. Naked. They are high above the city in a penthouse apartment. It's all part of a drug- and disco-fueled dream right out of a movie.

And the sex is exquisite: raw and sensuous, primal and exhausting, but romantic as well. Reciting haunting passages from Dryden, Gray, Byron, and Blake, the Disco King touches parts of his soul he never knew existed. Draws feelings and emotions from him in waves, using His voice, His touch, His mesmerizing gaze. Pulls pleasure out through his pores, his eyes, his lips, his cock. The Disco King devours him, leaving no inch of his body unexplored, no part of his mind unexposed. Orgasms are wrenched from him, more than he ever thought possible in one night, wringing him out until finally he collapses into blissful, dreamless sleep. From which he awakens into horror...

"Here you go, sweetie." Craig sets the snifter down on the bar, shattering the old man's reverie. He turns to stare at the bartender, temporarily disoriented. "She's pretty good, isn't she?" Craig says, nodding in the direction of the stage.

The old man closes his eyes and shakes his head. When he opens them again, they are focused, sharp, piercing. "Yes," he says. "She is...delightful."

Craig nods. "One of the best in the city. You picked a good night to visit us here at Winks. How long will you be in town?"

It's an assumption on the bartender's part, an attempt to gain information. The old man has not said more than a few words all evening. He lifts the snifter, takes a small sip, and inhales deeply, imagining the fire coursing through his body. Then the memory fades and he is left empty again. Wanting. His eyes fall on Craig. The bartender is patiently waiting for an answer.

"My business here is almost concluded."

Craig smiles. "Too bad. Phoenix has a lot to offer these days." He winks, knowingly. "If you know where to look."

"So I've discovered."

The bartender nods, then his attention is drawn away by another patron and the old man is left alone again in a sea of hunger. He sits back in his chair. The feeling of desperation is palpable to him, but he can't remember what that hunger feels like, can't remember much about what it's like to feel anything, anymore—except hatred. Looking up at the mirror, he focuses on the object of his obsession: the Disco King—the vampire who transformed him into...this. Tiredly, he lets his eyes wander across the mirror to the empty seat he now occupies.

It's been 25 years since he's seen his reflection: both a blessing and a curse. If he has to be what he is, after all, best to be spared the constant reminders a mirror might bring. He's never seen the wretched bag of bones other people see when they look at him. But he can see his hands and the rest of his emaciated body—the skeletal remains, stretched over with parchment. To the average eye he must look to be in his 80s or older. Inside, he's only 45— still young, by some standards. But youth is something that was denied him long ago, stolen from him in one brief night of ecstasy on a sultry summer night in 1978.

He looks up again, piercing the gloom to stare angrily at the raven-haired beauty holding court in the corner booth. The supreme irony of the situation brings an unfamiliar sourness to his mouth. Ironic that it is He, the vampire, who is visible in the mirror, rather than his victim. The old man hadn't expected that, figuring that if he had no reflection, it would only stand to reason that the creature that did this to him would also be so afflicted. It infuriates him to discover otherwise, but there sits the proof, still so young and vibrant, still desirable and full of energy—energy stolen from others, leaving behind a long trail of mysterious disappearances, emaciated corpses, and unanswered questions.

Why he himself is still here is a mystery to the old man. All the other victims had been dead when the creature had finished with them. Drained of all life. Not blood, as might be expected, if one were to believe the old myths. Rather, they had lost their essence, their spark. Why he himself was spared the finality of death, even after all these years, is beyond him. All he knows is that for a quarter of a century he's been trailing this abomination with nothing but questionable memories of a Man he only briefly knew to guide him. Watching television, reading newspapers, and studying scandal sheets, he was waiting for the next piece of the puzzle to fall into place, bringing him one step closer to an answer.

It's a trial that has grown cold so many times that the old man has known fear. More than once he has lost track of his prey— never for long, though. The creature didn't feed often, but it did need to feed. Every five years or so was all it took, plenty of time for trails to fade. But even the coldest of trails pulse with expectancy when you've been left with nothing but obsession to keep you alive. And it was always just a matter of time.

In fact, it was pure luck that had led him here to Phoenix. The fiend had gotten sloppy. Always, in the past, foul play was logically suspected when a young man disappeared. No clues could be found as to the reasons for the disappearance, but it was always pointed out that the victim in question had been "beautiful and full of life." They always had so much to live for, held so much promise, and friends and family always keenly felt their disappearances. Still, with no real leads, and no body to confirm the allegations of foul play, the case would be filed away. *Case closed—so sorry. It's just another mystery to puzzle over.*

But the last one had been different. The last victim had been preparing for a trip. And, for the first time since this nightmare had begun for the old man, the creature had gone against form and taken advantage of His victim's plans. It was doubtful if anyone even suspected foul play in His last assault. The young man simply flew away to Phoenix, as expected, and had yet to resurface. Not that unusual in these troubled times. Everyone was looking for an escape of some sort, and it wasn't like he had left that much in Portland to draw him back.

Eight months later, after studying familiar patterns and following one false lead after another, the old man found himself here, in a claustrophobic drag bar, so close to his prey that he could taste the eventual finality of his 25 years in purgatory. In reality, the old man hadn't tasted anything in decades. Couldn't taste anything, couldn't feel anything, merely existed, without dreams, without desires, without any of those things that sustained a normal human being. He was empty. A husk. A living scarecrow who was driven by vengeance. He was death for the deathless. And tonight would be his night.

Taking another sip at the tasteless amber liquid, the old man studies his prey. A beautiful blond boy is whispering something into His ear, eliciting laughter. The Disco King is so relaxed, so comfortable, so fresh. He wouldn't have to feed for another four years or so. He has all the time in the world. This is just one stop among many in His endless quest for meaningless pleasure and hedonistic thrills. So it comes as no surprise when He takes the blond boy by the hand and, gently prodding others out of His way, exits the booth.

The old man watches as concerned friends first question, then smile knowingly at Him as he passes. *This won't take long,* he can almost hear the Disco King saying. No need for alarm, He isn't deserting His admirers, just taking care of business. The boys in the booth chatter happily and return their attention to the show, whispering among themselves and watching as He and the blond boy make their way toward the back exit. None notice the decrepit old man who follows in the Disco King's wake.

~

The Disco King's head is thrown back in the languid buildup to sexual release when the old man enters the back alley. On his knees at His feet is the beautiful blond boy, eagerly devouring His sizable organ. For a moment the old man hesitates, eyes intent on the familiar dimensions of the gorgeous cock being licked and slobbered over by the young hustler's expert mouth.

The look of ecstasy on the boy's face is to be expected, for the

Disco King's cock is not only flawless in every detail, but such is the Man's glamour that the taste and smell of His flesh defies description. Like an aphrodisiac, the musk He emits envelopes the senses, heightening the experience beyond mere elicit coupling. It becomes something more, something beyond carnal, something intensely satisfying and fulfilling, something akin to a religious experience.

The young man is so caught up in the act, in fact, that he never feels the cold dry hand that clutches the nape of his neck, snapping his spine like so much dry kindling. The Disco King's eyes snap open and are razored into awareness by the murderer's burning gray eyes. His mouth drops open, but a clawlike hand wraps itself around His throat and the scream dies before it can escape.

"Remember me, Disco King?" the old man rasps. The look in His eyes says otherwise. "No, I don't suppose you would. It isn't every day that the predator comes face-to-face with long-discarded prey." Without relinquishing the hold he has on the vampire's eyes, the old man pulls the young hustler's slack mouth away from the Disco King—a trail of saliva stretching from glistening cock head to dead, wet lower lip—then tosses the body carelessly aside. Instantly, the free hand returns to wrap around the large spit-slicked organ, stroking it lovingly.

"It's been a long time since I've touched such perfection..."

"P...please..." the Disco King gasps. "Don't—"

"Don't?" the old man asks, leaning forward until he can smell the alcohol on the other's breath. "Don't what? Don't hurt you? Don't kill you? Don't touch you so intimately? Why not? They're all my right. I've waited a long time to do all those things. And more."

The terror in the Disco King's eyes fascinates the old man. He is, after all, an immortal. So long as He continues to feed, He should, it only stands to reason, live forever. The fact that He can know fear, however, is a bonus. It means that He is not impervious to harm. He is, in some way, vulnerable.

"How old are you, Disco King? How long have you been prey-ing on beautiful young men to sustain yourself?" Loosening his grip on the soft white throat, the old man prods Him with a sharp tug on His deflating cock.

The vampire yelps in response. "Why do you keep calling me that?"

"Calling you what?"

"Disco King?"

It's the old man's turn to look surprised. "Why? Because it's the only title I've ever known you by. You took everything from me, but you never told me your name. Just as, I'm sure, you've never told any of your victims your name. Why bother, after all? Why should the butcher give any consideration to...livestock?"

"No." The look in the Disco King's eyes changes, become less afraid and more...pained. "You've got it all wrong."

"Do I? How wrong have I *got* it? Look at me!" A sob catches in the old man's throat, unfamiliar and dry but surprising nonethe-less. "I was once young and beautiful, just like you. I was 20 years old when you robbed me of my youth. You left me behind, just as you have so many others—a withered husk of humanity!" Flecks of foamy spit shower the Disco King's face as the old man rants. "Something to be discovered and disposed of by those whose job it is to discard of the old and the homeless when they die, alone and uncared-for. The only difference is, when you left *me*, I was *still alive!*"

The old man pulls back, shaken. Tears have formed in the Disco King's eyes. Sadness has etched itself into every contour of His beautiful face. "Don't pull that shit on me, vampire. It won't work. I've had a long time to think about this day. I don't know how vulnerable you are, but I've every intention of making you suffer for your sins."

The Disco King closes His eyes, and large wet tears overflow onto His cheeks. "Suffering would be nothing new," He says in His strange Euro-American accent. "Coming from anyone else, those would be idle threats. I've waited a long time for you to come—"

"No tricks!" the old man snarls. "I won't let you rob me of my triumph. Shut up or I'll kill you where you stand!"

The Disco King gives a tired smile. "I'm sure you've figured out by now that I'm not that easily killed..."

Tightening his grip until the vampire's eyes begin to bulge and strangled gasps are all that escape from His throat, the old man leans forward. "Aren't you?"

Wrapping His own hand around the wrist of the older man, the Disco King squeezes until the grip on His throat loosens. The act angers the old man, and he reacts by yanking hard on the fleshy cock in his other hand.

"Please..." the Disco King gasps. "It shouldn't be this way. Tell me your name." His eyes drill pleadingly into the old man's steely grays, and something inside clicks.

Suddenly all the years of anger and spite seem to retreat from the old man, draining away into the warm Phoenix night. The grip he still has on the vampire's throat loosens, and his hand slides downward until he is leaning heavily on the hard, muscular chest. His other hand gently squeezes the flaccid organ one last time and drops away.

"I don't remember my name. You robbed me of that as well."

The Disco King nods. "As did He who came before me."

The old man looks up questioningly into the other's watery eyes. "You can't remember your name either?"

The Disco King shakes his head. "I've used many in my travels, but none are my own. When I take a...consort...I purposely withhold the lie. I believe they deserve that at least. I know it comes as small comfort, especially after so many years have passed, but believe me when I say, I've felt every minute of regret for all the lives I've taken. Even yours."

Anger briefly flares again in the old man's gray eyes, then is replaced by a heaviness he hasn't felt in years. "How would you know, if you can't even remember who I am?"

The Disco King closes his eyes. "New York. Summer. 1978. Studio 54. You were an artist. A photographer." Brilliant otherworldly eyes open, and the old man is transfixed. "You were beautiful then, a perfect specimen. Possessed of an exquisite grace that has never been duplicated by male or female, before or since."

The old man bows his head, and the silence between them becomes palpable. "Please tell me one thing," he finally whispers.

"Anything," the Disco King answers.

The old man's face is a mask of anguish when he raises it again. "Why me? Why did you spare me? Why not kill me like you did all the others?"

The Disco King looks mildly surprised. Then a slight smile twitches at the right side of His beautiful mouth. "I didn't spare you. You spared yourself."

The old man's mouth falls open, but he can't find the words. Thoughts ricochet around in his head like shrapnel, but nothing coherent will emerge from the chaos. Instead he lets his eyes ask the question.

"My consorts are carefully chosen," the Disco King sighs. "I choose them for their vitality, their spark of life, their creativity, and their ambition. To keep me sated, only the best will do. Every once in a great while, one comes along whose spirit is so bright, whose will to live so strong, that he can't be snuffed out, not even by one such as I. When that happens, the victim becomes the predator and the predator the prey. It is all part of the endless cycle. As it has been since the beginning."

The old man's head is bowed again, hanging tiredly, eyes closed. He listens as the words wash over him. He listens, but understanding is slow to dawn.

"Tell me," the Disco King whispers into the night, "how long has it been since you've cried?"

A heavy, soul-rattling sigh. "Too long…"

Placing a finger under the old man's chin, the Disco King raises his head and waits for his eyes to open. The other hand moves to the old man's face. The Disco King wipes at his cheek and lifts wet fingers for him to inspect. "I've waited a long time for you to come, my vengeful lover. Too many centuries have made me weary.

So much so, I thought you might never arrive. But you have and the cycle refreshes itself. You've learned how to sustain yourself, by preying on the weak. You do not want for money, and killing to get it has become second nature to you. You've become the perfect predator, and I your perfect prey. Like you, I was not ready before. I am ready now. Please, do what you came here to do. Release me."

"How?" the old man whispers, unfamiliar feelings muddling his thoughts.

"Take back that which was taken from you." Placing firm, young hands on the old man's bony shoulders, the Disco King now pushes him down onto his knees. Rising up to greet him, the vampire's beautiful cock finds its way to his lips, and the old man takes it into his mouth without hesitation. It is good, so very, very good. The smell, the taste, the incomparable feel of the silky flesh—better than he remembers it being 25 years before. Hungrily, he gives himself over to the urge and concentrates full attention on the Disco King's scepter, suckling from it as though it is the fount of life itself.

~

The statuesque black drag queen is back, this time growling out the Eartha Kitt song "I Want to Be Evil." Looking up into the mirror, the young Man pays brief attention to the deserted beauties growing restless at the Disco King's booth, then lets his gaze fall to the handsome young reflection staring back at Him. Piercing gray eyes study the long-forgotten contours of a vaguely familiar 20-year-old face.

"You're the second person to order this tonight," Craig says, placing a snifter of amber liquid on the bar. "The last guy was sitting right where you are. Weird, huh?"

The young Man smiles. "Yeah. Weird."

Craig cocks his head. "You sure you're old enough?"

"Want to see my ID again?"

The bartender hesitates, caught up in the glamour, then shakes his head. "Nah, that's OK. You're new to town, huh?"

"Just got in."

Craig winks. "Welcome to Phoenix."

Nodding in return, the young Man lifts the snifter to inhale the strong aroma, then takes a small sip and smiles, savoring the fire coursing through His body. It will be years before He feels the hunger creep in upon Him. There is so much to experience in that time, so much to catch up on, so much youth to savor and flesh to conquer.

But first, He thinks to Himself, *I will need a proper name.*

Saul's Shadow
Alexander Renault

Breathing is sacred. Many world religions believe it symbolizes the spirit and our connection to God. Without breath we are nothing, and we return to being nothing more than a handful of ashes thrown on the ground. Without breath we are nothing but dust on a breeze.

Saul has remained a mystery to me. You may find it strange that I can't recall our first meeting. But oh, I do recall our last. Thinking about that moment still sends a shiver through me.

I am a pharmacist. No, I was a pharmacist caught in a strange spell. Go ahead, laugh! All of this is silly from the outside, but I was a modern-day alchemist. I could not cure the way a physician is able to lay his hands upon a body, diagnose illness, and prescribe the proper medications. I swam in a pool much more shallow, but I was still able to heat, melt, and blend substances for any named medication, and a few yet to be named.

Born with a severe case of asthma, breath often eluded me while growing up. Trying to pull enough air into my lungs, I had fits that frightened my poor mother to exhaustion. Sometimes I turned bluish and fainted. Her brow always looked so furrowed in the candlelight by my little bed.

Yes, it is strange that I can no longer recall his face. My mind was blinded by Saul and I could see little else after we first met. I have no knowledge of where he came from or where he was going.

Saul was obviously much older than I, and he always laughed when I asked him his age. He often treated me as though I were a child. I was 26 when we met; I can no longer recall how old I am.

~

When I now think of Saul a heat invades my groin, and that uncommon feeling of a flushed face returns to me. He was not like a brother, because we had no rivalry. He was also not quite a father figure, because those relationships are often filled with scorn. I simply called him Saul, although we were both well aware of the inflection in my voice, the dark reverie, and knew I meant Master.

It is amazing how quickly one can fall under the spell of such a man. At first, a curious enigma, and then the obsession begins. He visits you in your dreams.

~

Saul came into the apothecary several days before the first dream, asking for laudanum. Even though he had no prescription I gave it to him without hesitation.

Before he turned to leave I thought, at first, that he smiled at me, but I could see no teeth, just the edges of his lips curling. I realized only after he was gone that his eyes had a blue spark and betrayed some bastardized affection.

~

The window is open and I can see my breath. I reach for the quilt, the one my mother made for me after her body turned on her but before her mind finally fluttered away like a black dove. I can't move, my wrists are bound, but my legs are free and freezing. My toes are turning blue, so I bend my knees. I feel the cold night air blowing up my night-shirt. I can't see the ceiling because the room is pitch-black, but I can feel those eyes on me moving over my body like rays of heat. I grow fright-ened, weary, and suddenly I make out the pupils, the crystalline pieces of blue. His lips are now wet, his face, his hands move closer, and the enor-mity of his body is suspended over me. The huge erection, the head of his thick cock, grows out of the blackest bush between his crushing thighs. A glistening strand of semen hangs from his piss slit, and I am embarrassed, red, and throbbing. The strand is stretching toward my face. I don't turn my head. I need his poison and take the stream, separating from the bulbous head of his thick cock and dripping into my mouth like the host body of Christ...

I wake covered in perspiration and am surprised when I reach to wipe sweat from my forehead and find my hands unbound.

~

You'd be wrong to believe my life was always abnormal and filled with supernatural intrigue. Is it so hard to think of someone like me living in the sunlight of our Lord's merciful face? That there was a marvelous sheen to my aura, and that I loved and was loved in return?

My wife's name was Sarah; our son, Jacob. I do not wish to divulge the details of their passing, but suffice to know they were both abruptly taken from me.

It was winter, the end of November. An early snow blanketed everything from an unexpected storm. After the strange snowstorm traveled through our small city, the temperature rose and it began to rain. My beloved family melted into the earth with the wet snow.

~

The dreams began in the spring, after I began to emerge from the stupor of my nightmare. Grief over the loss of Sarah and Jacob almost annihilated me.

Beyond recognition my face grew ashen, my hair sticking to my bedding, a swab of dark grease. I lay in bed all day, wondering why on earth she had to take the boy with her. Then again, what did it matter now?

I ate little and could not bear the sun on my face; I'd only go out in the evenings, after I'd emerged from my black chrysalis. The hunger first invaded me when the dreams began their daytime pursuit.

It began as a brush, a lingering hand upon my leg, or fingertips across my chest. There were certain places and times when men could meet in the dark Boston night.

Initially I recalled those moments simply as queer dreams, until my awareness brought me to a place where I could no longer hide. I was hungry for them, and they for me.

~

We met again on the street. I recognized him and felt my heart skip a beat, as though an electric shock entered my chest cavity and bounced around for several seconds before exiting through my perpetually chilly feet.

Yes, he was older than I. Perhaps he was in his mid 50s. The hair peeking out from under his hat was a gorgeous silver, matching his carefully trimmed beard. The man had unruly ringlets of gray hair falling from the back of his hat, just enough to be unfashionable for the time. He would have been nondescript except for the nakedness and intensity of his eyes. They bore into me like slick fingers. The eyelashes were too long and thick for so old a face, while the deep crow's-feet along the sides of his eyes told of advanced years and hardship. Then I heard the chthonic voice like the scratching of gravel underfoot.

"My name is Saul. Excuse me."

He walked around me and held my gaze until he was well past. His animal skin tippet flowed behind him. I think it was fox. It was just after dusk, and his dark clothes faded as he walked into the night.

~

I was well past mourning when the shock and anger began to abate. People in town still looked at me strangely; some went to another pharmacist on the other side of the city. I could read their apprehensive thoughts.

What kind of a man was I? Any man whose wife kills herself and their only child with medicine must be some kind of monster. A demon, perhaps?

As time passed, I cared less and less.

~

The sweat trickled from my underarms, legs, and my back was damp against the white sheet. My face must have been a mask of intense heat. When I looked up at the ceiling I saw Saul's eyes.

My nightshirt was drenched, and I felt hot, like when I almost died of scarlet fever as a child. At least it felt as though I was dying at the time. In my child's stupor I had imagined myself floating to heaven. Now I float elsewhere.

Saul's gaze did not frighten me anymore. I was relaxed in my heat, my thoughts drifting toward wonderment. What time is it? It is the dead of winter, so why am I perspiring?

I was unable to move, but was relieved that my wrists and legs were free. I could not tell if Saul was naked, because the room was dark. All I could see at first were those eyes, then a hand and finger pointing at me. His teeth shined brightly through the blackness, and I could see those thick red lips with arching corners.

It was as though his arm stretched eight or nine feet, the finger coming closer to my face. A sharp fingernail descended, and for a brief moment my anxiety shot through me like an arrow and I feared he would pluck out an eyeball. It would have been so easy for him.

The razor-sharp talon touched the center of my forehead then ran down over my nose. I was finally able to ascertain that he was not hurting me when it moved over my lips. No trickle of blood. Not yet.

As Saul dragged his fingernail down my neck and chest, I felt a strange pressure and heard a horrid ripping sound. I knew I was being disemboweled, but there was no pain, only the feel of his fingernail scraping the inside of my gut. This confused me, even in my stupor.

The monster broke his gaze as he looked down the length of my body. I swallowed hard and was terrified of seeing myself torn apart, my ravaged body opened like a gutted fish. But it was not horror or gore that took my breath away, but my nakedness. The frayed tear down the front of my old cotton nightshirt left me open and stripped. I never felt such exposure, but oddly, I was fully aroused, the head of my cock engorged and my shaft stretched and jutting over my abdomen.

The room began to spin, and I closed my eyes, feeling them roll into the back of my head. There was a great pressure on me, and I could feel that Saul cloaked me with his own naked and thickly haired body, his huge erection pressing against my thigh and belly.

It began as a slight tickle in my hanging testicles, which were against the nest of my bush and the cleft of my thighs. The warmth began to spread behind my sac. My orgasm was building under my perineum, and it felt almost inhuman. How could any mortal feel this?

The heat spread through me like spilled blood on a white carpet, increasing its intensity until my asshole clamped shut like a vice. I was rushing over the edge. Then I felt the agony of Saul's teeth sinking into my neck, like a snake biting into a soft, sleepy rodent. The pain did something to me—I came so hard that I was unable to utter a sound as Saul held me down with what felt like thousands of pounds of dead weight, crushing me into the mattress, his solid hips undulating heavily against me. I could not breathe, and it reminded me of my childhood asthma. It somehow intensified my pleasure.

I slipped out of time and felt like I was coming for 10 solid minutes. My ejaculation was a maelstrom of wet heat. I arched my back violently, further crushing myself against my captor, and I felt my own seed splash across my face as I tasted my own metallic jizz on my swelling, choking tongue.

Near the end of my lustful rush I opened my eyes. There was nothing there. No one. Closing my eyes again, I heard Saul whisper behind my left ear.

"Yes..."

Then I heard a faint laughter that seemed to be coming from outside my window.

~

I am lying on my back on the bed, my legs splayed and tied; I am trapped in a swirling haze as though I was full of poisonous mushrooms.

My wrists feel like they are bleeding strips of cloth that bind me to the headboard. He is here; Saul is smiling at me from overhead. I can see clearly through the darkness now that he is naked, as I am naked. He floats down upon me. I am so cold, and he warms me as he descends. Or does he cool me, his huge erection jabbing into my abdomen? I feel his large, scratchy, callused hands reach under me and firmly squeeze my buttocks. He rips the cloth strips from my ankles, freeing my legs. Then his hands move behind my knees, listing my hips upward. Saul lowers his face beneath me; I feel his slick, hot tongue upon my most private place. I squirm. I am turning inside out as Saul's mouth is pressed hard against me, licking my balls. My mind dives into the blackest waters. I no longer care if this is evil. His tongue moves up inside me, expanding straight up through me so that I can't fathom this moment. He looks up and smiles at me. He moves up onto me, lifting my knees, and then my hole is burning like a match stuck there, a raging torch, as I feel my rectum stretch. I am dying. He looks into my eyes and it is morphine. The tingle of pain leaves me, the sense of violation abandons me to this gutter thing, this vile devil I release. I move my hips against him as he violates my center with increasing thrusts, longer strokes. I feel the head of Saul's cock popping in and out, stabbing me; trying to kill me. I feel the full length of his shaft, his hairy balls banging against me. I hear a wet slapping sound of sweat and funk over and over until I am ready to pass out. His eyes continue their assault upon my mind while his cock destroys the inside of my body, his tongue filling my mouth. The jabs increase until Saul releases an unearthly cry like an animal in pain, my desire now a steaming kettle. Saul crushes what is left of me, his pistol crushing me in the center. Then, without warning, a pleasure rips through the middle of me repeatedly, like ripples flowing from the center of a pond, in slow motion, covering me. I feel his sharpest edge cutting me open as I ejaculate onto myself. My writs are bleeding and I feel Saul pour himself, shoot himself, inside my bowels, the pulsing spasm of this killer's ecstasy.

~

I was not bound when I woke but could tell I had been asleep a long time. Even though the shades were drawn I could hear the street noises below my bedroom window.

Cramping slightly as I rose, I realized my nightshirt was missing. My bottom was tender. Sitting up, I ran my hand over the dried sperm coating my stomach, crusted through my pubic hair.

In the center of my bed was a dark stain that was still wet to the touch: the blood of a new bride.

Osirus
Daniel Ritter

He looked like just another short, scraggly kid: nationality unknown, sitting on the pier in ripped-up jeans and a T-shirt that looked like it was from an Arabic rock concert. I don't know why I gave him a second look at all—not my type—but I did. Maybe it was the shirt—not much call for Arabic in Brazil.

"Got a light, man?" he asked. English, not Spanish, and definitely not a kid's voice.

"Sure," I said. I sat down next to him and got my lighter out. Wish I could say it was a Zippo, but it wasn't. He didn't seem to care one way or another. He put his hand over mine to steady it and sucked as the end of his cigarette started to glow. I took a look at him in the single streetlight and the flame. His skin was too pale to suit him, and his hair was long, the sort of blond that happens to brown hair after a year or two in the sun, and his eyes, I don't know what it was about his eyes. They were hazel with dark brows and lashes, hardly unique, but they grabbed me by the throat and paralyzed me.

A twitch of a smile danced over his lips. "Thanks, man."

I lit up too. I needed it. He said nothing for a minute. I couldn't think of anything to say, but I didn't want to leave. *Attracted* to him isn't the word. Too skinny. But his eyes. Jesus! The tropical air closed around me, trying to get under my clothes.

"Nice night," he said after a while.

"Yeah," I said. I liked the pier at night, when the noise and the crowds had gone. I came out there a lot, but I had never seen anyone else out there before.

"See that?" He pointed at the maze of stars overhead.

"What?" I was winning prizes for repartee, that was for sure. Damn it, I could usually manage to be a bit smoother than this but the heavens in the Southern Hemisphere were still strange to this American Midwestern boy.

"That's Sirius," he said. "Brightest star in the sky. The ancient Egyptians named it after Osirus, who was supposed to have the head of a dog, and they said the summer heat was because of the star. It brought the floods too. When they saw Osirus in the sky, they knew the Nile was about to go ape-shit."

"Oh," I said, still tongue-tied.

"The funny thing," he said, "is that the Dogon people of Mali believed that Sirius had a buddy, an invisible floaty made of a metal never found on Earth. This would be just another mythology, but it turns out that it's true. Sirius, what we see, is actually two stars, and one of them is a white dwarf. Not exactly invisible if you've got a good telescope, but definitely made of a metal unknown on Earth. The thing is, nobody knows if they just believed that since forever or if some dipshit anthropologist told them about it. No way to find out. You just have to take the facts and put them together in a way that makes sense."

He was tripping. That was my first thought, although it didn't fit with his eyes. It relaxed me a bit, although I still had nothing to say.

"I liked the Egyptians better," he said, filling the space left by my silence. "They were an imaginative bunch. They did a fantastic job of weaving myth and fact until you couldn't tell what world you walked in. It was almost seamless. I liked it there," he added. "It was a shitty life in some respects. I mean, if you made it to 40, you were an old man and a lucky bastard, but they had a way of thinking things through that seems to have gotten lost somehow. The difference between then and now...." He shook his head. "I'm not sure it's all an improvement, or maybe it's a trade-off. Yeah, I think it's a trade-off."

Definitely tripping. I liked him. "What's your name?" I asked, pleased that I was contributing something to the conversation.

Something about that struck him as funny. "Call me Wes," he said with a chuckle.

That wasn't the same as actually giving me his name, but I assumed it was short for something long or weird. I held out my hand. "I'm Noah."

His grip was warm and surprisingly strong, even though the hand he gave me might well have been a woman's for size, and the eyes met mine again; just a quick flicker, but I knew then that he wasn't high, and I was suddenly terrified. "Nice to meet you on such a splendid night, Noah." Then both grips were broken and I could breathe again.

"Are you hungry?" I asked. He looked like he must have been.

That was definitely funny. "No, man. You?"

"No."

"Cool. Hey, you know much about the Egyptians?"

"No," I said.

"Let me tell you about Osirus, man. He was the one who brought civilization to the Egyptians and gave them the White Man's Burden. They were supposed to go out and civilize the rest of the world, you know? He was law and order and music and all that shit, which tells you something about how the Egyptians saw music. Anyway, he had this evil brother, Set, who bumped him off and tore him into pieces. Osirus's wife, Isis, got totally bummed, and being a goddess and all, she tracked down the pieces and put him back together. Know how she did it?"

"No." Out of the grip of his eyes, I was convinced again that he was high. He could barely string his ideas together, and yet the picture was so vivid, as if the buzz was contagious.

The corner of his mouth flickered upward. "She sucked him off, man. The kiss of life. My favorite form of raising the dead."

Something about that struck him as funny too, because he laughed but at the same time a delicate, pale finger traced the seam of my jeans from knee to groin, raising buried flames in its wake. I jumped, my cock twitched abruptly to life, then he gave me the eyes, full wattage, and I was helpless. "You like blow jobs?"

"Yes." It came out in a hoarse whisper, and I cleared my throat, fighting for breath. The heat was bearing down on me suddenly, smothering me. "Yes."

"You game?"

No. This wasn't my style, this wasn't my thing, hit-and-run sex in public with someone I didn't know, he was too young, something was badly wrong here, but the rising tide in my jeans wasn't taking "no" for an answer. "Yes."

"She gave me lessons, you know," he said, that small hand covering my crotch, fingers caressing my balls through the denim, "or at least her high priestess did and in those days, that was close enough. You'd think it would be a guy who could suck dick the best, but there was nobody like Isis. She was the master."

He wasn't high, he was mentally ill, but he didn't fumble with button or zipper; they seemed to dissolve under his fingers. "Scared, Noah?"

I nodded, unable to speak or lie.

He eased me back onto the concrete, one hand down my pants and the other stroking my forehead as if I were a sick child. "Don't be. You're perfectly safe with me. There's nobody around for at least 500 yards and they're all staying in the light, but you, you came into the dark and look what you found? Don't be scared, baby, I'm not going to hurt you." He smiled, a brief flash of white teeth in the moonlight, then he bent his head and kissed me.

I howled into his mouth, arched against his hand, reached for him, every fear and hesitation forgotten. He had the key to heaven in there and I wanted it. I thought for a minute that I'd come in his hand, it was that intense, but as the minutes passed I realized that I hadn't, it was just the kiss, a kiss like an orgasm that never seemed to end even when he broke it off to look at me. The eyes were blazing; I was history. "That's better. See? I'm not going to hurt you. Now can I show you what I learned from Isis?"

I nodded.

He bent over me, pulled my jeans down over my ass, and my cock surged in anticipation. He sighed, and I felt the wet tip of a strong, warm tongue kiss me right where the head meets the shaft. I groaned as he hefted my balls in his hand and went to work.

It wasn't a blow job so much as a slow devotion. He kissed me, licked me, his thumb separating my balls, caressing each of them in turn as one finger played with my asshole. Hours seemed to pass before he even took the head into his hot mouth, and I twisted up into his face, tears in my eyes. He let me in inch by miserable inch, and I died a little when my cock hit the back of his throat. For all I knew, he was Isis and I was Osirus, being put back together again by my wife, or was it my sister? I knew the myth, just not well. Or maybe he was Osirus because there was nothing feminine in him in spite of his small size, and I was his. It had never been like this, never I would come and I didn't think I'd survive it, but he grabbed my hand and held on, anchored me, as I shot hard into his mouth, so many stars dancing in front of my eyes that I didn't know if they were open or closed.

"My turn," he said, and there was nothing of the stoner left in him. He rose to his knees, unzipped his jeans, he had nothing on underneath, and his cock rose hard and hungry out of his fly.

I sat up, drawn to it, and he grabbed me by the hair, almost but not quite painfully. "Suck me, Noah," he said, his voice just as hard, and he gave me no time to do anything but open my mouth.

The truth was, even sated, I was still hot for him, and I swallowed him greedily, wanting his taste and his smell. For though he looked unwashed, he had almost no body odor, just the faint musk of his crotch as if he had bathed only minutes ago. He was uncut and I loved the idea of his tender, exposed head at the mercy of my tongue. He moaned, stroked my hair, murmured to me in a language I couldn't even identify, much less understand. I gave him my best, lots of lip and spit and tongue. His body was small but his cock was quite respectable, enough so I had to concentrate hard to take him in all the way, and his balls felt thick and full in my hand. I dug the fingers of my free hand into the crack of his ass and felt the hard muscle flex as he thrust into my mouth. He was a small man but he was strong, nothing on him was wasted. I felt him tense, felt his balls draw up, oh yes, yes.

I risked a glance at him, wanting to see what his come face looked like, and if I hadn't been in the grip of it, I would have run from him. The cords in his neck stood out, power well beyond my own, barely restrained. His eyes were closed, but his teeth were clenched, his face twisted with it, and he looked just then as though he might have gotten lessons from Isis, he looked that ancient. I caught my breath and it was a good thing, because he was coming and I would have choked on it. Instead I closed my eyes and took it—sure I had seen something nobody could see and yet still live.

He let me go and I swallowed, wiping my mouth. His semen tasted faintly metallic. He sat back on his heels and held me, kissing my ear through my hair, and in spite of everything I felt safe in his arms. "Will I see you again?" I asked, not sure which answer would be worse.

He laughed and kissed my mouth. "I don't know," he said. "It's like the Dogon. You have to weigh the evidence and come to your own conclusion." Then he froze me with his eyes, stood, zipped up, and walked off down the pier. By the time I got my wits together, he had vanished.

I went home, but I didn't sleep until dawn.

The following afternoon it occurred to me that I'd just sucked off a total stranger without a condom. I spent six months imagining the worst, seeing a junkie in that lean, spare body, and in those six months I went over that night in my mind until the details were branded on the inside of my skull.

I did some barhopping, but my heart wasn't in it, and it wasn't just my virus anxiety either. Now that they were used to me, I was to the natives what I was to everyone back home, a Ph.D. who had-n't managed to turn it into big money. A failure. That, and Brazil, in spite of more liberal laws than other parts of Latin America, wasn't the easiest place in the world to be gay, and this definitely wasn't Rio. Nothing grabbed me, and I kept my hands to myself. It just didn't seem worth it, not in any sense.

Instead, I spent my time recording the lives and habits of the local parrots, hoping to save them from extinction. The birds, usually nodding acquaintances if not friends, seemed more inclined than usual to bite me. A mama, who usually tolerated my incessant weighing of her offspring with relatively good humor, screeched at me and ripped a three-inch gash into my forearm. It hurt like hell, but instead of being angry, I was grateful. She made me honest; the pain in my arm mirrored the pain inside. I went through life like a zombie, but I never went down to the pier. I didn't dare. Every time I closed my eyes, I saw Wes's.

When I got my test results, I stared at them, stunned. I'd been sure they would be positive, but as I read through the letter over and over again, his voice came back to me. *You're perfectly safe with me. I won't hurt you.*

What had I been afraid of?

That night I went down to the pier. It was winter and the concrete was damp with the day's rain. The clouds chased one another across the moon, but I knew that the Dog Star was nowhere to be seen. Not that time of year, anyway, and I was afraid that Wes, like the Nile, was drawn out by it. I didn't think I'd find him there but sat down anyway, heedless of my jeans, chain-smoking and kicking myself. He hadn't hurt me. In fact, he'd given me the head job of my life. OK, so he was a little loopy, but there was intelligence underneath it; the stories he told were grounded in a solid understanding of both history and myth. In retrospect, his face as he came became something more ordinary, or maybe it was longing that erased the memory of terror. I missed him. I missed his rambling. I missed his skilled wet mouth.

"Hey, man!"

I jumped; nearly fell over as I turned. It was Wes, in what might have been the same jeans but a different T-shirt, this one in

German. His hair had grown out a bit and the roots were dark.

"Hi," I said, stumbling over the word, chills running down my spine. How the fuck had he done that? I hadn't heard a single footstep. "What are you doing here?"

"You called, didn't you?" He sat down beside me and took out a cigarette. This time, he pulled my head around and lit up on my butt, and he looked young again, barely 18. "So I'm here."

I couldn't argue with that because there was nothing to argue with. "Where were you?" I asked.

"Berlin," he said. "Ever been?"

"No," I said.

"Oh, man! You should go. It's a hell of a place."

"Yeah?" During the last six months I'd imagined talking to him, but now that he was here, I was struck dumb. Again. I'd forgotten the fear, the sense that I was in the presence of something dangerous. Time had diluted him in my memory.

"Yeah. I love it. You know, before the Wall fell, it was two separate cities. Now they're trying to mesh and they don't always quite make it. You know what chimeras are, man?"

He was back into his myths. "Weren't they some kind of mixed-up monster?"

"Oh, yeah, but that wasn't what I was thinking of. I was thinking of human chimeras. It's where fraternal twins somehow get all mixed up into the same person. It's, like, the opposite of conjoined twins, where identical twins don't quite separate. Chimeras are even more rare, but you get the DNA of two people in the same body. There was a case recently where a woman gave birth to children who weren't genetically hers, and they found out that her ovaries were someone else's. Anyway, Berlin's like a chimera, you know? They've tried to erase as much of the physical evidence of the DDR as they could, but the culture still exists. You just have to know where to look to find it."

Again, I had nothing to say. Although I'd managed to go below the equator, I had never left the Western Hemisphere.

That was OK. Wes could talk enough for both of us. "It's

amazing. There's a bit of imperial Germany left there, a bit of East Germany, a bit of old West Germany, and then all the new stuff. They've always got new stuff. You lie on top of the Brandenburg Gate and it's like the whole fucking world's going by under you, you know? You should go someday. It's a great place to be gay, man." His half smile grew. "It's all there, everything, and even if you don't speak German, you can manage OK."

"Do you speak German?" I asked.

"Kind of," he said. "The problem is that my German is a few centuries too old. I sound like an asshole when I use it, so I tend to go with English or French. Mine are both within spitting distance of modern and you can get around in either one. I should probably learn modern German, but I'm too damned lazy."

There he went, off again in his own version of the world, but it bothered me less. Just being with him, regardless of the conversation, made me feel again: that mix of fear and anticipation that made every sense go into overdrive. I was itching to get my hands back on him.

"Want to take me home, man?" he asked, flashing me a hint of those astonishing eyes. Again, to him, conversation was foreplay.

"Yes," I said.

"Cool." He rose fluidly, effortlessly, and held out his hand. I took it, and he pulled me up effortlessly, the lean muscle in his forearm bulging.

He was short. He barely came up to my shoulder, and I'm no six-footer. He laced his fingers with mine until we got to the street, but even after he let go, I was hyperaware of him, where he was, where his body heat was. I had forgotten that tremendous energy that radiated out from him, like a magnet pulling me in. Oddly, others barely seemed to notice him. It was if he were invisible to everyone else, and that was fine by me.

I lived in a small apartment in a rathole not far from the pier. It stank of old carpet and somebody else's dogs, but he didn't seem to mind. Instead, he poked his nose into everything, making comments about books, CDs, my computer, and the crippled macaw in the cage by the window. "Hungry?" I asked.

Again, it was funny. "Hell no, man, I've already eaten. Go ahead, though, if you are."

"No," I said. In the light he looked about 15, not 18, and I was starting to panic again. Who the hell was he?

He came to me, put his hands on my shoulders, and looked me squarely in the eyes. The effect was predictable: My knees almost buckled, and what little will I had drained out of me. "Look, Noah," he said, and he didn't sound anything like 15. "I told you before that I wouldn't hurt you. You're perfectly safe with me."

I believed him. It wasn't a question of wanting to or not, I just did. In that state he could have done anything to me and I wouldn't have cared. This tiny wisp of a man pulled my face down to him, opened my mouth with his, and destroyed me.

That heady rush—just like before, unlike anything I had ever felt. No other lover compared. His small, strong hands ran up under my shirt, tweaked my nipples, tugged on the hair on my chest. Under his T-shirt he was a compact bundle of muscle, sinew, and bone—harder, in his own way, than the gym rats I'd slept with. Mostly, I was drunk on him, that bliss, once I let go of fear and doubt. As long as I trusted him, I was happy. "Bed," he whispered, and he led me there, even though it was my place.

Horizontal, the size difference was minimal, and in any case, I had no fear of hurting him. He stripped me with the same expertise he had used that night on the pier, and his mouth went where his hands had already been, sharp teeth capturing my nipples, pinching just enough to hurt. I yelped and he laughed, his tongue kissing me better. I pulled his shirt over his head and marveled at how that lean hairless torso, like a rock star's, could hold so much power. I couldn't see it in him, but I could feel it, waves of strength that washed over me like the ocean. He kept his eyes open as he kissed, and if I risked it I could get lost in them, lost in the ages, all of his history and myth and languages fused into something that burned with an incredible white heat.

I fumbled with his jeans and he slithered out of them, his

erection standing tall and ready, the foreskin still covering him. I reached out, pulled it back, and he sighed, let his head fall, looked almost perfectly human for a moment, then he rolled me to my back and straddled me, let his hard cock fall to mine.

If I'd thought a blow job from him was something, genital contact sent a spark leaping between us that sizzled in sweet agony then burst in my brain and my balls. When I was younger I had experimented with coke, but that rush was nothing like this. My hips bucked, looking for more, and he gave it to me, lowering his body to mine and letting our cocks rub together between our bellies. It was exquisite, and I could have come like that, but each time I started to, he stopped, resting, just kissing me, and I forgot all about orgasm and just kissed him back.

His hand reached back, snaked over my ass. "I want you, Noah," he said.

"Yes," I said, and the fear came back full force. This was a bad idea; he would kill me with it.

"You'll live through the night," he said. "I promise." He reached for the bedside table, for the bottle of lube, then looked me in the eye.

It was exactly what I needed. In those hazel galaxies I forgot my fear, forgot everything but desire, forgot that I even had a name. He eased his way inside and I forgot where I was. There was nothing else in the world that mattered. This was sex the way it was supposed to be, what it was meant to be, what I had been trying for with everyone else and had failed to reach. He slid in both easy and tight, not a breath of space to spare.

As he went into my body, he unleashed the full effect of those astonishing eyes on me, and it was as if a door had opened between our minds, and he went in there too. I don't know what he saw, but I saw eons in him, empires rising and falling like tides; smelled my own sweat and scent; heard the rush of my own lust-fueled blood in my veins, and I knew that it inflamed him. I felt my own skin under his hands, felt my ass clamped tight on his dick.

I knew then that he loved me, love at first sight; he had always been prone to it, especially after he became what he was and could read minds. More than one night he had followed me, learning my routines, even sat at my bedside watching me sleep, and he had set up that first meeting on the pier. It should have freaked me out, but he could also see my secret thoughts and desires, and rather than putting him off, they intrigued him. He didn't see failure in my meager salary and scarred hands. Instead he saw my fascination with the birds, my rejection of my father's avaricious workaholism, he saw wisdom in my caution rather than paranoia, he saw someone he could talk to and he needed that desperately. He would never hurt me, although he had hurt others, some in hideous ways, done without thinking things that were unthinkable. In the grip of it I forgave him, and the rush of his gratitude went straight to the base of my spine and coiled upward. I'd heard of guys who could come just from being fucked, and although I'd never even tried it, I thought it might be possible if he could hold on long enough.

And he did. He kept an even, steady stroke that went on and on forever, his eyes locked with mine. If I'd had a brain cell left, I would have wondered how he had managed to do it, but he just fucked me and watched me, a look of intense concentration on his face. I can't remember if he touched my cock or not, I was that far gone, and when he felt that I was almost there, his teeth flashed in a satisfied smile and he picked up his pace. It was a race now, one that nobody could possibly lose, but we came into the final stretch neck in neck and the whole world exploded inside me as the low murmur of his strange, secret language filled my ears. This time, I understood every word.

I woke up about an hour later to find him still awake, running his hands over my body. I was already hard, and I reached for him. He made a happy sound low in his throat and pulled me close, kissed me, and it was nearly all over before it began again.

The whole night was like that, a drift from sex to dream and back again. Wes, as far as I could tell, never slept. Every time I woke, he was looking at me.

The numbers on the clock got higher and I could feel him disengaging. "Don't go," I said. "I'll make breakfast."

He laughed. "No, man, it's cool. I just gotta go, is all. But thanks for the offer and I wish I could take you up on it."

"I think you should." Now that I had him home, I wanted him to stay.

"Hey, you know how to find me."

Go out on the pier at night? As his hold on me loosened, my fear returned. I had no idea who he was. This was crazy, I was crazy, he was no more than a kid. "Who are you?" I asked, afraid of his answer.

He shook his head. "Five hundred years ago, you would have known the night you met me. Now? I can't tell you. You have to work it out for yourself."

"Please don't go!" I said. I needed to talk to him, get to the bottom of this.

"I have to," he said, disentangling himself from me and getting out of bed.

I reached for him, but he turned his eyes on me and I couldn't move. I couldn't do anything except watch, helpless, as he dressed and turned to go.

"Wait!" I said, pulling the words out one by one. "How do I find you?"

He stood in my bedroom doorway, silhouetted against the light. "You just call. I'll be there." And he was gone.

I curled up under my blankets, shivering in the gray light of early dawn. Every time I got near it, my mind shied away like a frightened horse and had to be coaxed back step by step.

His incredible strength. His eyes. So he didn't go swooping around in black velvets, but who would? He would need to blend in at least a little.

His smile never uncovered the bottoms of his front teeth. Had it been my imagination, or had I felt needle-sharp points on my nipples? I looked; found a tiny, tiny scab.

He had bitten me.

Probably he was one of those guys who thought he was a vampire. Anyway, why would a real vampire want me? A nutjob I could believe. I'd had my share of them already.

Wes wasn't crazy.

He had to be crazy. Normal people didn't go around pretending to be vampires.

People who pretend to be vampires usually make a big fuss about it. They go swooping around in black velvet and too much eyeliner. They don't look like 15-year-old rock stars.

I promise you will live through the night.

Jesus!

OK, so what if he was. Where was he from? How old *was* he? I thought suddenly of the suits of medieval armor I had seen in museums, where the top of the helmets came up to my nose. Those guys were maybe, what, 5 foot 5? I was only 5 foot 8, and Wes was a good six inches shorter than I was. He was beyond short, but he didn't carry himself or behave like a small man.

Perhaps when he was born, he hadn't been.

What if everything he'd said about himself was true?

His German was a few centuries old, but the closest he'd come to dating himself was Egypt, when he said he'd learned to suck from a priestess of Isis. Then we were talking millennia, not centuries.

He was older than Christ.

He was fucking delusional. Or I was.

He thought food was funny. His sperm tasted like copper.

You just have to take the facts and put them together in a way that makes sense.

Did they let just anyone climb the Brandenburg Gate? I hardly thought so.

Something invisible to the naked eye, made of a metal not found on earth. That fit, at least in the sense that he wasn't something anyone from Earth would expect or even see unless they were lucky. Had he been telling me what he was?

What was a vampire? Not the demon things on *Buffy*, I

didn't think. The undead? What the hell did that mean anyway?

What else had he talked about? A chimera, a patchwork of things, not one thing or another. Was that what a vampire was? Or was it his patchwork of culture, language, and myth—not belonging anywhere anymore? If I asked him, would he tell me?

I didn't sleep for the next day and a half. It was another six months before I went out to the pier.

I didn't think it would do any good. I figured he would have forgotten about me by then. After all, I couldn't think why someone like him would care. But Osirus was in the sky, pulling me out as it pulled the Egyptian tides, and six months was enough to drown my terror and doubt in a sort of dull misery, enough to make me realize that there was no other option. No one else would love me like he did, not in any sense.

I sat looking up at the moon, smoking, waiting. Nothing. Hours passed. Around me I heard tropical night sounds, something I never quite got used to, but not his long-missed greeting. Fuck! I had taken too long to make up my mind. He was gone for good.

I got up, tears in my eyes—and he was standing just behind me. I damned near jumped out of my skin.

"Hey, man," he said softly.

I looked down at him. His hair had grown out seriously, and this time his T-shirt was in English, a Scottish punk band. "Why?" I asked. I was no longer afraid. Whatever he was, I was his and I knew it.

He turned the eyes on me. Yes. I was back where I belonged. "Some things don't change," he said, and for the first time I caught a hint of pain in him, something bleak and barren. It broke my heart.

"How old are you?" I asked.

"Not a clue," he said. "It was awhile before I started using a solar calendar, and by then there didn't seem any reason to keep track." His teeth flashed in a grin. Fangs? I couldn't tell. Part of me was still skeptical. Most of me no longer cared. Vampire or lunatic, either one was fine with me. "And don't ask me about the Resurrection," he said. "I was in China at the time. Nobody had the slightest idea that what was going on in Palestine was even remotely relevant."

"What about..." I began, but he put his hand over my mouth.

"There was a guy named Orpheus," he said. "Dude was a killer musician, could play the wild beasts to sleep and all that shit. Anyway, he married this beautiful girl, but she got bit by a snake and died. Orpheus decides this isn't going to work for him, so he goes to the underworld to beg his wife back. He plays so well that Hades agrees on one condition: He can lead her home, but he can't look back. Well, he's walking and walking, but he can't hear anything, or he just isn't sure, and he starts thinking that maybe she's not really there, that it's all a trick. So he turns back to check, and watches as her face dissolves. Not exactly happily ever after, you know?"

I nodded, feeling like a fool. I must have been asking him the same questions he'd been asked for centuries, questions he was probably sick to death of. If I wanted to keep him, I would have to keep my mouth shut.

"The ancient Greeks told pretty stories," he continued, as if this were just another one of his lectures, "but they were real shit-heads, you know? I mean, girls were married off at 15 or 16 to men twice their age who treated them like slaves and prisoners, and it was no fun being a guy either. Really macho culture, worse than Rome. It was a loveless life, unless you were fucking lucky and I wasn't, so I didn't stay long. It was about then that I got curious about what was on the other side of the ocean."

He might not have liked to answer questions, but he liked to talk, and he had his own notions of what was important. He also found something about it sexy, because his hand was creeping over my chest and his smile had taken on a speculative quirk.

"Look," I began, "are you planning on..." The sentence was so absurd that I couldn't finish it.

"Not up to me, man," he said, smiling. "That kind of thing needs full cooperation of the victim."

That was disconcerting. If he really was a vampire, I had some hard decisions to make down the line, and I didn't know what to do. No, I did. I knew exactly what to do. "Want to go home?" I asked.

He stood on tiptoe and kissed me, and I fell happily into that endless well of him. "Yeah, man. Let's go home."

Starlight

Jordan Castillo Price

Blood brought us together.

It was a night like any other night: dark and rich, full of possibility. I had already fed, and so I lingered deep in the park, far off the gravelly trails, watching the stars. I lay on the earth, my long black coat spread beneath me, hands woven together behind my head. They say you can't see the stars in the city, but they're wrong. If you get far enough from the streetlights and peer up between the trees, they're there, countless small lights flecking the indigo-black night sky.

My thoughts flashed red as the smell of blood bloomed nearby, instantly sharpening my senses. I heard a muffled scream, belatedly realizing I approached like a sleepwalker, drawn by the scent of life.

The sounds changed soon, from struggles and screams to tearing and crunching, underscored by a continuous low growl. But the scent of blood grew so strong, so overwhelming as I neared, that I could hardly hear.

I parted black tree boughs and found a small clearing where I saw him for the first time. I'd expected a predator animal of some sort, but he wore the shape of a man instead. Blood, black in the starlight, covered his nude body. Were it daylight, I'm sure the grass around him would have been painted red. But by starlight, I saw only him, his pale, sinuously muscled body dappled with dark, dark blood.

I stood, not even daring to breathe, and watched him feed. I'm not sure how he sensed me, but after a few moments he snapped to an eerie stillness, and then turned. His face was long and pointed, canine; his hands, in silhouette, splayed like great claws. And somehow, even in the shadows, even through my stillness, even in the dark of night, he saw me.

His lips curled and starlight glinted off his fangs. He growled.

The skin prickled up the back of my neck at that sound, but I stood my ground and watched. Stronger and faster than any mortal, I was unaccustomed to actually feeling threatened, practically invulnerable since my change centuries before. But the blood-covered beast before me was easily as magical as I—would I be immune to him as well? Perhaps not. The thought stirred my belly.

His eyes narrowed as he continued to growl, huge gobbets of bloody flesh falling away from his muzzle. His eyes were locked on me, challenging me or warning me away, I don't know. But finally, after a terribly long time, he broke the gaze. I can be still.

He reached down with his peculiarly human hands and shredded what was left of his prey's clothes. A set of keys and an empty beer can clinked against a stone. He grabbed up some other items from the prey's pockets and, in a silvery blur, was gone.

My chase instinct surged—strange, because I wasn't hungry, and yet a longing filled me that felt as sharp as hunger. I paused just long enough to glance at his prey, only partially eaten, belly open, ribs gleaming in the starlight. So different from the way I took my prey, so much more brutal. It intrigued me. Following the scent of fresh kill, I followed him.

Luckily, I'd seen which way he went, though my surprise had made my reactions slow. I put some distance between myself and the prey, and searched instead for the scent of the hunter. I picked up the blood-animal smell of him with little effort, as he was so covered in gore, and yet I marveled at how quickly he must have moved for me not to have overcome him yet. As quickly as me. That strange feeling fluttered in me again, and I stopped for a moment to consider it. Arousal. I stood for just that moment to savor it. It had been so long since I'd felt that.

Once I identified my motives, I pursued him still faster for fear of losing him. His trail snaked into the city, through a business district that slept, and into a poor, grimy neighborhood with warrens of filthy alleys. The smell of garbage nearly blotted him out for a moment, and I wondered again how he could be so incredibly fast. But then I picked up his scent again, noting that it was now less of gore and more of sharp, animalistic sweat.

I charged up a dimly lit street, nearly colliding with a group of smoking teenagers, then realized I'd lost his trail. I backtracked, lingering at the mouth of an alley, and then caught his scent again.

Alley, street, alley, I tracked him carefully, vaulting over tipped garbage cans and hulks of abandoned cars, ducking out of the view of mortals who should have been long asleep in their homes.

And finally, by the flickering light of a television that strobed through a window, I found him in a dead end.

He stood in the alley, man-shaped and clothed how, hands clenching and unclenching at his sides. He must have been there for at least a few moments, I thought, to have dressed, and wiped away the blood. Fast, so fast. My groin stirred along with the pit of my belly, and the sensation baffled me. I could hardly recall the last time I'd thought about sex, let alone responded physically to the notion.

"What are you?" he growled, breaking through my stunned realization.

I wanted to ask him the same thing. I thought I knew, but what was the polite word? I plucked my long coat into place, as it was askew from our chase, and stepped forward. I had to get a better look at him. That meant I had to let him see me.

"I am a blooddrinker," I said. "But my name is Joseph." Well, technically it is Yousef. But I do make some small allowances for modern society.

"A vampire." He stopped clenching his fists. I could see he wasn't totally finished dressing—his combat boots were unlaced, his belt hanging open. My eyes wanted to linger there, and then I decided it was probably rude to stare. I met his eyes. Even in the dimness of the alley, they were pale. Now, in his full man-shape, his hair was moon-pale too.

"And your name?" I asked for his name rather than his...species. To prove a point, I suppose.

He squinted at me, then wrinkled his nose. "Bite me, dead boy." He turned on the ball of one foot, crouched, and leaped. His jump cleared the two-story building that covered the end of the alley. He was gone.

Dawn prevented me from pursuing him further. That, and my own stupefaction.

I found myself back at that alley after sunset. A crumpled towel, stiff with blood, and a bloody, torn wallet marked the spot where I'd last seen him. I lifted the towel to my face. It smelled of old blood, the blood of his prey, but also of his sweat. I tore off a small piece for myself, stroking it between my thumb and forefinger, vowing to find him again.

I searched for weeks, combing the maze of alleys and streets, holding that scrap of fabric and breathing his scent to remind myself why I kept coming back. And just the scent of him became enough to arouse me.

I grew weary of searching for him among the mortals, and the mortals grew wary of me combing their neighborhood night after night. The teenagers tried to buy drugs from me. A police car trailed my wanderings. Frustrated, I returned to my roost and cursed him as the lethargy of daylight closed my eyes.

At sunset I awoke and cursed my own stupidity. I needed to search the parks.

In only two more nights, I found him. If I had been searching with only my eyes, I would have passed him by, but his scent drew me like a beacon. He looked like a regular mortal, sprawled on the park bench in his torn jeans, combat boots, and leather jacket. A fast-food bag lay beside him, and he idly swirled a french fry in a huge red pool of ketchup. "You missed a pretty sunset," he said to me around a mouthful of fries. He stared straight ahead, not turning to meet my eyes, and chewed with his mouth open.

I cursed the fact that no pithy retort would spring to mind because I could do nothing but rake the curve of his body with my eyes. I could see his profile clearly now, young and sharp, with a strong jaw and high cheekbones. He was perhaps a bit older than I was when I was turned, but probably less than 30. If he aged as mortals do. It was a strong face. Not classically handsome. Impertinent.

Then he swiveled his head to stare back at me, and oh, but he didn't move anything like a mortal, and I was rock-hard for him and my breaths were coming fast. His eyes were the palest amber.

"Well, Vampire Joe?" he said. "Whaddya want with me?"

"You still haven't told me your name."

He cocked his head to one side and regarded me, then dragged a fingertip through the ketchup and licked the thick redness off, eyes locked on mine. My teeth ached. Did he know what he was doing to me? Could he see it? Smell it? I stood statue-still. Surely he couldn't know.

"It's Danny."

My eyes followed his finger back to the ketchup, and again to his mouth. His tongue snaked out to swirl it. An image of shredded clothing and starlight on pale flesh flashed in my mind's eye.

"And you can eat...that?"

He glanced down at the crumpled wrappers, then looked back at me and smirked. "It's not filet mignon, but it'll do." He crumpled the ketchup-smeared papers in a ball and lobbed them at a nearby trash can, missing.

"May I join you?" I gestured to the bench.

He stared at me, blond eyebrows pulled together in a quizzical V. "Why?"

Mortals flocked to me like iron shavings to a lodestone, but this creature seemed quite immune to whatever charms mortals saw. And so of course I wanted him all the more.

"Don't you wonder?" I left it at that, to let him fill in the blanks. How we are different, how we are the same. How we would be together.

He stood—or more accurately, uncoiled from his careless slump on the bench. He stood as tall as me, all wiry energy. "Curiosity killed the cat. Joe."

I watched him walk away. Of course he had a fine ass too, slim and muscular. It figured.

The next prey I chose happened to be a man. And he happened to be blond. And rather tall. With a strong jaw.

He bent his long throat to me in an alley a few scant blocks from the club where I'd found him. He wore too much cologne— the scent burnt my nostrils. And he wasn't really blond; the peroxide had left him brassy. But I breathed in my scrap of towel and caught Daniel's scent, and took a long lick up that mortal throat, and found I was half hard. The arousal made me giddy. I wondered if I could actually take more from the mortal than my sustenance— not that I ever had, with a mortal.

My teeth sank into his soft (if overly fragranced) neck, his hot life pulsing under my lips, and I drank, blood coursing over my parched tongue. My gnawing thirst receded as his blood flowed down my throat, while the mortal moaned and stroked my long hair, grinding his crotch into my thigh.

I held him loosely, one hand on his low back, the other cupping his ass, and slowed my drinking after the initial surge, allowing my fantasy to spin out a little longer. Daniel, weaving his fingers through my hair, riding my thigh with his hard cock butting my hip. Daniel, who would moan my name as my hands ranged over his nipples. Daniel, whose canine blood would slake my thirst.

The mortal's moans turned to whimpers, and I stopped feeding. He was light-headed, and it would be greedy of me to take more. And his cologne was truly cloying. I clasped him to me and he trailed kisses over my cheek, his tongue darting toward my ear, and I bent my throat to him and he covered it with his slick kisses and ineffective mortal nips. I was glad he didn't try to kiss my mouth. Because the fantasy wouldn't hold together if he did—not at all.

I pushed the mortal away far enough to catch his eye and willed him to sleep, and immediately he drooped in my arms. I eased him to the ground, propping him against the brick building and folding his hands over his belly.

I turned to leave and froze. A blond figure blocked the alley's mouth.

"Wow. You don't kill yours?"

I stared stupidly. That scent, that clean animal scent. I'd thought it was all the scrap of fabric. But it was Daniel.

I gestured toward the mortal. "Would you like...?"

Daniel's eyes, pale in the ambient neon light, flickered toward my prey. "Nah. He's got way too much cologne on." His eyes came back to rest on me, and he was staring. I could detect a spike of something in his scent, feel his heart working a bit harder. Hunger, or lust?

I took a step toward him, slow and smooth, waiting to see if he would bolt. And then another. He stood his ground. I stopped with a hand's breadth between us, and stared into his eyes. Did he know about the hypnotic powers of my kind—and did they even affect his kind? The sound of his heart working filled my ears, and I was still hungry for him, though I had already fed. His eyes filled mine, huge. Then he blinked and shook his head. He thumbed a bit of blood from the corner of my mouth and licked his thumb.

He smirked. "I don't know how you can eat 'em after you let 'em hump you like that."

He was gone, leaving a trail of laughter in his wake.

In the following days I felt anxious. I'd never known another creature who could approach me without my hearing it, who could outdistance me, and break my gaze. I lurked in my lair, worried that he would sneak up on me if I set foot outside. Or hoping that he would, and then worrying that I wouldn't know what to do with him once he did.

And then I started to worry that he wouldn't find me again. I decided I had to find him.

I inhaled the scrap of towel, then left it in my lair, thinking he'd find it on my person and I'd have to try to explain it and would fail miserably. I hardly needed it now anyway. I could imagine his scent as a tangible thing.

I tried the neighborhood where I'd first trailed him, and then the area by the club, and then I began scouting the parks. His scent was freshest by the second park I scoped, a small area of green with a few thick patches of trees and late-night neighborhoods close by. I trailed him into a neighborhood, past a hot dog stand, and into a garishly lit arcade.

He leaned into a machine, concentrating on the screen while he worked a button with one hand and a lever with the other. He grinned as I stepped up beside him.

"Whaddaya say, Vampire Joe?" he asked, while the video game made fighting noises.

"Daniel," I murmured in return.

He stopped playing and fixed me with a stare. "That's Danny," he whispered.

Well, if he could call me "Vampire Joe"... It amused me to disturb him, finally. I suspect I was smirking now.

He caught himself and remembered to act nonchalant. He leaned against the video game and regarded me through half-lidded amber eyes.

"You could pass for human," I said.

He quirked one pointy eyebrow. "You say that as if you couldn't."

I knew my clothes and hairstyle were out-of-date. I could hardly keep up with the style of things from decade to decade, let alone year to year. "No, not really."

"Sure you could." He reached toward me—I froze—but he merely tucked a strand of hair behind my ear. "No one'd look twice at you in a goth club. Matter of fact, you'd be one of the tamer ones there."

His hand paused beside my hair and he almost dropped it, but then seemed to change his mind and stroked my cheek instead. I closed my eyes as his hot touch seared me. I shivered.

When I opened my eyes I saw a muscle in his jaw leap. His stare pinned me. I wondered if werefolk had hypnotic powers too. "What do your people call themselves?" I whispered.

"Lupen." He smiled a bit, without so much irony, I thought.

He glanced to the side. A trio of toughs were watching our exchange, a bit too baffled to do anything quite yet, though shortly they'd come after us with fists, chains, and baseball bats. Or worse, guns.

"We should go somewhere," I said.

"C'mon," he said, grinning fully now. "We can take them."

"But I don't want them."

His eyes met mine again, and he understood. "Right. We're outta here."

We left his game making noises with a full soda beside it on the floor, and headed for the park.

Once out of the mortals' line of sight, Daniel became a blur and I followed close behind. His scent blossomed around us as his leg muscles bunched and stretched, his body reveling in the pure joy of simply running. So feral, so beautiful.

We stopped within a grove of trees, illuminated by a waxing moon. He grinned wide, panting. "So. You can keep up with me. I'd kinda wondered there. You were pretty easy to lose that first night."

My need for him gripped me tight and I didn't bother trying to banter with him, crushing him against a tree instead. Our eyes bored into each other's, foreheads touching. I could still see he was grinning. I breathed him.

"You don't smell dead," he went on. "I kinda worried you would. But I guess you're undead, instead of dead."

Our chests pressed together. I could feel his heart pounding, heard the squeak of his leather jacket. I wedged my knee between his thighs to press us closer.

"Can we catch each other's curses? I mean, I've never heard of a vampiric werewolf, have you?"

"You talk too much," I said, bending my mouth to his.

At first I just pressed, feeling the heat of his lips, inhaling that clean smell that was so much sweeter than a regular mortal's. It was muskier but free of the sour taint of drugs and disease. He spread his lips and met my tongue with his. He moaned, his hands snaking into the front of my coat, finding their way under my shirt. I bent into his hot hands, the taste of his sweet mouth on mine heady in its unexpectedness. I had hardly dared dream it for weeks—and it was actually happening.

I realized I'd been clutching his hair hard, but he just gasped and flicked his tongue against my fangs, then shivered against me. I felt his teeth—sharp, all of them sharp, not just the canines. I nicked my tongue on them and we both moaned aloud.

"Seriously," he said, managing to pull back just enough to look at me. His arms remained locked around my ribs. He looked as tousled and dizzy as I felt. "How do you make someone a vampire? 'Cause I just tasted your blood."

I pressed my lips to his ear. "I would need to drain you to the cusp of death," I said, trailing my fingers down the side of his jaw, brushing his throat. "And then I would nurse you back to life with my blood."

His breath quickened in my ear and his hardness pressed into my thigh. "Right," he said shakily. "Well...don't do it."

"Trust me," I purred in his ear. He gasped and clutched hard at my sides. My hands found the neck of his T-shirt and grasped it, the fabric giving way with a tired sigh as it shredded from his body. He shrugged out of his leather jacket while he nipped at my jaw, biting his way back to my mouth, my lips. I trailed my fingers over his chest, finding some hair but not as much as one would expect on a werebeast.

His hands moved to my shirt, and buttons flew in all directions as he parted the front. I squirmed from my coat and shirt while he tried to help me with jerky tugs. His tongue found mine again and we both gasped, and my fingers grazed his nipples, hard and peaked. "Your hands are cold," he said into my mouth, pushing his hard cock against my thigh.

"Get used to it."

We worked at the waistbands of each other's jeans, though it would have been more efficient if we each removed our own. I caught him grinning still, and I knew he was aroused by the fact that, whatever we were doing, it was unheard-of. I had certainly never heard of a vampiric werewolf either. Our peoples had no history with one another, none at all.

Finally jeans were shoved around knees and he pushed back from the tree, toppling me down onto the damp grass, half on, half off my crumpled coat.

He pinned my hands beside my head, clutching each of my wrists in a preternaturally strong grip. He rubbed his cheek against my jaw, nuzzling my neck, grazing his lips over my collarbone. "Is it difficult to keep from biting me?" I asked.

He chuckled, trailing his tongue over my chest, which set me to trembling. "I don't fuck my food."

My hand was out of his grasp lightning-fast, and I had him by the hair. I forced him to look at me. "Nor do I."

His eyes narrowed. "I saw. Remember?"

I pulled his face closer. "I wasn't going to make love to him. It was just a game."

Daniel considered that statement, weighing it against what he'd seen outside the club. "Well, I suppose. Clothes stayed on and all that."

I don't know why it was so important to me that he believe me. I stared into his eyes.

"Funny, though. He looked a little like me. From a certain angle. If you squinted." Daniel grinned.

I relaxed my grip on his hair and coaxed his head down for another kiss. He let go of my other wrist while he propped himself up on one elbow, snaking the other hand between our bodies.

He took our hard cocks in his fist, and we both gasped, then crushed our mouths together harder. Jolts of sensation raced straight to my spine as I clutched at his hair, lost and floating and overwhelmed with wonder, because I was not kissed, I was not touched. I was a blooddrinker, separate, apart. Alone.

His sharp teeth nicked my lower lip and we both moaned again.

"You taste so fuckin' good," he whispered into my mouth, and my hips bucked up into his hand. He trailed hot kisses down my throat, mouthing my collarbone, my chest. He hovered over my nipple, hot breath stirring it. Then he flicked his wet tongue against me and I arched into his mouth.

His thumb stroked the underside of my cock, pressure even, sublime, while he sucked hard at my nipple, growling low in his throat. I couldn't stop clutching at his hair, helpless against the sensations that shot through me, my body bending first toward his mouth and then his hand, the whole of me writhing as I moaned.

He nipped a trail down my ribs, growling louder now, his thumb dipping to stroke at my balls. I stopped pulling at his hair and clutched at my coat instead as he dragged his sharp mouth down, down, his hot wet breath on my cock. His hand kneaded my scrotum as his wet, slick tongue flickered on me, and I clenched my teeth together and tried to stop from screaming his name, my hands plucking at my coat and pulling up tufts of grass all around it.

And then it was hot and wet all around me as my cock slid deep into his mouth, all the down to the root, his throat closing around the head. I stared down at him, and his amber eyes watched me, amused. He sucked me, head bobbing gently, eyes on mine, sharp teeth carefully covered with his lips, while I stared. The intensity peaked, and then it was almost as if I couldn't feel it—too much, all too much. My hips shook beneath him and he left off playing with my balls to hold my hips down, pressing hard enough to mark me with bruises.

He gave me a wink and pressed his face down hard, taking my cock in so wet, so deep, and then he growled and his throat vibrated around the head.

"Oh, God," I said, a strangled moan, and I wanted to stop him because it was too much, but I wanted it to never stop. Pleasure gathered deep in my spine, my balls tightening, and then, hot—wet—perfect. I bucked into his face, my cock pumping, and I was coming, so wet and slick, so hot in his mouth.

He slid his mouth off my cock and licked his lips, still grinning. I lay there, limp and stunned, enjoying the heavy wave of lethargy that followed my orgasm, almost as heavy as a sunrise, but much more delicious.

His cock lay on his thigh, thick and red and unsatisfied, and I shifted to take it in my hand. He caught me by the wrist, much quicker than me now. "No, not yet. Not now."

I raised an eyebrow.

Daniel rolled away, kicking off his boots and jeans. I wondered if he thought I could perform again that night. I wondered if I could myself. Blooddrinkers are notoriously slow to arouse, given that we propagate by blood rather than seed. But still, he was so alluring. Maybe I could.

He crawled up to my face and nuzzled my ear. "Watch my clothes for a little while."

"What?"

He crawled away, smirking, and rose up on all fours. Moonlight shone on his pale body, spine slightly arched, his limbs all muscle and sinew. "I told you. I don't fuck my food. And right now, I'm starving."

I watched as his spine lengthened and curved, his limbs shifting, hands and feet clutching. "Wait," I said, "don't go."

He looked at me, amber eyes haunting in a face turned wolfish. "Don't worry, Joseph," he said carefully, his voice resonating in that elongating snout. "I'll be back."

Silvery blond fur sprouted from his bare limbs, rolling over his body in a great, sleek wave, and his legs made a popping noise as his knees flexed back on themselves to bend the opposite way. His tongue lolled out as he panted, chest heaving with the effort of the change, and he arched his spine, threw his head back, and let out a howl that raised gooseflesh on my arms.

A flash of moonlight-colored fur, and he was gone.

I stared down at our discarded clothes, his scuffed boots

and worn leather jacket. My limbs were leaden with pleasure, but it was still many hours before dawn. I lay back on my coat and tucked my forearm under my head and sighed, looking up at the stars.

He'd called me Joseph. That was progress.

Darien Sucks
Jason Rubis

Lambert had long ago stopped wondering how the boys got into his apartment. It was enough that they were there almost every evening, waiting for him. Once the routine had established itself he gave up keeping late hours at the office and let his gym membership lapse. He all but ran home from the subway.

There were at least three of them most nights. The number varied, but the core group was always Sonny, Price, and a dark-skinned boy whose name Lambert never caught. They would be lying sprawled on his chairs and couch when he opened the door, playing his CDs and drinking his liquor. He used to feel a little pang of fear at that moment, when the door opened and he saw them there. It had eventually, like his curiosity about the boys' means of entry, simply stopped.

Most nights Sonny would start them off. He would saunter over to Lambert, thumbs in belt, cigarette dangling (he always had a cigarette). Lambert would smile. He couldn't help it, his mouth always bowed up in the same ridiculous, happy grin. Sonny just looked so *perfect*. A picture in a magazine. Sonny might strike him a light blow on the shoulder—a parody of camaraderie, only hard enough to send him stumbling back a step or two. Or he might slap his face, and that would hurt more, it would make tears jump in his eyes. But Sonny never went too far in that direction, he was always careful. Lambert appreciated that.

Sonny was tall, with a hard face and short black hair. His arms were scarred and strange with many tattoos, but his cock was long and uniformly pale and quite beautiful. He would in due course take it out and point wordlessly at it, the cigarette jerking humorously in his mouth.

During all this, Price would be giggling. His big body always reeked of something sweet and earthy. Lambert never quite identified the smell—it was like pot, but it wasn't pot. Whatever it was obviously put Price in a playful mood. When Lambert got Sonny in his mouth Price would shout for more liquor, or food, or to have the television channel changed. He would stomp. If Lambert tried to disengage himself so he could attend to Price, Sonny would slap his ears. When he went back to sucking, Price would come over and shout at him, kick him in the ass so that his head bumped forward and it would be a chore to keep the sucking pleasurable for Sonny. The dark boy rarely took part; he generally just lounged on the couch, watching the proceedings with a sleepy, beneficent smile.

Afterward, once Price had collapsed in red-faced giggles on the floor and Lambert was savoring the aftertaste of Sonny's cock, they might demand money—Lambert always made certain he had at least five fresh 20s in his wallet—and leave. On other nights, when the weather was bad (or, as Lambert liked to think, they were just perhaps feeling tender), they would stay a while. The three would take turns letting him suck them, then suffer him to lie naked and breathing and seeping on the floor at their feet. One might offer him a stroke. The dark boy sometimes got down and ran stubby dirty nails along his back with the same indulgent smile he might wear if he were scratching a dog, and that was wordlessly delicious.

They would talk among themselves then. Their range of conversation was limited. It was all about new cars on the market or the girls they had recently fucked or a bouncer in such and such a club who was, quote, looking to get his motherfucking face rearranged, unquote.

Sometimes they talked about Darien.

"Next time I see that bitch, swear to God, OK? I'm going to

fuck him so he sneezes my jizz the next two years, all right? Right? I'm going to *doom* that little cunt." Price never laughed when he talked about Darien. His beefy face grew red and there was a focus in his eyes Lambert never saw any other time.

Once Lambert asked—shyly—who Darien was. Sonny drew unhurriedly on his cigarette. When he exhaled, words came out with the smoke, hot and biting.

"Darien sucks, man. He'd suck shit right out your pink little bung hole. Price?"

"Dude."

"D'you say Darien's a bigger pussy'n even Phyllis here?"

They called Lambert "Phyllis" when they called him anything, because his Christian name was Philip. Lambert thought that was funny.

Price glowered. "Darien's like the pussy of the *world*, man. *Hate* that little prick."

"Not so loud, man," the dark boy whispered. Lambert saw the boys start and their eyes twitch as one toward the wall. For the barest instant, Lambert saw them show fear. It was strange, but it didn't last long, and afterward they were in a terrible mood.

Lambert never asked about Darien after that.

~

One Tuesday night in August, Lambert came home and found the apartment vacant. He waited patiently with the door open, but no one so much as knocked. It wasn't unheard-of for the boys to stay away a night or two, or even several, but for some reason their absence tonight made him nervous. Maybe they had gotten in some kind of trouble. Maybe they had grown tired of him. He spent the night in a nail-gnawing frenzy, too agitated to make himself a drink. He fell asleep on the couch, and when he woke at 5 the next morning, he was still alone.

They stayed away the next night as well, and the night after that. The weekend was hell. Lambert grew slowly resigned to their absence, but it left a hole in his life. He had few friends left in the city, and he had grown too used to the boys' company. Spending each night jerking off and watching television was driving him slowly crazy.

The escort agencies were the obvious answer but proved disappointing. For $200 Lambert received a visit from a sleek leather-sheathed gym bunny who refused to touch him. Instead, the man invited him to masturbate while he flexed his muscles and dispensed pointed tips on nutrition. After that, Lambert swore off escort agencies.

Finally, reluctantly, he ventured out to the bars. He was looking for the boys, though he didn't actually admit this to himself. He would stay slumped on his stool long enough to finish a single drink, then go out to the alleys, where the trade congregated. But the alleys were always all but empty. He knew none of the boys now and they were ugly things anyway—hardly boys at all. All were on the wrong side of 30 and unappealingly paunchy. Still, the ritual brought some excitement back into his life, and through it he rediscovered the pleasures of people-watching. Soon he was closing out every place he went to. No one seemed interested in him, but every now and then he managed to fall into a conversation, mostly with men his own age, and that satisfied him.

One night, two strange things happened.

The first happened on his way to the bar that had recently become his favorite. His route took him down a side street that, even at 9 on a Saturday night, was empty. As he walked along, thinking of nothing in particular, he happened to look up—at the side of an apartment building.

There was something *on* the building, next to a window near the topmost floor, a vague black shape flattened against the bricks. Even with the moon full and plenty of streetlights, Lambert couldn't figure out exactly what the shape was. Its strangeness vexed the eye, and he couldn't seem to look away. Oddest of all, it seemed to be moving, creeping slowly to the left, until it came to the edge of the building. Then it seemed to leap out, hanging in midair for just a moment before disappearing around the building with a sudden, somehow emphatic jerk.

Lambert stood blinking for a while, then got on his way. It had been a strange experience, but not enough so as to make any lasting impression. He had forgotten about it in a matter of moments.

The second odd thing happened after he'd finished that night's drinking and, feeling nostalgic, ventured out into the alley. It was empty, but there was graffito on the wall Lambert had not seen before: the words DARIEN SUCKS, not in spray paint but lines of white chalk that had been scraped over and over into the stone, so that the letters stood out with a kind of jagged ferocity.

"They sure do hate that Darien," a voice said, and Lambert started. An older gentleman was beside him, viewing the graffiti with impassive, somehow resigned eyes.

"Who?" Lambert asked.

"The boys. The ones that used to hang out back here, anyway. You'll notice there aren't a lot of 'em around anymore. That's his doing. Darien's. Selfish bitch." He laughed. He had a soft voice, so pleasant to the ear that his slurring was barely noticeable.

"I meant, who's Darien? Some friends of mine used to talk about him."

"Friends," the older gentleman said, with an insinuating smile.

"Yes, *friends*," Lambert snapped, flushing. "I'm talking about Darien. Who is he? Some pusher?" He felt proud of the effortless way he deployed the word.

"Pusher," the older gentleman said, stroking his stubbly chin. "You know, that's not a bad way to put it. He gives them things they think they want...things they think mean power, or, I don't know, freedom or what have you...but he's not giving, he's *selling*, it turns out, and at a higher price than they're prepared to pay. When he exacts that price...well. It's not pretty. Ugly ain't ever pretty."

"Does he go to the bars ever? Darien? Would I know him?" Lambert knew he was babbling; liquor had always had a way of making him chatty. "See, I think he may have hurt these friends of mine, and if he *did*—"

"Honey," the man said, touching Lambert's arm. "Don't. Just stop right there. Hurt your friends? He probably did. But there's nothing you can do about that. You can't *look* for Darien. If he wants you, he'll find you. And you wouldn't be any too happy about that, chances are."

He turned and walked quickly away. Lambert thought about going after him; the man might be his only hope of finding the boys. But he knew he wasn't up to getting any answers from him. Not in his current condition. The man would only laugh at him and keep walking, or maybe he would get frightened and call for help, and that would accomplish nothing. That would be rather embarrassing.

So Lambert stood silently, staring at the graffito. DARIEN SUCKS. He felt vaguely humiliated. He made up his mind that he would go looking for this Darien person the next night. He'd go to every bar in the city until he found him. He wouldn't wimp out next time.

~

As it happened, next time never came. As it turned out, the old gentleman was right. Because when Lambert got home half an hour later, Darien was there, belly-down on the couch. He had a CD on. Old Dolly Parton. He was moving his lips along with "Mule-Skinner Blues."

There was no question in Lambert's mind that this was Darien. He knew it with the drunken certainty one feels in dreams. But he would never have expected the terrible Darien to look like the man now occupying his couch.

Darien was a coquette gone to seed, his long blond hair thinning around a visible bald spot. He looked only slightly younger than Lambert. He was no longer truly pretty, though the prettiness was still in him, still floating close to the surface and keeping his slightly too long face appealing in an odd, sly way. Had Darien had been less fortunate in the looks department, Lambert realized, his face would have turned horsy by now. His outfit was too bright, too affectedly youthful to suit him. It showed off too much slack tanned skin.

"Darien," Lambert said, and then, a shade less steadily, "You're him." He was actually in a slightly worse state now than when he had left the bar. Vodka snuck up on you, he should have learned that years ago.

Darien turned his head so his cheek rested on one outstretched arm. Slowly he shut his eyes, then opened them again. Lambert found this oddly unsettling.

"I'm him, OK. And you're Phyllis." Darien's voice wasn't the camp lisp Lambert had prepared himself for; it was soft and faintly country-sounding. It sounded infinitely tired. There was no challenge or threat in it at all, nothing like nastiness.

Lambert moved slowly into the apartment, shutting the door behind him. He took care not to get too close to the couch.

"What did you do with the boys?" His voice sounded ridiculous to him: raspy and squeaking. But he got the question out and felt immediately stronger for it.

"Nothing. I'm looking for them, is the truth. Or Sonny, rather. I got just mad as fire when the others ran out on me, but they ain't worth the looking. They're stupid, see. Stupid to the solid marrow. Their kind never take to nightjaunting. Not without Momma along playing teacher. Sooner or later they'll take a chance they shouldn't, if they ain't already. Then—*pfft*. But Sonny—he's smart. Smart enough to figure the dark paths without Momma's help. I figure he'll be back by here sooner or later. Mind if I keep you company while I wait?" Darien's eyes opened and shut again, and this time Lambert realized why he found the movement so uncomfortable to watch: Except for this slow, somehow flirtatious winking, the pale-blue eyes didn't blink. Not once.

He turned off the CD player but still hung back from the couch. He wasn't afraid of Darien, but the crazy talk made him nervous, in a way that was slowly eroding his lingering drunkenness. He pressed on, even so, determined to get an answer before his courage evaporated.

"Who are you? The boys hate you. Everybody says so. They must have a reason."

Darien sat up suddenly, swinging his legs off the couch. He gave the cushion at his hip an inviting pat. His staring eyes seemed brighter now, as though he were noticing his host for the first time, and found him rather interesting. Perhaps rather attractive.

"Why you want to bother yourself about all that, now? That ain't nothing nice to talk about—bunch of silly little boys going out getting themselves hurt. Sit down here with me, let's us visit a little."

"No." Lambert was shaking all over.

"Aw, come on. Please? I'll tell you a story."

Darien's voice sounded wide awake now. It grew wheedling and honeyed, took on seductive cadences that disgusted Lambert. The man himself disgusted him. He was just an old simpering queen, the polar opposite of the boys' youth and strength and beauty. Darien was nothing to be afraid of. Why the boys should so dread him was a mystery.

"You want a story? I know some good ones, hon. Back from the old days. There were more forests in the old days, you know that? That's where all the good stories come from. The forests."

He had some kind of hold on the boys. He was blackmailing them, maybe. Or maybe he was a pusher. He gave them drugs and got them addicted, so they would do anything he said.

"I'll tell you about the old Queens of Night and their brave and handsome consorts. I'll tell you the whole history of those pretty ladies, 'bout their warring with the daytime world and what came of that—how they forged the dark paths and set their children on them, forever wandering, forever devout, in thrall forever to the Red Secret."

Darien was leaning toward Lambert, reaching for him with a soft, imploring hand. His unblinking eyes were pathetically eager as he babbled on and on. Silly old bitch. Lambert could take his arm and twist it. Make him squeal. Yes. He could *make* Darien tell him where the boys were.

Instead, he took Darien's cheeks in both hands and kissed him. It surprised him how he did it—thoughtlessly, but with the surety of a long-held, long-suppressed desire. Darien's mouth opened under Lambert's, and Lambert felt his tongue working into the soft wet space, thrusting with a huge ferocity.

There was a smell. It seemed to explode in the room, and it had no one source, though it seemed particularly strong on Damien's breath and skin. It hit Lambert's nose first like the sweet scent that lingered around Price, then suddenly prismed into many other scents. Lambert smelled something like the mushroom smell of cock, the rich stink of too long unwashed jeans. A moment later he was inhaling the salty smell of a locker room, the loamy stench of an ass well-fucked. It made his head spin and his cock strain at his trousers.

Memories flashed behind his eyes. Roland Marcos smirking and giving his crotch a contemptuous, surreptitious stroke as Lambert passed him in the dorm hallway. The taste of Alan Hess's balls and the sound of his laughter somewhere far overhead. Endless crushes, loves that never materialized. Magazine pages full of poses and heavy, laden balls; tender nipples, squirting cocks, pictures a much younger Philip Lambert had eaten visually until their every element was imprinted in his brain and guts.

There were other images too, many people and places he didn't recognize, but all of them, every one, about bodies and want and release. The shame these images might have once caused in Philip was gone now, barely a memory. They made him feel exultant, adoring, and adored.

It was quite marvelous.

And then suddenly, he was in Darien's arms, his head resting in his lap and being stroked. Darien looked...if not exactly younger, then infinitely more attractive, his little imperfections now charming. How was it Lambert had not noticed earlier how charming he was? His mouth was smeared with something dark and sticky-looking. Lambert chuckled. *She's smeared her lipstick.*

"That's right, sugar. You gonna do Momma good? Already have, haven't you? Yeah, you're a sweet little smackerel. A little taste of heaven. Might just have to keep you around a little longer."

Lambert grinned. He heard what Darien was saying, loud and clear. He was telling him how handsome he was, how strong and desirable, how utterly wonderful and worthy of love. It made a fierce joy in Lambert, so strong he felt the sting of tears.

Behind them somewhere a door was opening. No, not a door,

but a window. A window sliding open. And there was a voice some-where in the vicinity of the window, on the wrong side of it. A tiny, piping ghost voice wailing a song of loss and jealousy. It didn't sound much like Sonny at all.

Darien purred. "Aw, well now. Little birdie's come home to roost. You excuse me a minute, sugar? Momma got to go put little birdie in his cage. For good this time. Momma'll be right back. Don't you go nowhere now."

Lambert sighed as Darien slid from underneath him. He relaxed on the couch as soft sounds filled the room: hisses, cajolings, whis-pers, and weeping. Once there was a bright, sharp noise like glass breaking. Once he heard something irresistibly like the beating of enormous wings. And somewhere—in one of the other apartments, maybe—someone was watching a movie in which many people screamed in desperation and unending horror. Lambert paid none of this any attention.

Darien would be back soon. His sweet Darien, who would stay with him forever, and show him how strong he was.

He had never in his life, not once, ever felt so strong.

Hot Blooded
Thom Wolf

The last time that I saw him before the wretched call on Sunday morning, Aiden looked better than any time I could remember. He came over on Tuesday night, post-gym, with a vivid flush to his Latino complexion—a little out of breath, still hot. He grabbed my crotch in the doorway, squashing me in a keen grip, tongue thrusting into my mouth. When Aiden was this aroused his enthusiasm could get the better of him. Gripping both wrists, holding him back, I asked why he had come.

"I got my invitation," he said excitedly, face thrusting forward for a kiss. "The e-mail came this afternoon."

I mashed my mouth against his before asking, "Invitation?"

"To the bareback gang bang." He shook his wrists free, unbuttoning my shirt.

"Oh."

"I've trying to get on the list for nearly a year. This month I get my foot in the door."

Aiden was a cyberporn enthusiast, NorthEastBareback-PartyBoyz.com his favourite Web site. It was an amateurish home page, showcase to an expansive gallery of pictures and movie clips. The site members met once a month at a secret location, invitation-only, to fuck the life out of a reckless, chemed-up party boy, loading his orifices with potentially lethal spunk. It was a nihilistic group, one that I found deeply disturbing. The galleries on the site were not pleasant: wasted boys, wide-eyed and ravenous, relentlessly fucked by a plethora of unprotected gang bang participants. Extreme photographs displaying abused, spunk-dripping arseholes. I could just about grasp the appeal of this fantasy, but not the stark reality of sexual Russian roulette—a game, it appeared, that Aiden was intent on playing.

"Don't do it," I said, turning away from his lips, wanting to sound serious.

"Don't be daft. Do you know how long I'd have to wait to be asked again? Most likely another year, if I'm ever asked at all. I've wanted to take part in one of these parties for too long, I'm not giving it up."

"Why? It's insane."

"It's hot. Thirty guys fucking one bottom."

"Are you the bottom?"

"Unfortunately not. The list for guys wanting to bottom is even longer. I only get to fuck this time. Think how great that will be, all that spunk. Most of the tops are gonna shoot at least twice, the bottom is gonna be sodden with the stuff."

"It's a slow attempt at suicide."

"Don't be so dramatic. It's all consensual." He headed toward my bedroom. "I spent an extra hour in the gym tonight. I want to look good in the photographs." He undressed quickly, tossing his clothes about the room. Soon he was naked on the bed, on all fours, his creamy arse thrust high, his arsehole dark and inviting. I put on a condom and lubed his hole, giving him as much as I could of what he wanted: riding his tight, toned, totally insane arse. I fucked him hard and deep, not caring whether I hurt him—he obviously didn't. I pulled out, spun him over, held his ankles high and spread his legs like a wishbone, shoving hard into the gaping hole, up into his guts. He grinned, looking up at me with wide chocolate eyes, tightening his slippery hole. I knew that he was not with me, he was in another place, with 30 other men queuing eagerly to come-dump in his butt.

He rolled away afterward and lit a cigarette. It was dark outside and raining. I listened to the splash of tires below my window and wondered if there were any other way of stopping him. "I can arrange an orgy for you. I've done that kind of thing plenty of times. I know some guys. It wouldn't be 30, but you'd get to be the bottom—the only bottom—to around a dozen men."

Aiden exhaled, blowing smoke to the ceiling. "That's nice. But you know it's not the same."

"Not the same as killing yourself? You're only 28. What has given you this death wish?"

"Stop it. You know I want this. Don't spoil it. I'm not going to die."

Later that week he e-mailed a photograph of the boy who was to be the focus of the gang bang's attention. "Wanna dump a load in our come-hungry bottom?" a caption read. It was a blurred image, taken with a low-resolution camera, but it revealed a body of tight muscle and looks that exceeded those of the average group bottom. He lay across an unmade bed in an anonymous room, adopting an easy pose, one arm behind his head, the other across his stomach, his thighs open and wide. He wore pale-blue patterned boxers and nothing else. His skin, as much as the picture could reveal, was evenly tanned, and his hair was dark blond, heavy on top with agreeable sideburns. His fringe fell loosely across a handsome brow. His good looks increased my unease. What could be so wrong in this boy's life to produce such extreme behaviour? What had happened to set him on this trail of self-destruction and loathing?

The phone call came on Sunday morning, early, while I was still asleep. "Aiden," I said, struggling to focus, knowing inherently who the caller was. I was expecting to hear from him, knowing how excited he would be in the comedown, desperate to regale me with explicit details. I'd gone out the night before, found a brief distraction in a couple from Newcastle and a bottle of vodka, tried not to think of Aiden while I screwed the two of them.

A dry gasp came down the telephone.

"Oh, sorry," I said. "I thought this was someone else."

"It's me," the voice said, sounding like the caller was 100 years old. "It's Aiden. I need you."

There was a recognisable note in the unfamiliar voice. Twenty minutes later I was at his house. The front door was locked. I had my own key, but the door was bolted from the inside. I thumped on the frame. "Aiden, it's Ben." After a moment I heard movement behind the door; two bolts were withdrawn. "What's the matter with you." I stepped into the hallway, backing him toward the stairs. The curtains were closed. I reached for the light, flicked the switch, and gasped at what I saw.

Aiden, what should have been Aiden, blanched under my gaze. He turned his head and tried to hide his face behind his hands—old, liver-spotted hands. In the four days since I had seen him last, he had aged 40 years. His hair was thin and gray, steely whiskers curled around his ears. What I could see of his high forehead was weathered and wrinkled. I grabbed the old man's hands and uncovered his face—sad and worn and unrecognisable. But not quite: There was a flash of recognition in those sad brown eyes; like his voice on the telephone, a hint of him remained. A grotesque aged parody of the boy I knew.

"What happened to you?"

"Shut the door," he gasped. "Lock it. Hurry."

He sat nervously on the stairs, gnawing at his fingers, watching me lock and secure the front door. I turned to face him and moved closer, struggling to make sense of what I saw. He reached his hand. "Help me up."

The bones beneath his parched skin were brittle and sharp. He eased himself to standing, leaning some of his weight against me. His body was small; he had shrunk five or six inches since Tuesday. Without him saying, I knew that this—whatever this was—was a consequence of the gang bang. Aiden, with assistance, sat down on the sofa. In front of him, on the coffee table, stood his computer, open and switched on. He asked me to get him a drink.

"Water?"

"Whiskey."

I poured three fingers into a crystal tumbler and another three of vodka for myself. He took the glass in both hands and swallowed the contents in a couple of gulps. I poured him another and left the open bottle on the coffee table. "Well?" I sat beside him.

"They're all dead," he said coldly, his hands trembling as he attempted another mouthful. "At least I think they are. I got out before it was over, but I think I was the only one."

I was thinking drugs and some demented hallucinations. But there were no drugs I could think of that could age a man so rapidly in just a few hours. "I want you to tell me everything."

"Darius," he said. "The bottom. He did it. He killed them all. Don't look at me like that, Ben. I'm not lying. I'm not high. I'm not drunk either. What do you think this is? Clever makeup?" He held his hand—his old man's hand—in front of me. His fingers trembled.

"I'm listening, not judging."

Aiden took another swallow, grimacing as the whisky slipped down. "They e-mailed directions two hours before the party was due to start. It's what they always do, to keep it secret. The address was an apartment on the Quayside, behind the railway station. It was a nice place, modern and clean, not at all sleazy. I recognised the interior from the March gallery. There were 20 or so men already there when I arrived. They were naked or in their underwear, but the sex hadn't started yet."

"What about the bottom?"

Aiden swallowed. "He was there too. He was in the bathroom, getting ready. The bedroom was all set up with video equipment, and there was another guy taking pictures on his digital camera. It was a well-organised setup. The men were all good-looking, most of them in decent shape, from around 20 to 50 years old. The atmosphere was pungent with anticipation. There were drugs around, but most of us didn't need them. We were turned-on already."

Aiden leaned forward and clicked a couple of buttons on his computer. A photograph appeared on-screen: of a room, tastefully decorated in a fleshy shade of yellow. It was filled with men, a wide mix of ages and ethnic origins.

"What is this?"

"It was taken tonight."

"How?"

"I stole the digital camera as I was leaving." He pointed at the screen. "This is the last thing these men did before they died."

"Aiden, what are you talking about? How can they all be dead? What happened, did Darius have a knife? A gun?"

He sank back into the sofa. "Look at the photographs. You won't believe me otherwise."

I clicked through the images of bare torsos and smiling faces, of eyes that blazed with a lustful polish and dicks that were swollen and bound for a communal destination. The men, on the whole, were average to good-looking; none of them were ugly and none of them had the appearance of ill health. There was a shot of Aiden naked between two men, their arms around one another's shoulders, smoldering for the camera like a day-old barbecue. I felt a sudden sadness, unable to equate the image, this man in his prime, with the elderly creature sitting beside me. But they were unquestionably the same.

The primary location for the shot was a bedroom, tastefully decorated, unremarkable and bland; it could have been the set of any one of a million porn films. All personal touches had been removed from the room: pictures, books, toiletries. It was a clean space, made empty for the purpose of sex.

Aiden lit a cigarette with shaky fingers as I clicked on the next image. It was the bottom—Darius—the epitome of perfection. There was something of the porn star about him, something unattainable, elusive, as if he could only exist in a photographic image, never in the real world. He was on the bed, on all fours, ass up, framed exquisitely in a white jock, mirroring Aiden's favourite stance. He cast a head over his shoulder, toward the camera, and smiled, showing remarkable white teeth and a devilish expression. His countenance said everything: He was there to be ridden and he was ready for everyone.

"He's gorgeous." I didn't intend to say it aloud.

Aiden grunted. "He was. When he came out of the bathroom it was like someone upped the temperature in the bedroom. We all wanted him. There was a tussle between some of the more senior members to see who would have him first."

Next picture: an extreme close-up of Darius's arsehole. Ordinarily I find such explicit photographs unappealing, but the sight of his anus—so exposed and ethereal—caught my breath. Other hands parted his buttocks, prizing the tight cheeks. His hole was a small jewel, finely drawn and fleshy pink, no bigger than a fingernail. His crack and an inch of perineum, not concealed by the white pouch of his jock, was smooth and hairless. His skin glistened, as thought it had been oiled and polished.

I trawled through the gallery. The photographs soon became more explicit. Just three pictures on and Darius had a cock in his mouth: a fat, veiny shank that stretched his lips and caused his cheeks to bulge. With the cock in his mouth his eyes stayed focused on the camera, brown and blazing. Soon they were in his arse, another meaty piece with the shaft sank halfway inside his pink opening. Another picture and another man—two men—one in front and one behind. It was followed by a series of wide shots. Darius fucked by a variety of men in myriad positions. On hands and knees, impaled in the mouth and arse. On his side, knees into his chest, giving the camera utmost access to the penetrations. On his back, his ankles resting on the shoulders of another eager top man. A close shot of his hole, relaxed and open, oozing a thick white cream over his shiny skin.

Then it was Aiden's turn, in a missionary position. I felt him stiffen at my side as the image loaded. Aiden lay on top of Darius; the boy's knees were hooked around his elbows, and Aiden kissed him as they fucked.

"You got what you wanted," I said coldly. I was inexplicably jealous. Despite my feelings toward this gang bang and what I could see had become of Aiden, I regretted that I was not a part of it. Just this glimpse of Darius, a two-dimensional image, filled me with a fervour for him. I wanted to be a part of him, I wanted to fuck him like all these other men had done, fuck him and fill his arse with a bigger, thicker load than any of those bastards could muster.

"It was better than I ever expected," Aiden said slowly, "fucking him. When I put my dick inside him, stirring up his arse with the come of all those men, we transcended that room and everyone in it. Despite everything I'd seen, or the spunk that oozed out of him with each thrust, it was like I was the first."

I stared at the photograph of them together, at the kiss, and the contact in their eyes. For a long time neither of us spoke. I didn't move or try to change the picture.

Aiden groaned and clutched his side, his face twisted in pain. He was getting worse, aging before my eyes. His body was thinner and the skin looser than when I arrived.

"I'm nearly finished," he gasped. "Use these photographs. Warn people."

"About what? All I've seen so far is a series of homemade porn shots and a group of men old enough to know better."

Aiden's face dropped. For a moment he looked disappointed. Then he made the effort to move, unfastening his trousers, gasping as he raised his narrow hips from the sofa, shrugging his pants down his thighs. "Look," he said miserably.

The wound was situated at the top of his thigh, almost in the fold of his groin. Its jagged edges were glazed with a dark sticky substance. It was thick, like jelly—congealed blood forming a fragile clot across the wound. Aiden shuffled forward, bending over the computer. He clicked forward across several pictures. More sex shots, stopping at an image he could not look at.

I felt the world fall away as I looked at the photograph. Its imagery came direct from a nightmare: bodies, naked and vulnerable, doused in blood. Faces twisted in fear, grotesque parodies of the handsome men I had seen earlier. It was an orgy of panic. My hands shook as I viewed the remaining pictures: more blood and fear, savagery and violence. Then a photograph of Darius, blurred with movement. His lips curled away from startlingly sharp teeth, drooling gore across the lower half of his beautiful face.

"He turned about an hour in," Aiden choked. "We'd all taken a turn by then; all of us had fucked him. The come was dripping out of his backside. Some of the men were hard again, ready to load him some more. I was watching from the edge of the bed, hoping for another ride before he tired. Darius was on his hand and knees, spit-roasted. When the man he was sucking started to scream I didn't know what was happening, I thought maybe he was just getting overenthusiastic. But it wasn't a cry of ecstasy, it was agony. Then I saw the blood spurt down his legs."

"Oh, no."

"Darius began attacking. His speed was terrifying, reaching out to anyone around him, tearing with his hands and teeth. The groin and throat were his main areas of attack. Everyone was in a panic. He bit me as I made for the door. It happened so quickly. I realised then that he was drinking. He was drinking my blood." Aiden paused, wiping his eyes. "They were dying all around me. I don't know why, but he left me before I was dead, moving for someone else. I saw him tear a man's heart right out of his chest. He ripped the head from another and drank his blood from the stump of his neck."

"How the fuck did you get away from that?"

"I don't know. Survival instinct. When he was busy with the others I took the camera and I ran. When I got home I realised that I had not escaped at all. I've aged a lifetime overnight." His small body shook with sobs. "I'm dying, Ben."

"Yes," I said softly.

"Hold me," he said. "Please, until I go."

I turned off the computer, having seen enough, and lay beside him on the sofa. I held him—his tiny, fragile body—through the tears and panic. He pressed his body against me, pressing his hard-on. "Aiden, don't," I said.

"Please," he whispered. "It's the last thing I'll ever do."

It hurt, but he would not relent. I manoeuvred him into a comfortable position on his side, supported on cushions, and slipped his trousers down to the calf, caressing his thighs and the bony curve of his arse. I've heard the anus weakens with age, and I found myself entering him with little effort. He moaned, holding tight onto my hand, and we rocked slowly on the narrow edge of the sofa. I caressed his cock, stroking to the rhythm of my hips. It was all that I could do for him, fuck him softly and jerk him until the end. It did not take long; too soon I felt the warm spurt of his semen down the back of my fingers.

His body shuddered and gave another little spurt.

My tears wet the back of his neck with the last, climactic spurt.

Salvation
Matt Stedmann

I never planned to let him catch me. Maybe on some level I knew how it would end and wanted it, even then. It finally happened on a Sunday afternoon in Dupont Circle as the weather was turning cold, one of those days when the sun is bright yet the air carries a biting chill with it.

I squinted through dark sunglasses at the young man who stood at the end of the block, pretending to window-shop. He'd been following me for a month now. I'd spotted him first at a music store, glancing across the aisle to see a young, clean-cut man in a brown leather jacket. I'd admired his good looks for a moment and then quickly turned away as I clamped down on a rush of desire. A while later I was having a slice of pizza down the street when I noticed him sitting alone at a nearby table. A week later he'd been in the lobby of the same movie theater with me. A week after that it was the supermarket, then the gas station, the video store. He was always alone, always watching me.

If he was cruising me, he could just ask. I would say no, and that would be the end of it. At first it seemed suspicious, and finally it got downright scary. I considered going to the police, but what would I tell them? "Yes, Officer, I'm a gay man who's worried that I'm being followed by a handsome young man in his 20s who's apparently deeply interested in me for some unknown reason." Right.

But even I could tell from the intensity of his attention that this was more than simple cruising. He was almost...hunting me. I still don't know what impulse finally moved me to confront him that afternoon. With a sudden decisiveness I headed up the street toward him. He looked toward me, startled, and then turned away for a moment as if to flee. Instead, he turned to face me.

For the past month he'd been a figure seen at a distance, sometimes as only a silhouette. Up close he was more handsome than I had imagined. He looked youngish, in his early 20s, and was short with the stocky build of a wrestler. He was nicely tanned, and even in a distressed leather jacket he was the vision of all-American wholesomeness. His hair was that mixture of brown and blond that looks golden in the sunlight, set against hazel eyes. Those eyes were looking at me with a focused intent, as if he had some important message to impart to me.

"You've been following me," I said. He shrugged mutely. It hardly seemed worth saying. "Why?"

"I'm Scott," he said, stretching out his right hand and smiling disarmingly.

"Tony. Tony DeAngelo," I said after a moment's hesitation. His grip against mine was firm and warm, almost electric. I yanked my hand back.

Maybe this hadn't been such a good idea. "Look, Scott, what do you want from me?"

There was a wildness about him, an eldritch energy that I'd seen maybe only once before. "Maybe I just wanted to meet you," he said, leaning forward on the balls of his feet and smiling jauntily.

I laughed bitterly. At 30 I was hardly past my prime and still retained something of my dark good looks, but believe me, I wasn't used to being approached by muscular young men with a roguish gleam in their eye. Not anymore. "Try again," I said.

His smile disappeared as a new hunger came into his eyes. He licked his lips nervously and then looked me straight in the eye. "I want to give you something only I can give you."

"Oh," I said, "And what's that?"

He looked at me hungrily. "The taste of my blood."

"Sweet Jesus!" I gasped. Without volition I took a step back from him. "What?"

"You heard me." His gaze was intent. "I want it. From you."

My heart pounded loudly in my chest. "How did you know?" I glanced nervously at the passersby who were streaming by us, oblivious except for the few who were giving Scott admiring looks. How could he know? No one knew, no one except...

"Gary," he said to the confusion on my face.

"Gary?" I repeated stupidly. The last time I had seen Gary in the flesh had been four years ago, not counting the nightmares I had almost every night. They say you never forget your first time. You never forget your last time either.

"We were lovers." He shrugged. "For a while. He told me about what happened. About you. He didn't know who you were of course, or where you lived, or what you were. I had to figure all that out for myself. It's taken a couple of years."

He leaned close. "Gary had his chance. Now I want mine."

A cold spike of fear shot through me. "Stay away from me," I warned. "Just stay away. You don't know what you're asking." I held his eyes as I took first one step back, and then another. Then I turned on my heels and ran for my life.

~

So of course I ended up in a church. I had walked the city for hours, until the sky darkened to dusk. Finding the church empty, I slipped inside and sat within the echoing quietness, clenching my hands tight against the pew before me to still their trembling. I bowed my head and listened to the reassuring silence over the still-frantic beating of my heart.

I'd always loved being in church as a boy, loved the smoothness of the dark wood and the smell of the incense, the quiet and the vaulting echoes. Raised in a good Catholic family, I couldn't wait to become an altar boy.

Of course, the real reason I couldn't wait to be an altar boy was Father Antonio. Square-jawed and dark-eyed, I fell desperately in love with him at 15, in the unreserved and worshipful way that only a young man can. I glimpsed him once without his shirt, and the image of his pale skin covered with fine dark hairs that grew across his chest and trailed down to his belly would forever remain burned into my brain. I would have let him fuck me in a minute if he'd asked me, would have given all I owned in the world for the chance to drop to my knees and show him how much I worshipped him, worshipped the cock that I longed to see. I would lie in bed at night, imagining it, imagining how it would feel inside me and, most forbidden, how I would feel inside him.

Father Antonio was always talking about moderation and restraint, and how we mustn't give in to desires that might lead us down the path of evil. At those times, his dark eyes would bore deeply into mine, as if he could see the secret inside me. Years later, I wondered if it was a secret that he too shared.

I quickly forgot all about Father Antonio's lessons on moderation when I fled our small Virginia town at 22 for Washington, D.C. Suddenly, the world was full of men, handsome men, who were only too willing to buy drinks for an engaging 22-year-old. To say that I look Italian would be an understatement. No one ever took me for anything else. From the top of my curly dark head of hair and dark eyes, to the black hair that escaped from my shirt collar and covered my forearms, right down to my big hairy feet, I was the image of what everyone thought of as an Italian. If I looked any more Italian, I'd be in the Mafia. Lots of guys in the bars seemed to like what I had, and I threw myself into the life of the clubs without any vestige of restraint. That is how I ended up in an alley outside of Studzz one night four years later, the throbbing sounds of dance music leaking through the club's back door, with my back against the bricks of the alley wall and another man's hand shoved down the front of my pants.

He'd said his name was Miklos and that he was visiting from Europe, just in town for a few days. He had a trim goatee and a short punky haircut with the attitude and manic energy to match. There was an almost otherworldly presence about him, an aura of danger

and wildness that made every man's head turn when he walked into
the bar. He'd picked me out of the crowd, and we'd danced until the
sweat ran down our bodies. On the dance floor he'd been wild, whipping off his T-shirt to dance shirtless in tight black leather pants. He
gave himself over to the throbbing music, grinding his ass into my
groin and smiling up at me as I ran my hands over the sweat-soaked
hair and pierced nipples on his slender chest. He laid his head back
along my shoulder and shouted into my ear over the music, "Later.
If you're good."

When we slipped outside the club for a breath of fresh air he
was just as fierce. Miklos pushed me up against the wall and shoved
his tongue deep into my mouth as his hands went for the top of my
pants. As his fingers wrapped around my cock I went instantly hard
in his grip. He pressed me against the wall with the length of his
body as he pushed his tongue insistently into my mouth. Then he
broke the kiss and began to suck and bite at my neck, shoving his
tight leather-clad ass back into my hands.

I gasped out "No marks," but felt a sudden stabbing pain where
his mouth met my neck. At once I tried to push him away, but he
held me fast against the wall with maniacal strength. I felt his lips
working against my throat, and with stunned horror I realized that
the man was actually drinking my blood! A cold wash of terror
swept over me, but it was followed quickly by a new sensation.

Pleasure like I'd never felt before slammed into me. Sound and
hearing vanished in the onrushing wave of it. It was the triumph of
finally sucking my first cock, and the joy of laughing so hard you
can't stop. It was ripe red strawberries and juicy steak and the smell
of fresh-baked bread. It was every screaming, clawing orgasm I'd
ever had rolled into one. I could feel my life washing away into the
vast sea of it.

At the height of the ecstasy, when I was locked against myself
and helpless, pinned immobile beneath him against the alley wall,
something changed. The flow of my blood outward seemed to slow
and stop, and instead something began flowing out of him and into
me. A strange power was passing from him to me, and with it I

could hear his voice laughing maniacally inside my head. The rush of energy spread outward from my throat and rushed down my body. When it reached the soles of my feet a wave of heat swept over me as if I had just been dropped into a blast furnace. The heat rose higher and I could feel it burning through me, transforming me. A raw scream tore itself from my throat...

And beside me the alley door banged open against the wall. The force of it startled us both, breaking the trance, and he jumped back from me. Facing us were two muscle clones, their jaws agape and eyes wide in horror at the scene before them. "Jesus Christ!" the taller one exclaimed.

For a long moment we all stood there in a frozen tableau, the two of them still shocked, me propped weakly against the wall, and Miklos, facing me, now poised to flee. His neat goatee was stained red with my blood. It trailed down his chin and matted down the hairs of his chest. He gave me a sneering, hateful smile, and I could see the protruding canines in his upper jaw: stained carmine like the rest of his teeth. Then with an insane laugh he turned and fled, running down the alley so inhumanly fast that he seemed to disappear into the night. Clamping one hand against my neck, I collapsed against the wall, the two clubbers jumping forward in surprise to catch me as I fell.

I spent the next three days in bed, running a fever and wondering in a vaguely distracted way if I should try to get to a hospital. On the third day the fever broke, leaving me weak as a kitten but otherwise recovering. Sometime during my ordeal the bites on my neck had disappeared, leaving only smooth skin behind.

I didn't notice any change at first. I did seem to be cold most of the time and a little more sensitive to light; I took to wearing sunglasses almost everywhere. Otherwise, I chalked it up to random weirdness. The guy was just some freak I'd been unlucky enough to run into. But then I began to have strange...cravings. As if there were some longing inside me for something I couldn't quite name, the way I had always felt in Roanoke before Father Antonio. I stayed away from the clubs for a long time after that unlucky night, but one Saturday night I finally drifted back, drawn in part by the craving that was beginning to clamor increasingly loudly inside me. Thinking it was sex I wanted, I went hunting for it.

His name was Gary, and he was blond. He was a big guy, well over six feet, with that curious mix of hard muscle and well-padded-out flesh that some guys get after lots of heavy lifting. He had blue eyes that seemed to glow of their own accord and matched the electric-blue T-shirt that stretched tight against the muscles of his chest. His tree-trunk legs bulged against the thin fabric of the camouflage pants he wore, and his ass was tight and high and inviting.

We tore each other's clothes off on his living room floor before we could get to the bedroom, Gary fishing a condom out of his back pocket with a smile. Soon I was inside him, feeling the long length of my cock slide into him and feeling that surely this must be what I had been needing, when my gaze became transfixed by the pulse throbbing in his throat, the lovely line of the vein outlined beneath his alabaster skin. At the sight of it the siren song in my brain swelled, and I knew without thinking that this was what I had been craving. A rush of animal desire washed over me, obliterating reason. There was a tearing in my upper jaw and I felt the sharp points of my canines jab into my lower lip. With a snarl I launched myself into the promise of his outstretched throat; my only thought to take what I so desperately needed. I clamped my mouth to his neck, feeling the fangs punch through the skin, and for one blessed moment of relief the wonderful taste of him was on my tongue, hot and alive.

Then Gary was shouting, screaming in fury, squirming beneath me to shove me off him. I was holding on with an almost hysterical strength, desperate for just one more drop of his sweet blood, but he was bigger and stronger than me. I tried to hold onto him harder, and he struck me roughly on the side of the head, stunning me and shoving me to one side. My still-hard cock slid out of him as he pushed me off him. He backed away from me with one hand clamped to his neck, shouting obscenities as his handsome face twisted in horror and disgust. I lay there stunned but with my cock still rock-hard, unbelieving of what I had just tried to do, and all the while the taste of his blood was on my lips and tongue, *so good, so sweet...*

With a strangled cry I grabbed my jeans and shoes and ran out of his apartment and into the stairwell, not stopping to pull on my pants until I stumbled to a stop on the landing two floors below. My chest was heaving and sweat poured down my body; within I was chilled at the horror of what I had just tried to do. Shirtless, I walked the city for hours until early Sunday morning. Then I found the nearest church. I walked right up the long aisle between the pews and threw myself down on the cold hard stone floor before the altar and prayed as I had never before in my life, begging and sobbing as I pleaded for salvation.

A priest found me there and I ran again, back home to my apartment, where I locked the door tight. I didn't know what had happened to me, and I didn't want to. Whatever horrible hunger I'd been infected with, I knew that next time it would drive me to kill. I would have murdered Gary in another minute, would have sucked him dry in my craving for the indescribable pleasure of drinking his blood if his instinct for survival hadn't saved us at the last minute.

I suppose I should have had powers like in all the stories—to be able to fly, to magically heal myself, the same eldritch presence that Miklos had. But if such things came with drinking blood, I wanted no part of them.

I stopped going out to the bars and the clubs, stopped returning the glances I got from men on the street.

I jerked off a lot.

But each time I did I would feel the hunger swell anew within me even as I came, and find myself gasping, tongue extended as I strained for just one drop of precious blood. Afterward, mopping up the spent come, I would see Gary's horrified face in my mind's eye, and a cold hand of fear and shame would clutch at my vitals, reminding me of how close I'd come to becoming a killer. After a while, even jerking off wasn't worth it.

There were long summer nights when the electric smells of the night would drift through my lonely apartment window, tempting me to go out into the night. To run, to fuck, to finally slake my red thirst. On those nights I would think, *Just once. Just one taste.* But I knew that if I tried even once, I would become a thing of evil. I had barely escaped committing a mortal sin the last time blood had touched my lips. I hadn't killed Gary, but I knew what would happen next time.

In my nightmares I drained him dry until I woke screaming, the sheets sticky with sweat and come.

~

It had been four long years since that first fateful morning. Four years of denying myself the slaking of my hunger. Four years since I'd lain before an altar, sobbing. I looked up at the altar now and above it at Jesus impaled upon the crucifix, his arms outstretched. He'd suffered too. For a moment I sat there, gazing at his face, until I noticed the crimson blood staining his forehead and hands. False blood. Even from here I could tell it didn't smell right. With a sob of disgust I buried my face in my hands.

A soft voice startled me out of my reverie. "Can I help you?" I looked up to see a young priest standing beside my pew.

Mutely I shook my head.

"You seem to be in distress," he said gently. He nodded toward my face. "I just thought that you might want to talk."

I brought one hand up to brush at my face in surprise and realized that tears were streaming down my cheeks. I looked up at the priest. He was waiting patiently for me to say something, to tell him what trouble it was that had brought me there. His face was open and without guile. He smelled of sandalwood soap and incense and sexual frustration.

Muttering apologies, I fled into the dying gloom of evening.

~

Lost in my brooding thoughts, it wasn't until I was turning the key in the lock of my third-floor apartment that I heard the floor-boards of the old building creak behind me. I whirled to see Scott emerge from the shadows of the hallway.

"I knew you'd have to come back here eventually." He took a step closer. "I've been waiting for you."

"Stay away from me," I said, backing away. I stared transfixed at the vein throbbing at his open shirt collar and felt the bloodlust within me beginning to stir. "You don't know what you're risking."

He took another step closer, and the intoxicating scent of him arose around me. "I'm not afraid of you." He smelled of sunshine and healthy male sweat.

"No," I mumbled, stepping back again until my back was against the cold metal of the door. This time there was nowhere left for me to run. Scott deliberately leaned forward and slowly, force-fully, pressed his lips to mine. And as our lips touched, all at once my restraint finally crumbled and the hunger I'd held back all those nights rushed forth at last.

I reached out and drew him into my arms, crushing him to me. His hands groped my crotch, through the fabric of my jeans, and stroked the length of my cock, which had gone instantly hard. His mouth was warm and yielding beneath mine and his body was pli-able in my arms, open and surrendering to me, and I realized that he wanted me to take him here, right here in the hall of my apartment building, take him in the way that I wanted to take him...

With my last semblance of control I fumbled desperately behind me for the doorknob and it turned, slamming the door open and tumbling us both into the room and onto the floor. We were knocked apart by the impact, and I scrambled onto my knees and shoved the door shut. When I turned around, Scott was backing toward my bedroom door, shedding his leather jacket as he went. I followed him as he backed inside, only to be brought up short by the sight of him undressing.

The streetlights shone through the bedroom blinds, painting him in alternating stripes of light and shadow as he stepped back and drew his shirt off over his head. His chest was hairless and tight-ly muscular. I watched the play of light across his skin as he slid his jeans down over his hips, revealing a burst of hair and an erection that pointed unerringly at me like a compass. Then he kicked off his jeans and shoes and stood confidently naked before me.

That's when my mind finally registered the scars. They stood out red and angry across his tanned skin. There was one running underneath each knee and one that drew a thin, jagged, angry line across his torso. An odd, pale, puckered one marred the perfection of his right shoulder, and another ran along his left forearm. Yet they only emphasized the beauty of his body. He looked like an angel that had fallen from grace. I reached out for him like a man reaching for redemption.

His flesh beneath my hands was hot and smooth, his warmth flowing into me as I ran my hands over his back, his ass, his legs. Then his hands slipped beneath my shirt and he was running them hungrily over my chest, his fingers grabbing handfuls of hair. As I hurriedly stripped my shirt up over my head he leaned against me and I felt his tongue drag across my left nipple. My back arched with the pleasure of it, and then he was licking all of my chest in long strokes, slicking the hairs with his saliva. His hands were busy at my belt and soon he had my pants open, my cock springing up aching and hard. At once he fell to his knees and swallowed me into his mouth.

I had forgotten how good it felt. Scott's mouth on me was wet and warm, his lips soft yet with a whipcord strength in them. He drew his lips upward along the shaft, his tongue playing over across the head, and then swallowed me deeply into his throat as his fingers stroked my balls. Under the warm pressure of his mouth, my inhibitions slipped further away as my need mounted higher.

I pulled him to his feet and shoved him onto the bed, pausing only to get rid of my jeans. Then I was on him, pressing him down into the bed with my mouth locked to his as my hands roamed his body. His flesh was smooth where it wasn't scarred, and feverish everywhere as he leaned into my hands, urging me with his body to take him.

"I want you in me," he whispered in my ear, and at that my desire raged beyond all limits.

I raised myself on my elbows and clawed with one hand at the nightstand, pulling the drawer open and fishing frantically for the condoms and lube that I hoped would still be in there somewhere.

With surprising strength Scott grabbed my wrist and yanked it back to the bed, shaking his head in denial. I opened my mouth to protest, but Scott didn't wait. He wrapped his arms around my shoulders and with a strangled cry thrust upward, impaling himself on my cock. I froze in surprise, but Scott grabbed my ass and shoved me into him again at once. He pulled at my hips hungrily, insistently forcing me into him over and over until, driven by his urgency, I let go of my restraint and began to fuck him myself, pounding deeply into him with each stroke.

"Yeahhh," he moaned in my ear before releasing me and letting his shoulders fall back onto the bed.

His face beneath me was the most beautiful sight I have ever seen in my life. His angelic head was thrown back in ecstasy, pushed deep into the pillows each time I thrust into him. His arms were thrown out to the sides, like a sacrifice. The strong curve of his neck was exposed, calling to me.

I pushed my face against his throat until my mouth was barely an inch away from his skin, breathing hot onto him, and in answer he leaned his head farther back. I grabbed him by the side of the head, shoving him down into the pillows, then in a long, slow stroke licked along the side of his neck. His flesh was hot and slick, and I could feel the throbbing of his pulse beneath my tongue. His blood was there, separated from me by only a thin layer of skin, and now I could smell it too. It called to me, and I once again felt the odd pain in my jaw as my canines extended. At the last moment I hesitated, remembering Gary. The tips of my fangs were just touching Scott's skin as with my last shred of rational thought I held back from him, but then his hand came around the back of my neck, urging me to him. I opened my mouth wide and bit deep into his neck as he stiffened beneath me.

The blood, when it came at last, was hot and fresh, pouring down my throat like a golden elixir. I could feel it rushing deep into me, a river of pleasure that burned away the coldness in my core. Scott gave a long, shuddering moan of pleasure, and I felt his cock grow rock-hard between us. Any lingering shreds of doubt I might have had vanished in that moment, and I gave myself over freely to the hunger within me. I wanted him, wanted to consume all of him. I would drain him. I would drink all of his blood and it would kill him but I didn't care.

And he wanted me to do it.

Even as his blood poured out into me Scott was gasping in frenzied ecstasy, his legs wrapped around my ass, clutching me tightly and urging me to thrust deeper into him. He humped his own cock up into the hairs of my belly slick with his precome. His back arched once, twice, then again.

Scott began to thrash on the bed, his cries growing ever higher and more ecstatic. His hands were clamped around the back of my neck, crushing me to his throat with a superhuman strength. And then he came. Great gouts of come blasted out of him and showered us both. As he did, his insides tightened around me, hot and tight and slick, squeezing me again and again until I came too, feeling my warmth gush deep inside him. A rush of pleasure shot from my groin up my spine and exploded into my brain to meet the pleasure pouring into me from his throat. The force of it was blinding and it threw my head back as I screamed, losing my grip on his neck. Blood gushed from my open mouth as I cried out, covering us both in warm wetness.

Scott looked at me in stunned, dazed satisfaction and then smiled contentedly. Blood was still pulsing weakly from his throat, and I bent down to lick the wound, bathing it in my saliva. When I looked up again, his eyes had closed.

I had lain awake watching him lie unmoving for what seemed like hours, trying to tell, as I watched the slow rise and fall of his chest, if he was merely in a deep healing sleep or slowly dying from blood loss. I was afraid to move, both afraid to leave him and afraid to go for help. I kept my palm against his chest, feeling his heartbeat thrum beneath it. The last thing I saw before my own eyes closed at last was the contented smile on his beautiful lips.

~

I awoke to the smell of frying eggs and the sound of dishes clattering in the kitchen. I stretched lazily, astonished at how good I felt. For the first time in longer than I could remember, there was no need clawing inside me. I felt complete and whole.

I threw on a robe and slipped into the bathroom to throw water on my face, then stepped cautiously into the kitchen. Scott was busy at the stove, his hair still wet from the shower, a damp white towel wrapped tightly around his hips. Far from being dead, he seemed to glow with health, muscles flexing smoothly under his tanned skin as he puttered around the counter. Early-morning sunlight streamed through the narrow kitchen window, alternately highlighting the planes of his body. He looked even more beautiful, if possible, than he had the night before.

"Um...what are you doing?" I asked, a little at a loss for words.

"I'm making you breakfast, what does it look like?" He opened my refrigerator and poked through the bins. "Haven't you got any bacon?"

"I'm a vegetarian."

He gave me an amused, disbelieving look. I shrugged, non-plussed. "The blood doesn't...taste right. Look, you don't need to do this." I started to push into my kitchen.

"Stop." He laid one hand against my chest. "Everything's fine, I've got it under control. Go wait in the living room and I'll be out in a minute."

I went out and sat on the living room couch. The room was bright with the light streaming through the picture windows and gleaming off the hardwood floors. Nothing made sense anymore. For years I'd fought my thirst for blood, knowing it to be truly evil. But Scott had wanted that from me more than anything, enough to find me. I'd come damn close to killing him last night; only the overwhelming shock of our combined orgasm had distracted me from draining him. Yet this morning my erstwhile victim was happily cooking breakfast in my kitchen. And I felt better than I had in years.

My thoughts were interrupted as Scott came into the room,

balancing a tray. I looked up as he set down a plate of toast and eggs before me on the coffee table. There was also a large glass of tomato juice.

I looked up to find him smirking. "Tomato juice," I said. "I get it. Very funny."

He shrugged and began to dig into his eggs. "Hey, it was in your fridge."

I just stared at him. "How did you know?" I burst out at last. "Know what?"

"That I wouldn't..." I faltered, then looked him in the eye. "Kill you."

He grinned wildly. "I didn't. But if you want something badly enough, you have to be willing to take a risk to get it."

I gaped at him. "You're insane."

He set down his plate and took my hand, then drew it lightly over the scar on his chest. "I got this free-climbing a rock face in the Rockies. I fell 15 feet and gashed it open on a ledge." He pointed first to his forearm and then to his knees. "Scaling a razor-wire fence, doing a little nighttime sabotage with Queer Nation. Blew the knees out on a wicked downhill run in Aspen."

"And this?" I asked, fingering the strange scar on his shoulder.

"Gunshot wound." He smirked as I started in surprise, then shrugged. "Long story. The point is," he continued as he took my face in his hands, "risk is how you know you're alive. The bigger the risk, the bigger the thrill. And last night? That was the best!"

"You took more than one risk," I said, my mind reeling. "No condom."

He stretched his neck upward to show me where the bite marks were already disappearing. "I think you have powers you haven't even begun to explore. Yes, last night was dangerous—that's what made it so hot—but we're both still alive."

"It's *too* dangerous," I protested. "Next time I might go too far or even make you...like me."

"I'm not afraid of you, Tony. I'm not afraid of the risk." He moved quickly, sliding the warmth of his body over mine. He tugged at his towel until it came free, and laid his head against my chest as his hands slid beneath my robe. "And I'm not letting you get away from me."

I sat there with his damp hair smelling clean and fresh against my chest as my groin hardened beneath his hands. I watched the bright sunlight streaming into the room and slowly, reluctantly, at last, accepted the promise of salvation.

9821 Easton Drive
Max Pierce

"Marilyn...Judy...Sammy Davis Jr.—I served them all. Was in the Embassy Ballroom the night Bobby Kennedy was shot. Bloody mess that was."

While many people only dream of living in Los Angeles, I made it real. I'd escaped forever the cold winters of the Midwest for the land of palm trees and perpetual sunshine. Free of family expectations, I would forge a new life.

But my arrival was not without complication. Deciding to splurge before settling into work and an apartment and not checking the situation beforehand, I arrived at the fabled Ambassador Hotel on Wilshire Boulevard, only to learn it was closing and no rooms were available. This New Year's Eve would be its last hurrah, although no celebration was planned. I was one of the final patrons of a hotel who had entertained presidents and royalty, hosted the Academy Awards in its Cocoanut Grove, and had seen the highest highs and lowest lows of life. A mustachioed bartender, wearing a long-outgrown tuxedo jacket that accented his barrel chest and husky arms with black hair jutting from the white shirt cuffs, focused on the lows. "The Ambassador has been cursed ever since that night. People just stopped coming in...and the goddamn owners bled the place white—"

We were alone in the Palm Bar, I watched the clock's hands

creep to 9 and nursed a tall vodka while eating peanuts, all the while wishing Clark Gable or Vivien Leigh might wander through the deserted lobby and join me in a farewell toast to 1988 and this hotel. Instead, I remained a captive, listening to ghost stories as the wind appropriately whipped outside, rattling the old windows.

"The Spanish Patio—that's what we old-timers call it. Walk out there and you can feel eyes on you—but nobody's ever around."

A rustling noise in the lobby grabbed my attention from thoughts of why the rental car place at the end of the drive had closed at 6. There was a Hyatt two blocks west. I could walk there, but hefting my luggage would be no small feat.

A well-dressed woman with regal bearing swept into the bar, but my eyes did not miss the bartender crossing himself before clicking his heels and giving her a short bow. She surveyed the room with a haughty expression, and as I was the single occupant, she looked down her hawklike nose at me. She passed to a table overlooking what must have been a glorious garden that now resembled a tired salad. A sudden gust of wind awakened the branches of a faded rosebush, causing it to scratch at the window as if beckoning me outside.

"Champagne," she commanded.

The bartender bowed again, leaving us alone in the musty room.

"Would you join me?" It was not a question but a direction.

The wind whirled again, causing the lights to flicker.

"Looks like a wild night," I said, unsure of what to say. Her faded elegance complemented the hotel.

"The Santa Anas. They create havoc." She studied me. "That's what we call the winds, for they blow from the east."

"I'm used to the wind. I'm from Chicago."

"Visiting?"

I shook my head.

She looked down her nose. "You look like a young Roddy McDowall. Do you have a girlfriend?"

"Yes," I lied, "we're engaged." Not wishing to continue this questioning further, I added, "I begin work on Monday at an academy in Brentwood." Saying it aloud, I couldn't believe it. Beverly Hills, Bel-Air, and Brentwood. The "B" circuit, the bartender said.

"Is that the Lange School? I know it well." She surveyed my luggage stacked beside the bar. "You're not staying here?"

"I would, but the hotel is closing—"

"When I arrived from New Orleans at Union Station, a limousine brought me to this hotel." She looked away. "Life was different then."

"—and they aren't renting any rooms. Could you recommend—"

The bartender returned with a bottle I recognized from my table-waiting days: Dom Perignon, 1959. "Excuse me, sir," he interrupted, as he filled our glasses, "I checked with the manager, and although we are closing, we do have a room for you."

"Nonsense," the woman said, dismissing him with a wave. "This is a rat trap. Usually there's only hookers at this bar."

"Not recently," he stated, avoiding her intense gaze. "We will give you the room at no charge, sir."

I assumed she was one of those rich eccentrics whose grandsons I'd be teaching. A free room, even in a dusty place such as the Ambassador, was tough to turn down.

"I live no more than 15 minutes from the Langes. If you will celebrate this New Year's with me at my home, I will have my car take you there in the morning."

"That would be kind of you." Although she seemed to have more in common with Norma Desmond than Nancy Reagan, it would be better than a night in the Ambassador. Those ghost stories were getting to me, and the Dom Perignon hit me hard.

"Then let us go." She stood, taking the bottle of champagne, and I tried not to gape at the brilliant diamonds that dangled from her ears and around her slender wrists.

"My name is David, David Karr," I said, following her

through the red-carpeted lobby, passing rows of identical lamps that lit empty leather couches. A wizened porter, as shriveled as the bartender was burly, carried my bags, perhaps the last ones that would ever be taken out of the old place.

"I am Irene Graham Basilone."

I was still trying to picture Roddy McDowall when this new bit of trivia was thrown at me. My small knowledge of movies had made me ill-equipped for a pop quiz. She stopped and turned, waiting, possibly pleading with her eyes for me to recognize her.

"Of course." I answered, hoping I convinced her.

She took my arm as we walked past a row of abandoned shops to the exit, serenaded by piped-in music of a half century before. "Don't be fooled by my kindness." She shook a diamond-laden finger. "I'm a lonely old woman hungry for some intelligent conversation, and willing to risk inviting a stranger into her home to get it."

I laughed a bit too loud as I climbed into a black and blue Rolls Royce. As the car pulled away from the fading lights of the Ambassador, the Santa Anas twisted the palms in the night.

~

The Rolls turned onto Benedict Canyon Drive, just past the Beverly Hills Hotel and headed uphill. Mrs. Basilone gestured while reciting a litany of neighbors' names, some familiar, most not: Hedda Hopper, Pickfair ("I've become a recluse, like Mary"), Harold Lloyd ("a year-round Christmas tree, most odd"); Gilbert, Garbo, Jennifer Jones, and David O. Selznick, "and some rock star"; Valentino ("Doris Duke owns Falcon Lair, though no one doubts he still visits") and Sharon Tate.

"After those murders, life changed here in Los Angeles," she said, sounding not unlike the bartender at the Ambassador.

Another winding turn or two and we were on a narrow road that clung to the hillside. How the Rolls fit through that tiny space, I wasn't certain.

"I've lived at 9821 Easton Drive since 1946, through three husbands. My third was Tony Basilone." When I gave a half smile, she frowned. "The MGM director. Back then, we contract players called it "Metro." You know Tony's name, don't you?'

I shook my head, tired of pretending.

My ignorance agitated her. "*Moonlight in Manhattan? The War Years? A Bell for Cordelia?* I was Cordelia. After that, Mr. Mayer gave me Myrna Loy's old dressing room. I'd earned it, he said."

Thankfully, the car stopped at an arched door. Her rustic home was built into the canyon, towering three levels above and two below like bramble. Inviting lights beamed from several windows. Although I suspected she had been gone from the screen for some time, Irene Basilone must not have to worry about her electricity bill. The wind still danced around us, and I followed her quick entry through the door.

We stood in a large reception room, dressed in a Spanish colonial theme complete with hanging tapestries and twin suits of armor flanking the doorway. A glance to the left revealed a dining room, decorated in Early American, complete with a portrait of a colonial maiden smiling over the buffet. The subject's eyes were familiar.

Mrs. Basilone beamed. "The musical version of *Quality Street,* directed by my husband. They said I was better than Hepburn or Marion."

A stout woman with close-cropped copper hair stood at the bottom of a staircase perfect for dueling. Her dour expression was the only cold spot in the warm room.

My hostess touched my back. "Carlotta will show you upstairs. Dinner will be served in about 10 minutes."

Without saying a word, Carlotta ascended the stone steps and I followed. Passing above the dining room, I saw two place settings.

"I must be intruding. I see Mrs. Basilone was expecting a guest."

"No one is expected. Madame always has a second place set. In case..." Her scotch-on-the-rocks voice stopped in mid sentence, and I pondered the use of the word "Madame." Norma Desmond came to mind again.

My room was to the right at the top of the stairs. Opulently furnished, I had stepped out of Old Spain into Cleopatra's Egypt, had Cleopatra lived in the art deco period. Carlotta studied me, unlike the weary warmth of Mrs. Basilone. Her companion's hazel eyes were icy.

"I shall leave you."

Feeling uncomfortable, and with the warm room stuffy, I walked over to a set of French doors that led to a small balcony. I stepped outside and drank in the night air, sage and eucalyptus—unfamiliar scents, but Mrs. Basilone informed me of them as we traveled up the hill. The hillside rose above the house, and before me yawned the canyon and the twinkling lights of Los Angeles.

Turning to go back in, two levels below I saw a man, dressed in a tuxedo and pacing the terrace. I could not see his face, nor was he aware of my presence.

I came back into the bedroom, finding Carlotta tapping her foot. "You can see Catalina Island in the daytime. Come, we don't want to keep Madame waiting."

"You said no one was expected, but I saw a man on the terrace below. He...didn't look like an employee."

"I am the only servant at 9821 Easton Drive." She arched a penciled eyebrow and left the room. I was certain of what I saw, or at least I thought I was. I ran back onto the terrace, but he had vanished. Perhaps the wind and cypress trees played a trick on me.

~

Mrs. Basilone polished off two bottles of red wine as I ate. The meal, which consisted of a hearty potato soup, steak with vegetables, and chocolate cake, was so delicious I almost forgave Carlotta's creepy demeanor.

"Carlotta tells me you saw a man on the terrace below."

"I thought I did, but I must have been mistaken."

"You were not," she said, as if chiding me for doubting my own judgment. "He is my son."

The pleasant dinner had turned uneasy in seconds. "It's none—"

"I wanted you to think I was a lonely old woman. Now you know I lied. I have a son. He is...ill."

"I'm sorry."

"His illness has destroyed my own sanity."

I didn't want to continue this conversation. I wished I could leave.

"I can't stand the sight of him. Completely mad, he is. He has his own suite of rooms—" She made a semi-acknowledgment of a door beside the fireplace. "—and Carlotta takes care of him."

On cue, Carlotta materialized from wherever she had been lurking and clutched her employer's hand. "Madame, do not—"

I said, "You never see him? There must be some treatment available."

"I wish he were dead."

This remark stunned me. I had questioned Mrs. Basilone's mental state since we met and now was alarmed for my safety. However, she had been drinking heavily, and I rationalized that perhaps she was reciting dialogue from one of her films, for she seemed not to be speaking to me or Carlotta but to one of the large ornate mirrors that hung throughout the house.

Mrs. Basilone drifted into her past. "Once there were happy times here. Life. People came to visit and stayed for weeks. We traveled to New York, London. Now, because of him, I see no one. It is all his fault."

She focused on me as if I had just appeared before her, or if I had forgotten my line during the middle of an important scene in one of her films. "I'm feeling rather tired. If you will excuse me, I will say good night."

With that, she departed, Carlotta clucking behind her. I sighed in relief. A grandfather clock chimed 10. I looked as if I would be sleeping through New Year's.

~

The Santa Anas woke me around 11, opening the French

doors and spitting leaves across the floor. I got up to close the doors and looked out at the moonlight-drenched hills. It was so clear, those who derided Los Angeles for its smog had never been here in December. I looked down to see Mrs. Basilone's son standing atop the stone railing and regarding the brush and rock-laden valley beneath him. He had removed his tuxedo jacket, shirt, and shoes.

"Don't!" I called, but the wind carried my voice backward instead of down.

He would jump, I knew it. Perhaps that was what his mother wished, but I could not allow it. Stepping back into the room, I grabbed a china vase and aimed it downward. The piece hit my imaginary mark on the flagstone terrace and shattered behind him.

He jerked his head up, surprised. The moon had shifted, flooding with light my location above him on the small balcony. The wind stopped as if holding its breath. I held out my palm. "Please don't jump. I'll come down there."

Not wanting to go downstairs in my bedclothes, I discarded my boxers and pulled on a pair of jeans and my shirt. I spied a sterling silver letter opener on the desk and tucked it in my pocket. If he was crazy and attacked me, I'd not hesitate to use it. After peeking around and making sure neither Carlotta nor Mrs. Basilone roamed the halls, I crept down the stairs, crossed the dining room, and went through the small door to the left of the fireplace.

I stood in a small library, shelves of books built above me, but there was no sign of him. Fearful to call out, I debated taking one of two doors that led deeper into the massive house, when I heard his voice.

"Who are you, and what are you doing here?"

His face was hidden by the shadow of a tall lamp, I could only see dense brown hair covering a well-developed chest, and thick forearms.

"I was afraid you might jump."

"Who are you?"

"My name is David. I'm a guest—"

"Come here."

I hesitated. He remained in the shadows.

His brusque tone softened. "Please come here. You see—" He extended his left leg, revealing a shackle clamped firm around his ankle. "—I can't come to you."

It was an ornate restraint; like everything in this odd house, it could have been used as a prop. But this was not a soundstage, and I was horrified at this primitive device. Mrs. Basilone must be as disturbed as her son.

He turned on the tall lamp beside him. "And I could not jump, though I'd like to, unless I wanted to hang upside down off the terrace."

"Like a bat," I suggested, inching forward. With the light bathing him, I lost some of my fear. He was quite handsome, with tousled brown hair and chestnut eyes above a clean-shaven face. I guessed him to be about my age, 31.

"Why do you say that?" he snapped, and I stopped, keeping the long reading table as a barrier between us.

"Can you name something else that hangs upside down?" I countered, irritated. He had the same imperious attitude as his mother. "Since you are in no danger, I'll leave. I'm sorry to disturb you."

"But I am in danger. Don't you think it's odd to see a man shackled like some type of animal?"

With his thick body hair, I wanted to comment he could have been mistaken for a wolf, but if he was insane, I didn't want to provoke him. "Your mother said—"

"That I'm crazy. She's told my friends that I'm dead." His angular face and broad shoulders fell slack. "I suppose I might as well be."

I reached across the table and touched his arm. Beneath the soft hair, I felt hard muscle.

"Why would she do such a thing, if it—" I was putting my foot in my mouth.

"That's because this house, our Malibu and Palm Springs homes, and several acres of property in downtown Los Angeles are mine. My father left them to me, but this way, she controls everything." His sharp eyes assessed me, and he added, "Come from behind that table and I'll show you the other reason."

I remained in place and rested my hand on the letter opener hidden in my pocket.

"Don't worry, I won't bite you." He offered his hand and the soft voice returned. "I'm Pietro."

Pietro Basilone had a firm handshake. I came around the table to him.

We were pretty well-matched for height; however, his body showed the effects of regular exercise, probably weightlifting, whereas my concession to health was an attempted run once a week. Or every two weeks. If I worked out more, or he less, we might pass for blood relatives. If he wrestled me to the ground I might have trouble. I clutched the letter opener in my pocket as he put his hands on my shoulders. Then he kissed me—full on the lips.

"This is the other reason. Mother, you see, doesn't want a gay son."

Busy with finishing college, obtaining my teaching degree, and looking for work, I'd little time for social interaction with anyone, and I'd repressed my own same-sex leanings for so long I'd almost forgotten they were there. But with Pietro's kiss, the pent-up demand came flooding back—direct to my center.

A glance at his waist showed he had needs as well. He took my hand and led me into his quarters, the sound of metal scraping on tile reminding us that he was a prisoner in his own home.

His rooms were well-furnished. I looked beyond, into a smaller room equipped as a gym, as I'd suspected, with two benches, free weights and machines, treadmill and, to the side, what looked like a tanning bed. I could see Pietro had no lack of material comforts.

"It's almost midnight. Care to celebrate?" He opened a small refrigerator in his exercise room and produced a bottle of champagne and two glasses.

I nodded, but I stared at the gold shackle around his leg.

Seeing my questioning look, he added, "They feed me sleeping pills to knock me out. I'm asleep most of the time. But for the past few nights I've tossed the food without Carlotta realizing it. Tonight, you see, is the anniversary of my father's death, and I thought Mother might be planning something especially evil. She usually only brings women home for company."

Before I could inquire if his mother was a lesbian, Pietro put his finger to my lips and unbuttoned my Levi's. With confident hands he reached into the fabric and exposed me to him. Then, pulling me by my own full flesh, he guided me to a wing chair. With one tug my jeans were off. I was embarrassed at the complete lack of self-control I had over my own body, but it had been an eternity since I'd last had sex with anyone other than myself.

Curious if he was as perfect beneath his black wool trousers as he was on the outside, I reached out and tugged at the zipper, feeling a bit giddy from the champagne and this unexpected turn of events. But Pietro walked off, returning with a pair of scissors.

"You'll have to cut them off me. Do you mind?"

I shook my head and nipped the scissors on the left cuff. Once severed, the fabric ripped in a deliciously wicked fashion up to his waist. Unlike me, Pietro wore Calvin Klein white briefs that accentuated his tanned skin and hirsute legs. Not wearing underwear, I felt wonderfully whorish.

He stood before me, removing his briefs in one motion. His finely sculpted body was as if he modeled for one of the statues lining the terrace. I felt odd—in my past the sex roles were clearly defined, but in Pietro, who possessed a sturdy but nonthreatening masculinity, I saw my own male potential, and an equal.

As he turned around, I got a clear view of his back, which tapered in a perfect V shape I did not share, down to a narrow waist. His backside was covered with the same dark hair as on his chest and arms, and I became seized with an animalistic desire to penetrate him, to force my hardness inside his body and make this ideal example of male beauty squeal like a girl. Boldly I stood up, wondering if he had condoms.

He turned back to face me, my eyes drawn down to his impressive yet not outrageous sexual equipment hanging before me that had not been discernable in either his trousers or the briefs. I was sorry these rooms were devoid of the giant mirrors that were in the rest of the house. I would have liked to have our reflections joined, but perhaps Pietro Basilone was not as vain as he should be, although he showed no inhibitions.

He pressed against my chest with his hand, and I sat back in the plush velvet chair. Pietro dropped to his knees and in one gulp took me into his mouth. His hands traveled up my body and he tugged firm on my nipples, grappling the light brown hair that I had on my chest, as I positioned my fingers in his earlobes to hold him steady. Each of us searched the other's eyes as he wrapped his tongue around and around my cock; instead of an insecure man needing to dominate to prove his superiority, I saw a partner only eager to please. I envisioned Pietro with both legs and arms restrained, being kept naked in my room. I imagined him minus the pelt that defined him as male, seeing his taut muscles unprotected and available for inspection.

His mouth was exquisite, and electric sensations began traveling up my legs to their apex. He abandoned my nipples and now concentrated on my forearms and fingers, working them back and forth as if he were operating a loom. At no time did I see him reach for himself, but I observed his cock had thickened considerably and a thin strand of clear liquid extended from its tip to the floor.

The tension traveled inside me rapid-fire, and I knew I could hold on no more. He must have tasted this foreshadowing as well, for he nodded, his eyes encouraging me to enjoy release. Then, in a display of expert timing, he released his mouth lock on me, and we both jumped as I exploded a powerful geyser that coated his chest and belly. As I arched my back and collapsed into the chair, he took himself in hand and began pistoning himself. He stood before me performing like a prize stallion and groaning deeper as he approached orgasm, while I manipulated his body with a confidence and aggression I hadn't owned before. Again I fantasized of him chained and naked: his ass, cock, and balls denuded of fur and available for my taking.

The wind stirred up again, and through the open windows the tree branches moved in rhythm to Pietro's hand. I wondered if, in the distance, someone watched us. Our eyes were locked onto each other as I became him, feeling his enviable cock in my own hands; inhaling his musky scent, the sweat on his muscular chest mixed with another man's semen; feeling a sense of hunger. Hunger, an odd thought. The lack of food, for fear it was drugged. That must be what he was thinking. I wanted to feed Pietro, then invade him, and have him invade me. Over and over.

I decided to offer my backside to him when Pietro groaned loud, long, and with finality, looking up at the ceiling before returning his vision to me. I glanced down to see his ankle was tight against the restraint, with a bit of blood where he had chafed against it. His stout legs were spread wide; feet planted firm on the ground, hips thrusting, he released a shower of male energy that smelled of brine and coated my chest and cock, which was beginning to harden again. He continued pumping, milking the last drops onto the stone floor like a desperate man. I stood up, pulled him into me, and we collapsed as one onto the bed.

~

"Will you help me?" he asked as he stroked his fingers across my ribs, making me giggle.

He had demonstrated nothing like his mother had intimated. How odd that a woman who worked in films, and known other gay people, would reject her own son, particularly since he gave no impression of effeminacy.

"What can I do? Do you want me to call the police? A friend?"

"No. Carlotta has told me my mother keeps the key to this shackle in a box on her dressing table. I need you to go up there and get it."

"But—"

He pressed a finger to my lips, and I licked the brown hair on the lower part.

"How much wine did she drink at dinner?"

Seeing the answer in my eyes, he continued, "When she's asleep she's like a dead person."

I was amazed at how easily I took to thieving. I padded up the stairs and to the opposite end of the hall where Mrs. Basilone slept, her snores providing navigation. Atop an antique bureau a small mahogany chest rested, and the gold key hung on the inside. Within three minutes I was back downstairs and handing it to him.

"I will not forget your kindness," Pietro said, but there was a new gleam of hunger in his eyes that made me a little uncomfortable. It was the same intensity he had shown while we were having sex, but it was no longer directed at me. He bent down and inserted the key in the lock. It clicked.

"What have you done, child?" Mrs. Basilone's voice drowned out the sound of the shackle being thrown aside.

Pietro put his hand on my back. "Go to your room, David, lock the door, and wait. I'll be there...as soon as I take care of this."

As I tried to scoot past her, Mrs. Basilone grabbed me. "You stupid—"

"Let him go." He paused, and the house shuddered. "Mother, come here."

I ran. Instead of heading upstairs, I went for the front door. If necessary I would run down the canyon to Sunset and get help. I opened the door, and with the wind rushing in, Carlotta stood before me. Her now-unkempt hair and wild eyes made me question if she also was mad.

"You let him out, didn't you? I warned the old woman. 'Bring only girls home, he'll dispose of them with no fuss,' I said. But no, she wanted to torment him. Show him what he couldn't have. But you, you spoiled all that. Did he fuck you first? Did you suck his dick? He's insatiable, you know."

I was horrified at her line of questioning and vulgar words. It was like an awful dream, or a bad movie I couldn't turn off.

She ripped my shirt open and grabbed my neck, clawing. "Where's the mark? Where is it?"

I heard an awful scream from behind the fireplace. Terrified, I broke away from Carlotta, who laughed maniacally as I raced down Easton Drive. At the turn onto Benedict Canyon, I tripped on a rock and tumbled into a clump of sage, knocking myself out. The daylight awoke me.

Vampire Joe
Bob Vickery

You wouldn't believe how fuckin' hungry I get when I first wake up. It's always like this, no matter how much I feed the night before. I crawl out from inside the refrigerator carton I found two weeks ago behind an appliance store and sit on the floor, scratching my head. I look around. Fourteen days in this rented room hasn't warmed me up to it; the place still looks like a junkie's nightmare. I never was like one of those affected Anne Rice vampire queens, all that tragic posturing and Louis Quatorze decor, but I do have some appreciation for the finer things. I can remember nice apartments, with fireplaces and bay windows overlooking parks and furniture bought new from Italian showrooms. And honest-to-God coffins for crissakes, made out of mahogany, with satin linings and bronze fittings. I stare at the ribbons of paint peeling from the walls, the ratty, Salvation Army furniture, the orange-crate tables. The psycho case in the room next door is screaming at his crack-addict girl-friend about something, and she's screaming back. This is all so depressing. If I could afford it, and if I could find a shrink that prac-ticed at nighttime, I'd get therapy. I have some real quality-of-life issues here. Immortality is not what it's cracked up to be.

My belly growls, and I realize that I've got to take care of busi-ness. I assess the situation. *What do I feel like tonight?* I ask myself. *Tex-Mex? Thai? Italian?* No, definitely not Italian, I had that last night. I think his name was Gino. I stretch and climb to my feet. Tonight, I feel like *seafood*.

I hail a cab outside and tell the driver to take me to the waterfront. It's winter, the evenings start early this time of year; and the cab darts and weaves through rush-hour traffic. The store windows are all lit up with Christmas decorations, and the sidewalks are crowded with shoppers. I stare glumly out the cab window. *When was the last time I celebrated Christmas?* I wondered. I can't remember. Certainly not since I joined the ranks of the undead. As the cab nears the docks the Christmas decorations get more beat up, until they're reduced to an occasional string of lights in some shabby shop window. The cabbie's got the radio on, and "The Little Drummer Boy" pours out of the back speakers. "Can you turn that down?" I ask irritably. The cabbie looks at me in the rearview mirror and after a couple of beats twists the volume knob to low.

We drive down streets flanked with dark warehouses and empty loading docks. It must have rained during the day, while I was sleeping in my cardboard box, because there's pools of water in the potholes, catching the reflection of the occasional streetlamp. The traffic has thinned to next to nothing, but I notice one car seems to be dogging us. I feel my throat tighten. *Van Helsing!* I think, feeling the old dread. It can't be. I've painstakingly covered my tracks since our last encounter two weeks ago—there's no *way* that old bastard could have found me again. But I know enough never to underestimate him. I wait a couple of blocks before I dare sneak another glance out the back window. The street behind us is now deserted, and I let myself relax a bit. But only a bit. You never can tell with that son of a bitch. It sucks belonging to the last minority it's OK to oppress.

I can only see the back of the cabbie's head: the greased-back black hair, the thick neck, the muscular forearms resting on the steering wheel. The eyes that glance at me in the rearview mirror are brown and melancholy. I glance at his ID on the dashboard and notice that his name is Vaslo. *Hungarian?* I wonder. *Polish?* I consider feeding on him, and I toy with the image of his body's hot fluids flooding into my mouth, how they would taste before I swallowed. Sweet Jesus, but that's a delectable thought! But with him driving, I can't maintain eye contact long enough to hypnotize him. *Let it go,* I think. *There's plenty of others.*

Vaslo drops me off at the entrance to a waterfront bar. As I pay him I look him straight in the face, taking in once more the sad eyes; the sensuous, well-formed mouth; the strong chin. Out of habit I hold his gaze as I pull my wallet out, and after a few seconds his eyes glaze and his mouth falls open. The hunger roars through my body. But we're on a public street, cars are cruising by, and I can see pedestrians half a block away. My hunger is tempting me to take dangerous risks. I throw the bills on the front seat. "Here," I snarl. "Now beat it!" His body jerks, and he blinks his eyes. I tear myself away and walk to the door without looking back.

The bar's a dump, but I'm not one to let aesthetics get in the way. I stand in the doorway, my eyes doing a slow sweep of the place. Because of the cold night outside, the room is overheated; the warm air rushes up to my nostrils, heavy with the scent of cigarette smoke, stale beer, and unwashed bodies. Saliva pools in my mouth.

I settle on the two sailors leaning against the bar, talking. My eyes scan them as I approach the bar: The one on the right is short and dark, with a tight muscular body and angry eyes that dart around the bar as he drinks his beer. I can tell he's a firecracker. His buddy is taller and leaner, with sandy hair and a mild expression. They strike me as unlikely companions.

When I'm beside them, I motion to the bartender. "Whatever you got on tap," I say. "And fresh drinks for my two friends as well."

The sailors turn their heads and look at me, the shorter one suspiciously, the other merely curious. After a beat, they give their orders to the bartender. By the second round they start warming up to me, and on the third we're all the best of friends. The sandy-haired guy is Luke, and his angry little buddy is Nick. I focus my thoughts as we talk, gently probing into their minds, setting things up to hypnotize them. I stop. *Hell,* I think. *I bet I can take these guys on without cheating.* There's always more sport to simple seduction.

I smile and pour on the charm, feigning interest while they fill me in on the sailor's life: how the Hong Kong girls compare to Thais, which ports have the best whorehouses, the stories behind their various tattoos. Subtly at first, but then with increasing blatancy, I nudge the conversation along toward sex. They're both only too willing to follow that thread, and soon there's a tension among us that starts to crackle like ozone before a lightning strike.

"It must be tough on you guys," I finally say, "being at sea for weeks at a time. I bet by the time you hit a port you're ready for whatever it takes to get your rocks off."

Nick and Luke both shoot me a hard look. They can sense that we've crossed a line, that we're not making idle conversation anymore. "Yeah," Nick says slowly. "It gets to be a real problem sometimes."

I let the silence hang in the air for a moment. "I can take care of your problem, if you want," I say carefully. My eyes dart to Luke's face and then back to Nick's. "For both of you."

Nick and Luke exchange glances. Nick raises one eyebrow, and after a beat, Luke gives a small nod. They both turn their eyes on me again. I jerk my head toward the back door beyond the pool tables. "Follow me," I say. My tone is calm, but the hunger is pounding inside of me like a wrecking ball.

We walk out the bar's back door into the alley behind it. The cold winter night bites into us. I don't waste time on preliminaries, but drop to my knees in front of the two sailors. I reach up and unbuckle first Luke's belt, then Nick's, unzip their flies, and then pull down their trousers. The two men watch me, Nick's dark eyes narrowed, Luke's gaze more calm and steady. I pull back slightly and take in what's for dinner tonight. Nick's dick swings heavily between his muscular thighs: thick, dark, uncut, and meaty. Luke's is pinker, blue-veined, with a fleshy red dick head and balls that hang low and ripe.

I start with Luke, burying my face into his balls, smelling their pungent odor of musk and sweat, feeling their hairs tickle my nose. I open my mouth and slide his dick in, slowly bobbing my head up and down. Luke's dick soon swells to full hardness, filling my mouth impressively. Luke sighs and begins pumping his hips, fucking my face with slow, easy strokes. I reach up and twist his nipples, not gently. Luke groans, and his dick gives a sharp throb in my mouth.

I spit in my other hand and start beating Nick off, sliding the silky foreskin up and down the shaft. Nick's dick is thick and fleshy, and I can barely get my fingers around it. I pull Luke's dick out of my mouth and beat off both men together, a dick in each hand. Luke's low-hangers swing heavily between his legs, but Nick's are pulled up tighter, closely hugging the base of his dick shaft. I look up at the two sailors as I stroke their cocks, probing into their minds, tickling the pleasure centers in their brains. Nick gives a star-tled gasp of pleasure and Luke's knees buckle. They stare down at me, astonished, and I grin back at them.

I alternate working over the two dicks in front of me, sucking on Nick's for a while, teasing him, bringing him to the brink, and then switching back to Luke's. I slide my hand under Nick's shirt, feeling the hard bands of his abs, the smoothness of his skin under my fingertips, the rough little nubs of his nipples stiff from the cold. My other hand squeezes the muscles of Luke's ass, feeling them clench and unclench as his dick slides in and out of my mouth. I've got the two of them wound up tighter than a top, and their cocks twitch in front of me, wet from my saliva, arcing up, about as hard as cocks get. Every time my mouth sweeps down their cocks I stare up into their eyes and enter their minds, tickling their pleasure cen-ters with increasing intensity. Luke gives off a little whimper with each downward slide of my mouth, and Nick groans loudly when I switch my attentions to him. I feel like I'm drawing music out of the two instruments of flesh in front of me, working them both with the skill of a virtuoso.

Their excitement ripples into my mind...I can *sense* it—feel its pulse in my brain—ratcheting up my hunger to higher and higher levels. It's hell for me as well to tease them like this, to bring them to the brink of shooting only to draw them back again, but the self-torture excites me, whips me into a frenzy of expectation.

Nick pumps his hips frantically, his moans bouncing off the alley's brick walls, and when I switch to Luke's dick again, Nick whimpers in frustration. Soon Luke is groaning again, tremors shaking his body as I work his dick ravenously while Nick watches us with feverish eyes.

I reach the point where I can't take the torment of the hunger anymore. I slide my mouth down Luke's dick shaft as I push into his mind with the one word: *now!* Luke gives a mighty groan and his body spasms. His dick throbs in my mouth and I feel his hot load gush down my throat. I suck on his dick like a baby on its mother's tit, squeezing every last drop out, savoring the thick sweet cream of his load; it's like a milkshake, and I close my eyes with the sheer sharp pleasure of it. Strength flows into my body as Luke crumples to his knees.

Nick is next. I skin back his dick and run my tongue around the flared head, as my other hand slides under his shirt, squeezing the hard muscles of his torso. I leave his dick full in my mouth for a moment, my nose buried in his crinkly black pubes, his heavy balls pressed against my chin, the balls that hold that sweet, sweet load of his that will soon be gushing down my throat. I squeeze his nipples again, and he groans. "Yeah," he croons, "That's right. Play with my titties." I reach behind and run my hands over his ass, feeling the firm flesh under my fingertips. I pull his cheeks apart and worm my finger up his asshole at the same moment that my mouth slides down his dick. Nick's body shudders and he cries out as his hot sperm splatters down my throat to join Luke's load. It's hot and spicy, with the faintest undertaste of chile and basil, and I gulp it down thirstily.

I'm sucking out the last drop from Nick's swollen dick when the door leading to the bar is suddenly flung open. Light streams into the alley, silhouetting the bodies of three men crowded in the doorway. I recognize Van Helsing and his gang immediately. *Shit!* I think. I jump to my feet, shoving Nick aside, and run down the alley. "Grab that cocksucker!" I hear Van Helsing shout, and then there's the sounds of footsteps in pursuit.

I fling the garbage cans down behind me; there's the crash of someone falling over them, but I don't look back. The entrance to the alley is ahead of me—it seems to stretch out at an impossibly far distance, and the footsteps are gaining. I still feel groggy from my recent feeding, my coordination is off, and I stumble and fall. Someone lunges out toward me, and I kick out, landing my foot in his belly. He grunts and doubles over, and I scramble to my feet again, lurching forward. *I'll never get away*, I think desperately.

I stumble out of the alley, and miraculously there's a cab by the curb, with the door open. "Get in," someone shouts, and I dive into the backseat. The cab roars off, tires squealing and the door still open. I look back and see Van Helsing standing on the curb, his face twisted in rage.

I reach over and slam the door shut as the cab races down the street. Vaslo's eyes glance back at me in the rearview mirror. He winks, and then shifts his gaze to the road ahead. I'm too dazed to say anything for a while. I lean back into the cab's seat and smooth my hair down. A glance out the rear window shows that the streets are empty, but I keep my optimism in check. Vaslo tears down streets and back alleys, the car lurching from side to side. My stomach clenches, but I don't ask him to slow down. He finally careens into a dark alley and slams on the brakes. I lurch forward, grabbing hold of the seat in front of me. Vaslo turns his head toward me, grinning. "I think we lost your friend," he says. He speaks in a heavy Eastern European accent.

I pull myself up. "Don't be too sure. He has a habit of popping up unexpectedly."

"Yeah, I know. I know all about Van Helsing."

I stare at Vaslo, letting a few beats go by. "You're full of surprises," I finally say. I take a deep breath and let it out. "What else do you know?"

"I know you're a..." Vaslo spits out some unintelligible word.

"What the hell does that mean?"

"It's Romanian. It means 'sperm eater.' " Vaslo stretches his arms above his head. "One of the lesser known types of vampires.

The ones that don't feed on blood." He pauses and risks a quick glance at me. "The ones that don't kill their prey."

"Jeez," I mutter. I give a humorless laugh. "And I thought I was so good at passing."

"I knew after you paid me," Vaslo says calmly. I notice that he's not looking me in the eyes as he talks but over my left shoulder. *This guy's no dummy*, I think. *He knows I need eye contact to hypnotize him.* "I know what it's like to be hypnotized by a sperm eater." He reaches into his shirt pocket, pulls a cigarette out and lights it. He inhales deeply and lets out a cloud of smoke. "I was the lover of a sperm eater once. Back in Moldavia. I was always his first. I'd wait by his coffin when evening first started coming on, and he would wake up and drain me dry." Vaslo's eyes soften in memory. "The best blow jobs I ever had." He risks another quick glance at me and grins. "That little mental trick you sperm eaters have, pushing into a man's mind right when he starts shooting, is fucking amazing."

"What happened to him?" I ask.

Vaslo's eyes harden. "Van Helsing killed him. His men cornered him and locked him in a room until he starved. I was in the local pub when Van Helsing came in days later and bragged about it."

"Jesus," I say softly.

Vaslo takes another long drag from his cigarette and exhales. We don't say anything for a long time. I hear a TV blaring from one of the windows facing the alley. "I can understand killing the blood drinkers," he finally says. "They're a public menace, and it's either us or them. But the sperm eaters harm no one." He shakes his head. "But Van Helsing is fanatical about vampires. He wants them all dead."

"No shit," I say. "The bastard's been tracking me for months. He's inhuman."

Vaslo gives a bark of laughter. "You're one to talk."

To my surprise, this stings. "Hey, I may be one of the walking dead," I say, "but I still got feelings."

Vaslo doesn't seem to notice my injured tone. "When I saw him walk into the bar with his goons, I knew it was you he was after.

That's why I waited with the door open and the engine running."

"You know, you can look me in the eye," I say. "I won't hypnotize you. I promise."

Vaslo turns his gaze toward me. "What's your name?" he asks.

"Joe." Vaslo raises his eyebrows, and I laugh. "We're not all named Dracula, you know."

Vaslo reaches down and starts the engine. "Let's go," he says.

"Where?" I ask. I find Vaslo's habit of taking charge disconcerting.

"To my apartment," Vaslo says. "I'm willing to bet Van Helsing has your place staked out. It won't be safe to go back there." I can't dispute the logic of this, and say nothing. "Besides," Vaslo grins, cupping his basket. "I imagine you'll want another chance to feed."

In spite of my recent feeding, hunger still flicks lightly through my body. "Why do we have to wait until we get back to your place?" I ask.

Vaslo shoots me a sharp look. "What," he asks, "you mean get it on right now?"

I grin. "You got a problem with that?"

Vaslo slowly shakes his head. "No," he says. "Not at all." He switches off the engine and gets out of the cab. In less than a minute he's in the backseat with me, with his pants down around his ankles.

I bend my head down toward his lap, but he stops me. "Kiss me, first," he says. "Let's put a little romance in this. I'm not a fast-food joint."

I look at him, startled. "All right," I finally say.

Vaslo cups the back of my neck with his hand and pulls me toward him. We kiss. Vaslo pulls back and looks at me. "I can tell you don't do this a lot," he says. I can't think of anything to say in response. "Relax," Vaslo says. "Open your mouth a little." He kisses me again, and I do as he tells me. He slips his tongue into my mouth as his lips work against mine. Soon I feel his hands sliding over my body, tugging my flesh, tweaking my nipples. The flame of my hunger fans high again. I run my tongue down the length of his torso and swallow his dick, which is like a torpedo: a sleek, small head that swells out into a fat tube. I pull back the foreskin and slide my mouth down it, inch by inch, until my nose is pressed against his pubes. I hold that position for a few beats, letting myself get acquainted with the size and texture of his dick in my mouth, how it fills me, how the head pushes against the back of my throat. Vaslo starts the action, pumping his hips slowly, twining his fingers through my hair, and gently tugging my head back and forth. I wrap my hand around his balls and give them a good tug as my mouth swoops down his thick shaft. I look up, and when my eyes meet Vaslo's I probe into his mind until I find the pleasure center. I give it a sharp push. Vaslo gasps. "Sweet Jesus," he murmurs.

I quicken my pace, bobbing my head rapidly, sliding my lips down the velvety skin of Vaslo's dick. Vaslo thrusts his hips up to meet each descent of my mouth. He shifts his body and now he's on top of me, his dick still thrusting in and out of my mouth, his balls slapping against my chin. His hands clasp the sides of my head, holding it still as he impales my mouth, our eyes locked. He gives a deep thrust and leaves his dick full down my throat, triggering my gag reflex. I reach up and tweak his nipples hard. Vaslo groans and resumes fucking my face.

When I sense by the throb of Vaslo's dick and the tightness of his balls that he's ready to shoot, I give another hard push into his mind. Vaslo cries out, and his body shudders. His dick pulses in my mouth, pumping out his thick load as I suck mightily. I close my eyes with pleasure from the taste of it: currents and spices, fruit and honey, with a slight hint of cloves.

Vaslo lies wedged in the corner of the taxi's backseat, panting. A last drop of come seeps out of his dick head, and I bend down and lick it off. Vaslo gently runs his fingers through my hair, and I look up into his eyes. "What about you?" he says. "Don't you want to come too?"

I shake my head. "This is my way of feeding, Vaslo. Sperm eaters never come."

Vaslo raises an eyebrow. "Never?"

I hesitate. *Should I tell him?* I wonder. I think about how he saved me from Van Helsing, how I owe him my life. "Almost never," I finally say. "The only time a sperm eater comes is when he's creating another sperm eater. He does that by fucking a mortal and shooting a load up his ass." I look at Vaslo. "Didn't your vampire boyfriend in Moldavia explain this to you?"

Vaslo doesn't say anything for a while. He shakes his head slowly. "I'd ask. But he refused to talk about it."

"I'm not surprised," I say. I give a short laugh. "I'm giving away a trade secret here, Vaslo. It's considered bad form for a vampire to reveal this to a mortal."

Vaslo is looking straight ahead, lost in some thought. He shakes his head and focuses his gaze on me. "Let's go," he says. "I'll take you back to my place." He climbs back into the driver's seat and backs out of the alley.

Vaslo drives us through a maze of streets, and we eventually wind up on a dark tree-lined street bordering Dolores Park. He slows down to a crawl. "I live a little further down, at the end of the block," he says. He leans forward, peering through the windshield. "Everything looks OK," he says tentatively.

The street seems deserted all right, but I feel a nagging sense of dread. I tell myself it's my frayed nerves. Vaslo cruises down past a line of parked cars, and the dread explodes like a sunburst in my brain. "Get us out of here!" I snarl. "We're in danger!"

Lights suddenly blaze on all around us, and I hear the sound of car engines roaring to life. "Shit!" Vaslo exclaims. A van pulls out in front of us and jackknifes across the street, blocking us. Vaslo throws the cab in reverse, but two police cars come tearing up behind us, sirens screaming and lights flashing. Vaslo guns the accelerator and plows into them. There's the sound of metal crashing on metal, and I'm thrown hard against the side of the car.

"Get out!" Vaslo shouts. "Make a run for it!"

I yank open the door, but before I can even place my feet on the ground, I feel hands grab my arms and pull me out of the backseat. Three men descend upon me, and in a matter of seconds I find myself pinned down on the street, face up, helplessly struggling. I try to stare into their eyes, but my attackers know enough to avoid eye contact. Behind them, two of Van Helsing's men are beating the shit out of Vaslo. He slumps to the pavement.

A man walks slowly up to me. He stops and squats down. "Hello, Joe," he says.

I look into Van Helsing's face, but, like the others, he carefully avoids eye contact. My throat tightens with dread. Van Helsing straightens up and nods to the men. "Put him in the car." Vaslo groans and props himself up on his elbow. One of Van Helsing's men kicks him, and Vaslo doubles over with a grunt. "That's enough!" Van Helsing snaps. "He's human. Save that for the vampire."

"Look," I say, making my words fast and urgent. "It'll be daylight in a couple of hours. Keep me laid out here until the sun rises. Make it quick."

Van Helsing chuckles, and he looks at me with an expression that seems almost affectionate. "Joe, my friend," he says softly. "I've invested way too much time and energy on you to finish you off so quickly." He lays his hand on my cheek. "We're going to drag this out as long as possible."

Visitations Dawn Till Dusk
Thomas S. Roche

Charles Ray Quinn was kidnapped by the dead, sprung from prison by his posse of blood suckers, snatched from the jaws of the State by a crew of killers from beyond the grave. A giant gang of homosexual flesh eaters, blood drinkers and kink meisters busted their way into his cell in the asylum and dragged him away, rescuing him from confinement, doing a serious redecorating job on those bland white walls, and dining cheerfully on a few security guards along the way just for kicks.

At least, that's the way the story went. Bony told it to me with his best Vincent Price voice as he pleaded with me to drive him up north.

I cringed from his coercion as I sat awkwardly against the wall on the opposite side of the tiny room, ignoring the invitation in Bony's slightly spread legs. My legs were stretched out and crossed, in part because I wanted to hide my hard-on if I developed one, since I always did when Bony was around. Especially because I could tell already he was horny as a fucker, and that he felt bad about busting in on me like this—throwing pebbles at my window at 1 in the morning on a weeknight, bringing $3 vodka and that familiar smell that called back memories I didn't want to have.

In classic Bony style, he filled all the available space in my life and then some. He had opened his duffel bag and spread clothes across all the room's broken folding chairs while looking for the vodka. In falling headlong onto my bed, he caused a gruesome crack, which I had thought (and, just for a moment, hoped) that it might have been his spine. The bed hadn't fallen apart yet, but somewhere in there lurked a Bony Crack in a hidden plank in that cheap bed frame that would, the laws of physics required, not disintegrate until after Bony had slept a good night's sleep and departed.

Scattering droplets of vodka across my pillow, Bony took a deep, messy swig and stretched himself out across all of my filthy double bed, arms and legs creating a vortex that either he was trying to coax me into or I was trying to coax myself—I still wasn't sure.

"Come on," he begged, stretched out across my dirty comforter with his cock distending his stretch jeans in just the familiar way that always made my guts hurt. "I can't believe you haven't heard of this guy."

"I've heard of him," I said testily. "I just don't give a fuck."

"Yeah, serial killers were never your speed," he said, smiling. "More like the Village People." I didn't respond, but he saw my nostrils flare. "Come on, Mikey, you don't have to be at work until, what, 7:30? Just a quick drive up north."

"It's an hour and a half away," I said. "I don't even know if my car will make it."

Bony made a crying face and rubbed mock tears from his eye. "My car won't make it! It's far away! Come on, puss boy, I came all the way to California! The least you can do is drive me up to this asshole's grave!"

"Golden Gate Transit offers free bus rides after midnight," I growled.

Bony sat up so fast, I cringed as he hurtled at me. My room was so small that he could perch on the edge of the bed and lean toward me, and with his long, angular frame he was right in my face. I could smell him: road dirt and male stink. It made my fucking dick hard, and I hated that. Or is it that I loved it? As far as that goes, when some drunk asshole is verbally abusing me, I never can tell the difference. Bony got the look of absolute wonder on his face, like he was telling me some deep, profound secret of human nature, which I guess in a way he was. "This guy," Bony said, "killed eight people, sucked their blood, ate their goddamn brains, and then—then, fuckin' Mikey, are you listening to me? Then he ate their fucking dicks. How can you not love that?"

"I thought he was a vampire," I said.

"Yeah, well, that's one story. Vampire, cannibal, brain-eating zombie, still at large, cult member, dead in the Russian River, whatever. This guy's got more theories about him than JFK. But whatever you think, either he ate those people or one of his buddies did. Then they desecrated the fuck out of all these graves in the cemetery across the county road from the asylum. But only the male ones."

"So he was gay," I said.

"Yeah, Charles Ray Quinn was a faggot, don't you know anything? I think he fuckin' ate them. I think he drank their blood and fucked them in the ass." Bony started to laugh hysterically—drunken, jittery-cigarette-jones laughter. "I think he sucked their blood right out of their fucking dicks," he said, "and when he was done he just put his teeth together and ripped. Two pints of blood and four ounces of brain matter. Some of them were missing," Bony told me, his voice low and husky. "Ripped their skulls right open. The ME says probably with a crowbar."

"I love it when you talk dirty," I said.

Bony laughed like I was the sickest fuck in the world, and I looked down, red-faced that I'd even said it. It was like he'd won; I'd finally made the barest hint of an overture, and he knew he fucking had me. I didn't even look up. I just felt his hand twining in my hair and dragging me forward. Pushing me down into his crotch.

"Yeah," he said, grinding his hard-on into my face. I could scent his cock even through the filthy material. If my cock hadn't already been hard, it would have been from the first moment I glanced up at him, looking down at me ready to suck him.

"Come on," he said. "You know what you want."

"What do I want?" I asked him, sighing deeply, face pressed

against his crotch but arms hanging limp at my sides. The uneven hardwood floors dug into my knees.

His smile was three fifths contempt and two fifths the kind of deep, profound, aching need that kept me down there taking his shit, taking his abuse, taking his cock since we were younger than young and he first noticed I got a hard-on when he wrestled me.

"Come on," he said.

"Just don't talk," I said, and brought my hands up to his belt.

Bony's cock, long and lanky like him, came free and hard into my mouth. His uncut head tasted sharp from days or months on the road, but I didn't recoil from the taste. I gulped it down. I took his long, thin cock down my throat—all the way, lips wrapped around the shaft and tongue pressed hard against the underside. For an instant, as I felt my lips brushing his pubic hair, his scent filling my nostrils, I thought how Bony was the nine inches all those fucking older AOL guys I kept trying to hook up with claimed to be.

And he could slap me the way I wanted.

His hips ground up against me, forcing his cock down my face. I hated that I was down here, but my cock was hard. How many times had I sucked this fucking bastard's prick? Bony was the god-damn punk Casanova, cutting a swath through every belly-ringed bitch in Charleston. I swear, he bagged a new girl every weekend. He would always come over after his dates and push me down onto my knees, and I would know from the way his prick was rock-hard and throbbing, dripping precome, filthy and skanky with puss but veined and full with blood, that he hadn't been able to come. He was always close but no cigar. He needed my fucking throat to bring him over the edge.

I remembered doing it right after he'd taken Chasey Simon's virginity; I tasted pussy and blood that made me want to puke. Then there was the time Bony came over looking all freaked out and guilty, and it took him longer than usual to get hard. He said he'd had a date with Chasey—but she was in Atlanta that weekend, and besides, he'd already broken up with her. When I put my mouth on Bony's cock that night, I tasted ass.

Bony's hands gripped my hair but let me do all the work. My head bobbed up and down, eyes flashing up at him to see the pleasure and contempt on his face. My hand pulled open my own belt and disappeared into my pants; I was working my cock when Bony growled, "Don't fuckin' jerk off while you're doin' it!"

I just looked up at him and kept stroking it. I half expected Bony to whip his dick out of my mouth and smack me, but he didn't. Instead, Bony got that panicked look he'd gotten the night he told me he wanted to take me out and watch me bag one of those loose bitches at the Cooper Street warehouse, because he wasn't so fuckin' sure I was straight anymore and he thought I better prove it.

"I'm not straight," I told him, and I saw him blanch as he realized that it had been a faggot who was sucking his dick all these years.

I had never once stroked my cock while sucking him off. That would have been too gay for him, and that fucking mattered to me once upon a time. Now I didn't give a shit. It had been a year that I'd been out in California, and all Bony ever called me for was to tell me about some bitch he'd just fucked in Philly or Chicago or Boston and tell me all about her while he jerked off. It had been three months since his last call, and since then, I'd actually had another guy suck *my* fucking dick, miracle of miracles. Like $3 vodka, Bony was a commodity I had started to outgrow.

If he wanted to fuck my fucking face he could do it while I jerked off.

I kept stroking my cock while Bony looked down at me, scared but hard. Harder than ever. He looked terrified, but his hips were pumping against me, forcing his filthy cock down my throat. He reached out, fumbling, for the flask of cheap vodka he'd left back on the pillow. He spilled half of it getting it to his mouth, but he gulped the rest in a long, steady stream. He threw the empty flask hard against the wall, where it broke. Then he seized my hair and started grinding his hips up against me. His cock pumped down my throat. I relaxed into him and just let him fuck my face, the way he used to. But there was something different about it this time.

He had never made sounds like this. He had never looked down at my face while he did it, meeting my eyes. He always looked away, or at a porn magazine, or at the video screen as it played some butt-fuck porno he'd stolen from his father.

Now Bony fucked me like he wanted to fuck me. A minute ago he'd been telling me I liked the fucking Village People. Now he was looking down at me as I stroked my cock faster, as I sucked his dick, as I let him fuck my throat.

I fucking shot so hard I coated his big black combat boots. Hot streams exploded down my throat and Bony cried out, gasping, throwing himself onto the bed as I rode him, my mouth clamped around his cock head, drinking him.

"Fuck, fuck, fuck, fuck, fuck," he said in that way guys do when they come so hard it feels like the top of their head blew off.

His hand was thrown across his eyes. He was shaking a little.

I licked his cock clean and zipped up my pants. I didn't even offer to wipe off his fucking boots, but then Bony didn't notice. He was too busy shaking and shivering on the bed.

I went into the bathroom and took a piss. When I came out Bony was up and putting on his coat. His eyes and face were red, and when he spoke his voice sounded all weird and stuffy.

"Get your fucking car keys," he said, and this time I just shrugged and grabbed my jacket.

~

Tomorrow's lunch money was all I had to pay for gas from west Oakland across the Richmond-San Rafael Bridge and up into southern Sonoma. But with Bony wigging like he was, I wasn't going to argue. Fucking middle of the night, and I'm driving my homeless best friend (friend?) up into the goddamn wine country to pay homage to a serial killer. A *faggot* serial killer.

"You visited a lot of these graves?" I asked.

"Some," said Bony, sounding drunk and completely out of it. I know I'm a good cocksucker—I mean, blowing his mind was one thing, but reducing him to a vegetable?

"Any other faggots?" I said, trying to make the word sound dirty as possible, hoping it would shake Bony out of his funk.

"Faggots?" he asked. "What do you mean?"

I felt guilty about it as soon as I said it, like I was using the *n* word or some shit like that. My fuckin' PC muscles clenched up and I thought I was going to puke.

I couldn't say the word a second time. "You know. G...g...gay serial killers. You know. Ones who killed guys? Gay ones."

He looked at me all sad and weird, drunk and freaked-out. He shook his head.

We wound up into the hills. Bony gave me directions in a monotone, leading us off the freeway and onto county roads. He didn't have the directions written down. He knew them by heart.

We drove past a freaky-looking building on a hill, half castle, half dormitory.

"What's that place?" I asked him.

"The asylum. That's the place they busted him out of."

"Who?"

"His gang," said Bony, sounding like a zombie. "His cult. When they killed all the guards. And desecrated the corpses."

"Whatever," I said.

"Pull up here."

I stopped the car in front of an old iron gate with a sign that said VISITATION HOURS DAWN TILL DUSK.

I looked at Bony, puzzled.

"This is his grave?" I asked. "I thought they never found his body. I thought he was missing, or 'at large' or something."

"This is where they desecrated them," he said, his voice flat. "Don't you know anything?"

"Not about serial killers," I said. "You're the fucking obsessed weird freak."

Bony didn't answer, just got out of the car, and I listened to the click-whine-chunk of the ancient Nova's door. I locked the car door behind him and got out the driver's side. He was already halfway over the iron fence. It took me longer than him to climb over; Bony was a much more accomplished trespasser than me.

By the time I dropped to the ground on the other side and cursed at my pained ankles, Bony was nowhere to be seen. It was a foggy night, and the winding paths stretched out into nowhere, crosses and stars of David scattered rhythmically around in the wisps of stony gray. I started running after him, with no idea where he was.

"Bony?" I shouted. "Bony, where the fuck are you? Don't give me this shit....Bony!"

I ran down a path as the fog rolled in, deeper, a tule fog like a big blanket of smoke. It was a pitch-dark night and I hadn't brought a flashlight. I stumbled through the dark, tiptoeing around freshly dug earth and scattered flowers, walking across stone monuments and slippery marble markers. I dug in my pocket for pennies to throw, but I had none. Just a quarter I was scared to give up because I couldn't remember how much the toll was going back across the bridge.

"Bony! Where the fuck are you, you fucking asshole. Don't fuck around!"

I slipped across a fog-slick marble gravestone and went down, cursing, smacking my knee so hard I thought for a minute I must have broken it. I laid half sprawled across the flat marble slab, slapping it with my open palm as the pain coursed through me. "Fuck, fuck, fuck, fuck, fuck me," I spat, still kneeling, waiting for the pain to subside and praying that I hadn't fucked myself up.

That's when Bony's coat went over my head, and I felt his hard body behind me pushing my face into the marble slab.

I tried to get up, but his weight was on me, bearing me down onto the grave. I already couldn't see shit in the pitch-black night, but now with Bony's coat over my head all I could do was smell him and curse at him. He wrestled me the way he always had when we were growing up—holding me down, his cock getting hard and grinding into my ass. I felt his hands under me, ripping at my belt.

"Bony," I said. "Knock it the fuck off, dipshit!"

He didn't say a word. He got my belt open and yanked down my pants. I could feel him long and hard in the crack of my ass, pushing through my Jockeys. I could feel his cock head nudging my ass.

He reached into my Jockeys and grabbed my cock—hard already.

He took that as his cue to pull my shorts down to my knees and climb on top of me, working his own pants open.

"What the fuck are you doing?" I asked him, and felt his cock between my cheeks. His head was thick and swollen, pressing against my dry asshole. He pulled his overcoat up to the back of my head and gripped my hair, forcing my face into the stink of his coat. I could feel the hard bite of his teeth at the back of my neck, biting in beneath. I struggled a little, not believing this could be happening. He was going to fuck me.

"Use some spit or something," I said weakly. "I've....I've never been fucked."

He drove into me hard at the moment he bit the back of my neck. I screamed, pain surging through my body. His cock ripped right into my ass, dry, unlubed, feeling like it was going into my fucking throat. But I still pushed back onto him, like I hoped getting it deeper would stop the pain.

It did, a little, but not much. He tore at the flesh of my neck as he pounded me, his cock opening up my ass. I couldn't hear him moaning; I couldn't hear anything except the slapping of his body against my ass and of mine against the marble slab. I shut my eyes tight and didn't dare look up at him. I buried my face in his overcoat and drank in his smell while his cock reamed me. He bit deeper at my throat and I swear I felt flesh tearing.

Through it all, my cock was still hard. The thrusts of his body pounded it against the stone, and it felt like this one time when this guy online made me slap my dick until I came. Only this time I had Bony's dick in my ass to push me forward, closer to orgasm.

I started crying as he pounded me; I shut my eyes tighter to hide the tears and bit into his overcoat as he ripped the flesh at the back of my neck. He didn't groan when he exploded inside me, just bit deeper into my throat. But I could feel his cock suddenly going all slick, and I thought for a moment maybe my ass was bleeding—but it was just the hot, sudden flood of salty come. It had to be.

Then his weight was off me, and Bony left me sobbing there stretched across some stranger's grave.

I pushed myself up onto my hands and knees, my whole lower body aching with the pain in my ass. Come was leaking down the backs of my thighs, and even if I'd had a light I would have been too scared to look down and see if it was mixed with blood. When I put my hand to the back of my neck, that was wet too, and I tried to tell myself it was just Bony's drool. But when I touched my hand to my mouth, I tasted iron.

I reached my hand down, blood-sticky, and started to stroke my cock. Two pumps—that's about what it took for me to shoot my load all over the marble slab.

Then I cried some more, pants down around my ankles, soft cock pressed to marble. I clutched Bony's overcoat, and smelled it, inhaling him as I waited for him to come back to me.

He didn't.

When the fog started to lighten and the sun began to burn it off—that was the first time I realized how motherfucking cold I was. I had been stretched there with my ass in the air, for how many hours I didn't know. I struggled my way up to my feet and pulled up my pants, buckled my belt, took Bony's overcoat and put it on over my own leather jacket. It was so long it dragged on the ground.

The fog was burning off quickly, and I could see the grave I'd been lying on.

MADELINE RENEE QUINN
BELOVED MOTHER OF CHARLES

"Bony?" I shouted.

I looked for him. I wandered through the fog as it burned around me, lifting in thin wisps to the heavens. He wasn't anywhere. My ass hurt like goddamn fire. There was blood running down my back. I tried to climb over the fence again but my ass hurt too fucking much. I finally found a little stretched space in the iron gate where some homeless guy or juvenile delinquents had pried it open with a crow-bar, and I managed to make it out.

The passenger-side door of my car was wide open, the interior light on, the door-open sound going *ding ding ding ding* as I broke into a pained trot and made it to the car, expecting to find Bony in the backseat, passed out and probably puking.

Nothing. Just a year's worth of California trash—fast-food wrappers, Coke bottles. I shut the door and squirmed my way into the driver's seat.

Fuck him.

~

That was it, I guess, for Bony and me. I don't know if he just decided to stop calling me or what. I made a couple of calls to track Chasey Simons down; he had called me a few months ago and bragged she'd put out for him when he'd been in town even though she had some law school boyfriend at the college she was attending up north. I found her in Boston. She told me she hadn't seen him and hoped she never did. She thought San Francisco was a cool town, or at least that's what she'd heard. Maybe she'd come out and visit me some time.

I've still got the scars across the back of my neck—ripped little abrasions that never healed right. Shaped like Bony's mouth but with big gashes where his little canines should have been. Sometimes they itch when I get horny.

A few months ago I took Bony's coat in to a dry cleaner's near my work and had them alter it so it would be short enough for me to wear.

"But don't clean it," I told them. "Promise me, promise me you won't dry-clean it."

But they did. All I've got is the stink of chemical where Bony's scent once was. Sometimes I close my eyes and try to think of what he smelled like. I remember a poem I once wrote about the drunk asshole. I said he smelled like vodka and cigarettes, sweat and sex, whiskey and public transportation.

I think those words to myself when I try to remember him. But all I can smell is blood.

Bad Blood
Wes Ferguson

Slade snapped awake with a sudden chill. Something had startled him, but the blackness in his mind gave way to no dreams. He slowly sat up in bed, thinking for a moment.

His brothers lay on either side of him, each a mirror of the other: spread out on their stomachs and comfortably naked, legs hopelessly tangled in the covers. With their pale and perfectly smooth round bottoms propped up in the moonlight, it was enough to make Slade pause in mid thought and admire their beauty. The twins were extremely masculine yet boyish-looking, as they were, like Slade, quite young. They had large and stocky builds in contrast to his slender frame, and their light blond hair was messed from sleep. He also slept in the nude with them, and found himself staring up at the mirror above their bed for some time, admiring how his own chest and defined torso looked nestled between their muscular backs.

It seemed that he was hypersexual now, as though his carnal lust had increased at least tenfold, as all of his senses had intensified beyond anything he could have ever imagined. Each minute sensation brought him more pleasure, and as he lay in bed between his brothers the swell of his blood flushed his body with a sweeping heat. He became fully engorged, and moved the tips of his fingers delicately over the length of his erection, swirling his thumb around his swollen head, then stroking downward with the back of his hand. He grasped both his hands around his shaft and held still, quietly drawing a breath and aching with desire.

Again he paused for thought. He looked toward the window across the room and remembered the cold chill that woke him from his sleep. He eyes rolled over his brothers' naked backsides again, quickly, and Slade moved out of bed with only the sound of silk sheets coming back to rest where he once lay.

He crossed the room to look at the large vineyard that spread across the property outside. Still waking, he stretched to his full height, a little over six feet, and brushed his hand through his thick jet-black hair. He knew his younger brothers wouldn't have felt such a chill, for it did not come from the open window. He shut it anyway and began to search the vineyard.

Carefully his eyes moved from the back of the lot over to each side and back again. Slowly he adjusted his vision onto each row of vines, combing them from end to end before moving on to the next thicket of twisted greenery. Then, he saw it.

The chill ran down his arm again, and he focused his powerful eyes on a single vine in the massive vineyard, rocking back and forth as if being pulled by some unseen hands. Slade blinked, and the leaves on the vine came into perfect focus.

There, hidden by the post, a white rabbit with oversize paws tugged sharply at the vine and gnawed feverishly on the stalk. The rabbit's red eyes suddenly shifted directly toward Slade, and it instantly froze in place. Certainly a small woodland creature could not sense the undead from several hundred yards away?

Slade wasn't too sure on the rules. He had only been initiated a few months ago, and much of the Vampire folklore he grew up with turned out to be, as he often put it, complete bullshit. An animal possessing some kind of hypersensitivity to his presence was another uncertainty, as much of his life was now.

Even so, he knew his mission. That much was clear. He turned to wake his new brothers. Suddenly something clicked in his mind, and he stopped.

He returned to the window and found the rabbit, still frozen in place. He looked closer. The rabbit's eyes were looking in Slade's direction but focused on something at ground level. His arm tingled from shoulder to wrist as his eyes caught the movement of a young boy walking across the vineyard. He wondered how he could have missed something so obvious; being caught up in the details, he often overlooked what was in plain sight. The boy moved toward the thicket of trees at the edge of the property, pausing every few steps to look at the house. Before the boy was at the proper angle to see him, Slade moved out of view and over to the foot of the bed.

There, he stood for a moment and again gazed upon his brother's naked skin in the early-morning moonlight. The floor was cold on his bare feet, but a surge of heat rushed him as he looked at his brothers. It was almost a compulsion to take in every inch of their bodies as they lay asleep unaware that he watched. They had only been together for a few weeks, their training complete and bodies adjusted to the demon blood that now flowed freely within them.

This came after discovering he was the last in a long bloodline of Vampires. His father, whom he had never known, was also born half-human and half-demon. The curse and gift of their family crest was a mystery slowly unraveling itself as Slade learned the truth behind the myth. He had only needed a trickle of demon blood to cross his lips and his own dormant powers suddenly sprang to life. A startled young man soon discovered that Vampires are born, not made.

But he had no time for these thoughts now, as it was imperative that their location, even their existence, be kept secret from the outside world. He changed into a pair of black cargo pants and T-shirt, then stepped into his boots and smoothed his hair back with his hands. The boy had reached the edge of the trees, and Slade could hear the patter of the rabbit's feet run off in the other direction. He was already downstairs and moved toward the front of the house.

The boy walked along the edge of the trees, looking over his shoulder at the back of the large house on the hill above the vineyard. The sun was rising fast above the mountains, and as he walked the night gave way to daylight, the moon still visible in the distance. He looked back over his shoulder once more and cut through the trees on the path back to the main road. Just as he came to the center of the thicket of trees, he stopped dead in his tracks. There before him stood a man in black, casually leaning with his arm against a tree. The boy knew immediately that he'd found what he was looking for, and a nervous energy swirled in his stomach as the man stared at him intently.

Slade glared out of the top of his eyes, slowly scanning his prey up and down. He guessed the boy must be 17 or so, a few years younger than he was. Even so, he knew what he must do to protect the blood. He held on to a small hope that it would not come to such drastic measures.

Unlike his new brothers, this young man was not a descendant of Vampires. Slade could sense the boy's pure human form, one that would only be corrupted by the demon life force that flowed through his own veins. He knew the man-child had wondered intentionally into their midst, perhaps enchanted by the allure of false myths surrounding his kind. Slade could not make him a Vampire. To do so would only drive the boy mad, the demon blood slowly taking over his body like a virus, eventually destroying his frail flesh from the inside out.

Slade feared letting the boy go might make others aware of their presence in the old vineyard. This was something, above all else, that he could not risk. However, since the boy came of his own free will, it seemed that his presence would not be missed by the outside world. Perhaps the choice had already been made.

Though these thoughts spun around in his mind with mixed emotion, Slade showed no visible sign of inner conflict. Instead, his burning glare only lured the boy further into the web. It was an insatiable charm neither of them could control.

All too aware of the Vampire's eyes upon him, the boy at first became self-conscious and unsure of himself. He waited for his master to make the first move. As the seconds ticked like hours on the clock, he felt a surge of boldness within him. Suddenly, he spoke.

"I know what you are," He said in a low, even tone, without a trace of innocence. His own voice sounded distant to him, words coming out of his mouth as though spoken by someone else. His vision focused only on the dark and beautiful stranger in front of him; everything else in view became soft as though brushed over with watercolors.

Slade understood, and took on his role in this grim fantasy. Without dismissing the boy's claim he acknowledged the truth of his nature. "If so," he said playfully, "would I be out in the daylight?"

The boy daringly shot back without thinking; with a rushed breath he blurted, "You're in the shadow of that tree."

Slade smiled devilishly and stepped out into the daylight. In an almost pompous fashion, he pulled off his shirt and flexed, with his arms by his side, ripples of muscle cutting into his slender frame. The warm glow of the sun spread across his chest. To the east, the thin outline of the moon stood against the pale-blue morning sky. He knew as long as the moon was visible no natural force could harm him.

He leveled his eyes at the boy. "And what about you?" He asked under his breath, close to a growl.

Not at all confused by the demonstration, the boy stepped forward and sank to his knees in the clearing. His eyes fluttered shut as the sun beamed down on him through the opening in the canopy. He sat for a moment.

When he opened his eyes, Slade was gone. He paused, regaining his vision as clouds rolled overhead. A slow crawl of darkness from the shadows overtook him as the clouds covered the sun above. He felt a chill slowly trickle down the back of his neck.

Slade moved in behind him. The morning mist hung in the air, and the boy could feel droplets of dew seeping into his pants from the grass his knees rested on. A still, cold hush settled over them.

Slade held tight behind the boy, hips flush against his buttocks. Slade pressed his hand on the boy's chest, feeling the rapid heartbeat echo through his own body. The boy's head fell back onto his shoulder and pressed against him cheek to cheek. The boy's lips parted and he let out a small, anxious sigh. Slade moved his other hand down to the buckle of the boy's belt.

The boy closed his eyes as his belt clinked against the ground. He gasped lightly as Slade slid his hand below the band of his briefs, fingertips resting in soft brown hair. He reached behind him and closed his hand around Slade's engorged sex. It was much larger than any he'd experienced so far.

The boy guided Slade between the spread cheeks of his backside. Slade pressed forward and the boy's anus twitched, then he bent over slightly. Slade flexed again and sent a small shiver through the boy as he began to enter him.

The boy let out a moan as Slade slid into his tight mound. A fit of pleasure overtook him, and he arched his back and pushed himself farther back, pressing against Slade's pelvic bone.

Slade stood over him and wedged his hips forward, letting the boy feel the full bearing of his weight. He pushed the boy's shoulders forward and spread his legs wide, keeping one hand on his waist to support him. Slade drew back and slid in and out of the boy with force. The slap of his body meeting the boy's was punctuated each time by a sharp moan. Slade thrust forward harder, angry for what he knew he must do.

The boy braced himself against the ground as Slade pushed his shoulders forward and thrust into the boy from behind. Each pulse sent the boy into intense delight as he moaned with anticipation. He doubled over, clawing at the ground, as Slade continued to thrust forcefully behind him. Again and again Slade drew himself back and drove into the boy. With each powerful thrust against his prostate the boy grew closer to climax, his swollen sex so engorged it ached. The boy writhed and drew short of breath, intoxicated.

Slade pulled the boy's arms back and pressed into the nape of his exposed neck. His nose resting under the boy's ear, he slowly opened his mouth and kissed the boy one final time before biting into his neck. The boy's arm twitched, shocked at the force as Slade's powerful jaws tore open his throat.

A trickle of blood spilled down the boy's neck; suddenly a memory flashed into Slade's brain. He thought back to when he first tasted the blood of another: His eyes flushed red, as they did now. He sank his teeth further into the boy's flesh: This time when blood splashed Slade's tongue, the sweet taste of the innocent washed into his mouth for the first time.

He knew then that this was something he could never tell his brothers. Even though he acted to protect them, it was difficult to explain and fully understand. Slade continued to rhythmically move his hips back and fourth, overtaking his willing victim, slowing draining him.

The boy released and let his pleasure course through him as the last of his lifeblood spilled from his body. Slade moved his blood-filled mouth close to the boy's ear, and though his lips moved, he did not breathe a word.

"Yes, master," the boy cried softly before falling to the ground, dead.

Learning the Alphabet
Patrick Califia

Like many stories about the lust of one man for another, this one begins with a predatory older man in leather stalking a younger man who is ignorant of his destiny. But the two men this story concerns were not in a leather bar, nor were they headed for a bondage fete. These were streets that natives of New York City did not brave. It was 1971 in Alphabet City, the lower east side of Manhattan.

From the sidewalk, it wasn't always easy to tell that this was a place where pizza deliveries and house calls from the cops didn't happen. The streets were silent: no children playing and few cars. The occasional corner store had large bald patches on its shelves. From time to time there was a more dramatic reminder of the area's evil reputation—an entire row of elegant brownstones with panels of plywood nailed over the broken windows and doors; a single house that had literally exploded, and then had simply been left in that condition, with blocks of stone and plaster shrapnel scattered in the street.

Who was more dangerous here? Ulric wondered. The brown-skinned people, the drug dealers, the other criminals, the punks, the young and angry queers, the artists, the junkies, or the junkies who were also artists? It was, he thought, the kind of neighborhood where housing projects looked well-kept. He ought to know: He was looking at one right now. Some architect on the city's payroll had indulged in a Spanish Civil War–era Cubist fantasy. The brightly colored assortment of severe, square, and rectangular shapes had no relationship to the older, more ornate 1890s buildings around them.

This housing project was surrounded by several feet of what could have been a lawn if grass had not been permanently discouraged by garbage, children running wild, and the occasional junked car. A tall wrought iron fence topped with razor wire surrounded the compound. But the residents had broken bars off to make a gap wide enough for two men to walk side by side. There was already an official gate, of course, but this was something the inhabitants had made: a rebellion against the fence, which might have been erected for their protection but looked and felt like something built to keep them penned. What would it be like to be a young boy here, to grow up behind bars and know that you had a 90% chance of being put in an even worse cage when you became a man?

Ulric's people had been tall and muscular. He was less heavy-set than his mother's brother and most of his peers. He had been changed when he had barely attained manhood, his body not yet thickened with the muscle of middle age. But on these streets, he had nothing to fear. In hand-to-hand combat he was strong and fast enough to take on a group of fighters, and a knife or a bullet would not kill him. He had demonstrated all of these facts when various desperate men and one crazed woman had tried to rob him, rape him, or chase him out of the neighborhood.

Now he was a part of it, as unwelcome as arson or a methamphetamine lab; like them, as unchangeable as bad weather. There was even a bodega where the resident *santero* sold a charm against him: a miniature of Ochosi the Hunter's bow and arrow, fashioned in pewter. The charm appeared to work because only the Spanish-speaking people knew about it, and Ulric did not like to take victims who were already being fucked over. Good Catholics and devotees of Santeria alike could frequently be found with the amulet around their necks because it was well-known that where he walked, corpses would tumble.

The black men who strolled these streets with feral grace were unbearably handsome, and Ulric would have lived in this neighborhood to watch them, even if he had to hunt elsewhere. He loved to linger in the shadows and listen to the cadence of Cuban or Puerto Rican Spanish. Perhaps he could have fed elsewhere and then used his erection with a man whose features showed the Native American contributions to his bloodline. But his self-control usually vanished in the presence of an open vein; Ulric fucked the same men that he killed.

When night fell, winter or summer, Ulric hit the streets dressed in black leather, wearing his unfashionably long hair in loose curls around his shoulders. He had big gold earrings and daggers in his jacket and boots and mouth, and he was driven by a hunger as inescapable as Alphabet City's poverty and madness. On this particular evening he had followed someone to the housing project. Someone who was as white as he was. A young man who had listened to Lou Reed and the Velvet Underground with a little too much high school fervency. Cannon was trying to score. He had his short black hair up in spikes and wore black eyeliner. His T-shirt and jeans were black, and he wore boots much like Ulric's own. But he had no leather jacket. The jacket had been traded for the cash that he hoped to trade for heroin. A lot of heroin. This young man intended to kill himself tonight, and he wanted to go out banging.

Ulric had seen Cannon before. He kept idle track of the young white people who scrabbled for drug money and squatted in various abandoned buildings. He had even sampled some of the drugs that they prized so highly, hoping that one of them might quiet the fire in his veins that forced him to hunt and feed each night. Alas, the same body that made him virtually immortal also identified and nullified the drugs, just as it would ruthlessly and eliminate a viral infection or heal a cut that had gone to his bone. He knew that Cannon had a girlfriend. She had died yesterday, doing too much of a score that, Cannon had warned her, was way stronger than the usual stuff. Cannon must have loved her much to give up his leather jacket, let alone his life, for her.

But if that were so, why did Cannon make so much money in Times Square? It was an odd job for a heterosexual. Jackie and Cannon were there almost every day, looking like twins. The girlfriend was a pickpocket, and she occasionally persuaded a motherly tourist to give her "bus money" home to New Jersey or Kansas. (The more gullible the tourist, the more distant her fictional destination.) But Cannon was a hustler. He went into porn shops, bars, hotel rooms, and cars and came out with enough cash to keep living fast and loose. Was he fast and loose? That was what Ulric wanted to know. Because he preferred it slow and tight.

Cannon's grief had fucked up his usual street smarts. He was about to let himself be led into one of the buildings. There, Ulric knew, he would be relieved of his cash and given a beating that would only make him wish he was dead. Like a sinister night watchman, Ulric came along, gently touching the minds of those who saw him, bidding them forget and go elsewhere. No sentinel gave the alarm when he slid behind Cannon and the three men who were conning him. Ulric didn't judge them for trying to get paid without handing over the merchandise. Selling the same stuff twice meant twice the profits. But he had a prior claim on their patsy. Like the wolf that he became when using a human form was not to his advantage, Ulric's territorial instincts were strong.

The five of them went up the stairs. Ulric stepped ahead and held the apartment door open for everyone. As he quietly shut the door—a polite and literally invisible butler—one of the dealers grabbed Cannon from behind and pinned his arms. A second man began to go through his pockets. Ulric sent the third member of the conspiracy into the bedroom to retrieve all of their stash.

It was more than enough heroin to keep an entire squat of gutter punks high for a week. "I'll be taking that," Ulric said, slinging the strap of the camera bag over his shoulder. "And this," he said, taking Cannon away from his assailants.

The young man barely had time to register his anger at the assault or his surprise at being rescued before the two of them were back on the street and walking briskly away from the housing project. The three burly black men who had tried to jack him up were sound asleep on the floor of the apartment. Ulric was irritable from the effort it had taken to remove the incident from their minds. He hated the greasy feel of other people's personalities and memories. So he was in no mood to play nice when Cannon slipped out of his embrace and bolted.

COME HERE.

Ulric usually would have retrieved his victim physically, but he was still in the mode of exerting mental control. The thought he threw at Cannon stopped the grief-stricken punk in his tracks. But he fought against its compulsion, his invisible being thrashing like a hooked shark, and Ulric was impressed by his strength. NOW! he insisted. Cannon came toward him as if he were swimming through newly poured, wet, sludgy concrete. Ulric took a firm grip on his hair and towed him along to the punk's most recent lair.

"I'm going to do you where you live, man," he told Cannon, shaking his head, deliberately hurting and provoking him. "I'm going to fuck you on the same bed where your chick bought it."

"No, you're not," Cannon blustered, ego wounded by the awkward, bent-over posture Ulric had imposed on him as much as by the pain in his scalp. "I'll shiv you. You'll be the one who buys it." He tried to punch Ulric and failed, his fists flailing. "Let me go!" he cried, and was humiliated by the childish and querulous sound of his own voice.

"OK," Ulric said, and released him. Cannon shot off to his left, crossing the street diagonally. Luckily there was little traffic; Cannon had not looked both ways before leaping off the curb.

CRAWL TO MY HAND AND KISS IT.

This time, Ulric threw more of his strength into the call. When Cannon struggled to him on filthy, bruised knees and put his lips to his hand, Ulric felt all of his victim's outrage and astonishment. And something else. Arousal. Unlike Jackie, Ulric knew that Cannon did a lot more for his tricks than let them suck his dick. That arrogant rock star mouth was almost as sweet as his dimpled bum promised to be.

"Shall I make you crawl the rest of the way?" Ulric asked.

"No," Cannon said. He stood up cautiously and brushed off his black jeans. "I'll come with you on my own two feet."

"Then run," Ulric said, and shoved him in the direction of his squat. "Run! If you can beat me there, I will let you go."

Cannon wanted to run away, but he didn't want to play this game with Ulric. He didn't want to make any move that could be mistaken for a desire to go on living. If Ulric was his executor, he would accept that, he told himself, stubbornly clenching his jaw and planting his feet. It was what he had gone looking for after he sold his jacket: a death that would carry him to the place where Jackie waited. So let this crazy man kill him here, without any demeaning games.

Then Ulric spun him around and forced his chosen prey to stare at his naked hunger. He hissed at Cannon, and there was nothing human in that sound, or in the red-eyed and fanged visage that seemed lit from within by a green, unhealthy phosphorescence. Ulric was all teeth and claws, a hunter as primitive and vigorous as a bear or an eagle. Nothing as clean and quick as a bullet was waiting for Cannon. "What the fuck are you, man?" the junkie sputtered. Then he was cutting pavement with his booted feet, running so fast it looked like he expected to launch himself into the air and fly.

Ulric strolled after him, speeding up only enough to keep him in sight. When Cannon was close to the appropriate alley, Ulric wrapped himself in ebony magic and slid by him, worming his way between a Dumpster and a wall of uncollected garbage bags to reach the piece of plywood the punks had wiggled loose from the back door of a brownstone. He waited until Cannon could see him, then ripped the plywood off the building and threw it over the young man's head. It went over the fence, over the yard next door, and was still flying with enough force to break windows when it hit the third building down.

"You lose," he told Cannon and dragged him into the fetid darkness. The floor at their feet came to life, rustling over their boots as a mob of squealing rats fled the derelict building. Anyone watching from the street would have seen a storm cloud of pigeons ascend from the roof. Only the insects remained, their patience in inverse proportion to their short lives.

Cannon and Jackie had dragged their salvaged mattress up a flight of stairs and shoved it under the windows that faced the street. The stairs were littered with the empty wine bottles that Cannon normally arranged behind them, booby-trapping the stairs so he and his lover would know if anyone tried to sneak up on them. The bed was relatively clean and covered with layers of rich-colored fabric, the red, brown, and orange paisley Indian prints that Jackie loved. There were two sofa pillows to prop them up when they wanted to sit up to fix, and a bunch of other large pillows strewn across the room to make extra seating for a party. Jackie had done some artwork on the walls, murals of women in bondage and men with guns, overlaid by unsettling mosaics made of eyes and teeth cut out of magazines. She had even set up a small kitchen with milk crates, a Coleman stove and metal picnic plates and cups.

But the hunger in Ulric left him with little sympathy for this shattered domesticity. He picked the young man up and threw him onto the bed. "Stay put," he warned him, and took a cigarette lighter out of his pocket. Guided by his night vision, he moved around the makeshift loft, lighting candles. When he turned back to the bed Cannon was sitting there cross-legged, watching him warily. The candle flames were repeated in miniature upon the punk's enlarged pupils. Before Ulric took his place beside him, he found the breakfast tray where Cannon and Jackie stashed their spoons, an alcohol lamp, a box of cotton balls, vials of sterile water, strips of rubber tubing, and syringes.

"What are you doing?" Cannon asked stupidly as Ulric lit the lamp, unfolded one of the paper packets of dope, and dumped a generous amount of it into a spoon along with a squirt of sterile water.

"Cooking your first shot," Ulric said, gently agitating the spoon so the powder would dissolve in the bubbling water. "Pull off a cotton," he ordered, handing him a new marshmallow-shaped wad of the stuff. Behind him, Cannon silently twirled off a tight bit of cotton. When he leaned forward to drop it in the spoon, Ulric caught his scent, hauntingly masculine and tragically mortal. Cannon was so full of grief and blood and lost chances.

"Are you going to get high before you kill me?" Cannon asked quietly.

"I can't get high," Ulric said shortly, annoyed with him. "Pump your arm up and tie off."

The hustler moved with alacrity. Suicide could wait until the rush was over, apparently. In less than a minute he was prepped, swabbing above and below the crook of his elbow with an alcohol wipe. He and Jackie had done this right; they often made contemptuous comments about the stupid junkies who gave themselves tracks and abscesses. They only shared needles with each other. Ulric thought briefly about adding a little of his own blood to Cannon's hit, but there was no reason to prolong his suffering. Cannon had doomed himself. Sooner or later the meat grinder of the street would turn him into hamburger. No sense in wasting the salty liquor that surged through his veins and made his heart plump.

Still, he would show Cannon this brief mercy, his favorite anodyne. Taking the young man's arm across his knee, he deftly tapped into a vein and pushed the junk home. Cannon gasped as the warm joyous surge of smack went up the back of his neck and out the top of his head. "That's good shit," he said inanely, and didn't fight Ulric when the vampire slid his arm around him and helped him to lay back.

While Cannon's muscles went slack with bliss, Ulric began to kiss him. He also unbuttoned his shirt. Cannon's skin was as pale as Hollywood's version of a vampire. *China White,* Ulric thought, and brushed his nipples. Cannon's body responded to Ulric's hands and to the mental suggestions he sent him. The rush lasted longer than he had any right to expect, and was tinged with eroticism that quickly became urgent. This was different than getting done by a furtive married salesman or a slumming executive who was committed to the corporate closet. Ulric wanted him with a pagan strength that had never been contaminated with homophobia. Chicks didn't touch Cannon this way either. Ulric wanted his whole body, and he wanted to fuck him, not be fucked.

Gutting Cannon's inhibitions, Ulric soon had his delicious victim undressed. Cannon was well-named. His cock was unusually thick, and his ball sac was heavy, bulging with two big balls. Getting a hard-on when he was high was normally hit-or-miss, but Ulric used his own hand and mouth to good effect, and soon Cannon's cock was jutting into the air, bold and stiff as a foot-high mohawk. The vampire detected a tendril of Cannon's fear about having his cock bitten, and made it dissolve and fade away. Then Cannon simply doted on having Ulric suck his dick. The immortal savored the taste of Cannon's first gift of precome, one more sign of his surrender to Ulric's spell of erotic ecstasy. He came off Cannon's cock and forced the boy to kiss him, let him taste his own dick drool on Ulric's tongue. He also let Cannon's tongue probe his fangs, and he allowed the young man to keep some of the fear and adrenaline that flooded him. Fear would subtly change the flavor of his blood, make it zing in Ulric's mouth and body.

"Now it's my turn," Ulric said, and undid the snaps at the crotch of his leather pants. His own cock was limp, and would stay that way until he tapped the boy.

"I don't suck dick," Cannon said, laying back with his arms over his head. The tufts of black hair in his armpits were an invitation to chew on him. He put one hand around his hard cock and pointed it at Ulric. "Do me some more, man. Come on. You know you like it."

Ulric shook his head. "Don't give yourself airs," he said, and slapped Cannon hard. If his head had not already been cushioned by a pillow, his neck would have snapped back. When Cannon opened his mouth to curse at him, Ulric slapped him again. The punk's lower lip bled, and Ulric gathered him up and licked it avidly. Cannon struggled, but could not escape, and once more he was reminded that Ulric's strength exceeded his own. "You taste better than apple brandy or mead," Ulric hissed, and threw Cannon back down on the bed.

Once more he went to the alcohol lamp and spoon. Cannon was soon at his elbow, fascinated by the process of preparing a shot. Ulric laughed at him. "Do you want this?" he asked, showing Cannon the loaded needle.

"Yes," Cannon said. "You know I do."

"Then suck my dick," Ulric replied.

As Cannon quickly bent, thinking to service him, Ulric caught him by the throat, drew him into a crushing embrace, and bit his throat. The hunt had been maddening, hours of foreplay, invisible cock-and-ball torture. As Cannon's blood fled down his throat, Ulric's cock began to fill out and come to the party. "I wouldn't want to stuff a piece of limp meat into your mouth," Ulric said, and put Cannon down on his dick, hand on the back of his neck.

Dizzy from being bitten, seduced by Ulric's psychic power, Cannon found an odd desire in himself to give this stranger a hell of a blow job. *Cocky fucker. Let him see what it felt like to be driven out of your mind.* If he could make Ulric lose control, or make Ulric want him or like him, might he be able to escape? Ulric smelled so good and his cock felt so right in Cannon's mouth that he didn't even think about the irony of his strategy. What was he going to escape to—death by his own hand? Hadn't that been the plan a few hours ago?

The lanky, long-haired stranger's cock was a forbidden savory. Ulric hovered in Colin's mind, observing him without altering his response. The other man was a good cocksucker. His attitude toward Ulric's hard dick was worshipful. His mouth melted over it, bathing it in hot saliva. He sucked slowly, built pressure bit by bit, coaxing every possible bit of sensation out of Ulric's cock head and shaft. With one hand he guided the cock down his throat, where there was no perceptible resistance, and with the other he fondled Ulric's ball sac, stretching his nuts enough to make Ulric gasp and thrust more deeply into his mouth. Why would someone who loved dick this much pretend to be a piece of straight trade? Ulric said out loud, "You love doing this, don't you, Cannon?"

The punk shook his head, laughing at himself, rolling his eyes in protest. Ulric got the mental image of a girl in the backseat of a car, holding her panties in one hand and covering her pussy with the other. "Please don't fuck me," she said. Ulric smiled involuntarily then came back to the business at hand. He shifted his position so that he could reach Cannon's cock. He grasped it below the head and ran his thumb over it, smearing precome all over the sensitive, spongy mushroom. Cannon tried to fuck his hand, but Ulric only tightened his grip and moved his thumb to the junction of nerves below the head, on the bottom side of Cannon's cock. The suction on Ulric's dick became more intense and sustained, and Cannon moved his head back and forth, giving Ulric permission to fuck his face. That required Ulric to stop teasing the bright red tip of Cannon's sex and grab him by the ears instead. The rougher Ulric got with the kid, the harder both of their cocks became.

But if he were to come, he needed more of Cannon's blood. Ulric was floating in the midst of a familiar dilemma. Bloodlust and the keen desire to put Cannon on his back and pierce his butt hole were at war. Most gay men tortured themselves by prolonging sex as long as possible without coming, and ran the risk of not being able to get off at all if they delayed orgasm too frequently. Ulric was resisting the need to drain every drop of Cannon's blood, absorb every bit of the vital energy that animated him, and feel the explosion of satiation that would only come when Cannon's heart stopped drumming. Could he stave off the need to kill long enough to come? Fucking dead boys didn't usually work. He needed to see their faces reacting to the gut punch of his big dick.

Ulric pushed Cannon off his cock and sat him up, wrapped the tourniquet around his arm, and told him to yank it snug. "Now for your reward," he said, sending Cannon pacifying and soothing thoughts. The heroin went home once more, and Cannon slumped, eyes rolling wildly. For a moment, Ulric was afraid he had overdosed the kid, but no. Cannon was getting into the intense feelings of liberation and fearlessness. The rules that governed proper conversation, sober sex, no longer applied. He had no inhibitions now and grabbed Ulric's face to kiss him. "I think I fucking love you, man," he said, licking Ulric's sharp left fang. "Good smack, a big mean dick, what else do I need? I want you. I do. I want you so much, I...can't tell you."

"Shut up," Ulric said fondly, and flattened Cannon on the squalid bed. He loosened and removed his own clothing, wanting to feel Cannon's hands on his naked back and buttocks. He stretched out on top of him and returned his kisses with fervor. Their hard cocks nudged each other like blunt spears, but only Cannon's leaked. Ulric's body was stingy with its fluids. He would come without ejaculating just as he could not shed tears when he wept after a poignant kill.

"I wish you could get high with me," Cannon whispered. "Do you know this is the first time I've ever done this? Had a man in my bed with no money on the nightstand. No agenda. Free to do whatever I wanted with him." He had apparently forgotten who was the boss. But Ulric didn't need to remind him yet.

Mouth-to-mouth kissing turned to nuzzling each other's necks and chests. Ulric opened the other side of Cannon's throat. Cannon's hair gel crackled against the palm of his hand as he manipulated the position of his head. "I am high," he confessed, and opened his mind to the boy beneath him. Cannon's eyes widened as he was hit with wave after wave of pleasure that made the best sex and the best dope he had ever taken seem as bland as banana pudding. "This is my drug," Ulric said, and lifted his head, showing his victim his bloody muzzle. He kissed Cannon without licking his teeth clean, made the boy taste his own blood.

Cannon began to shake and his heels beat out a rapid tattoo on the mattress. Ulric went into his mind and body, trying to return everything to equilibrium. But Cannon hung on to the link between them, fought against its closing with more raw power than he had shown when he tried to physically resist being kidnapped, raped, and killed. "Don't take it away," he sobbed. "Please, man, don't take it away. I'm a junkie and I can't live without this. I can't. Don't you understand? It makes everything OK. No fear, no doubt, no anger, no shame, just...scarlet redemption."

"Don't worry, you won't have to live without it," Ulric said. He licked Cannon's nipples while he groped along the side of the mattress for the tube of lubricant they used when Cannon screwed Jackie in the ass. He found a battery-operated vibrator before he got the tube of K-Y and wondered who it had fucked last, the boy or the girl of this strung-out couple. Cannon's mind still clawed at him, demanding admission. He begrudgingly sent him a trickle of his own need and gratification. The boy calmed down, but he began to chant "Fuck me, fuck me, fuck me" in a low, dirty voice that Ulric was pretty sure no client had ever heard.

"If you want to be fucked, lift those legs and spread 'em," Ulric ordered. "Come on. Let me see that fuzzy dimpled butt of yours open. Oh, yes. Make that asshole wink at me, Cannon."

His cock was as hard as a living partner could make it. Why not fuck Cannon dry? Why was it OK to kill him, but not OK to hurt him unnecessarily? Ulric smiled at himself and briskly lubricated his cock. The feel of lubricant sliding around inside of Cannon would mimic ejaculation. He would miss the feeling of shooting a bit less.

It wasn't exactly easy to get into Cannon, but the coppery smell of his blood and the boy's glazed and happy eyes made the slow insertion worthwhile. Ulric's hunting instinct was clamoring at him to strike and take everything now, now, now! But he teased himself and the boy beneath him by gradually working the fat head of his cock past a sphincter that wanted to be violated and did not have quite enough experience to gape open at will. The vampire amped up their rapport, and all of Cannon's resistance fled. Ulric slid into him and gasped at the sensation of being surrounded by smooth, swollen, and vulnerable flesh. Cannon's hands dug into his shoulders and the punk threw his feet around Ulric's waist, drawing him in even deeper. "If I could, I'd get your fuckin' balls in me," Cannon said, eye to eye with his killer. "You got me, dude, you got me where I live. Oh, God, fuck me blind and stupid."

Ulric would have been doing exactly that even if Cannon had not requested it. He brought one of Cannon's hands down to his crotch and encouraged him to stroke his own cock in time to Ulric's hips. Together they drove Cannon to a place where everything that was sweetest and happiest about him was distilled. Ulric drank in his existence, then tilted Cannon's head back and raped his carotid artery. The other bites had struck only veins. This strike was different. The blood spurted as if Cannon could not give it up to Ulric fast enough. It was too much to swallow, yet he took it all in. Ulric felt as if the tissues in his mouth and throat were absorbing blood at a rapid rate, just as his soul was being assailed and enriched by Cannon's unraveling aura.

In exchange for this bounty, he drove his cock into Cannon with a calculated savagery that kept him on the edge of coming for so long that the spike-haired boy bit his tongue. Ulric told him he was a cunt, slapped him, and ordered him to shoot. He got what he wanted, and a wealth of tasty sobs as well. The white blood was thick between them, and the smell of Cannon's come was so enticing that Ulric came without warning, shaking and shouting as the weird sensation of an orgasm without ejaculation possessed him.

"Never been this good before, never, never," Cannon raved. "Kill me now. I'm ready to go. Please. Please. Kill me now."

Ulric's psychic connection to Cannon slammed shut. He was suddenly imprisoned in his own body, no longer awash in shared sensations, the mingled thrill of being fucked and screwing Cannon's near-virginal ass. It was harsh to feel his loneliness restored so suddenly. It pissed him off so much that he nearly administered the killing blow to Cannon's heart. But his own heart wasn't in it, and he quickly realized that something strange had happened. He was replete, full to the brim, and the drive to hunt no longer raved in every cell of his body. He could seek a new hiding place, allow dawn to send him to sleep, and stay in one place quietly till night fell again and the drama had to begin once more.

"No," he said, rolling off Cannon. "I don't believe I will." He reached for his leather pants and hoisted them on, shrugged on the T-shirt. He was trying to stuff his feet into boots without bothering with his socks when Cannon came after him, clawing at him like an angry girl who wanted to scratch his face and pull his hair. Ulric stopped him with the palm of his hand against his face and shoved him down to the bed. "Stop it," he said sharply, and got his boots on.

"You're going to leave me like this?" Cannon demanded. "You promised to *kill* me, man!"

"So you've got a reprieve!" Ulric shouted.

"But now that I know—now that I've seen it, felt it—if you won't kill me, make me like you! Let me be that way, have those feelings, I *have* to be like you."

"Not in a million years," Ulric said. "This is my hunting ground. I can't share it, and I won't give it up to a novice. I never wanted to be this way, Cannon, and I won't spawn any miserable descendants."

"What have I got to live for if you won't help me?"

"I picked you out because you wanted to die! If you were going to be dead by morning anyway, where was the harm in me taking what I need from you? At least I could offer you a happy death. But you were too good, Cannon. So blame that tight little butt of yours. I got what I needed from you without killing you. If you want to die, you will have to do it yourself." He picked up the plastic bag full of smack and tossed it onto Cannon's naked stomach. "Here. It's all yours."

"And it's shit!" Cannon stood up, taking care to keep beyond Ulric's reach. "I can't do that garbage anymore. It's nothing compared to what you've got."

When Ulric got to the top of the stairs, Cannon was also there on his knees, grabbing at his hand. Who knew a mortal could move so fast? "Please," Cannon said. "I am begging you. I'll go someplace else. You'll never see me again."

Ulric stopped and extricated his fingers from Cannon's grasp. Dawn was uncomfortably close, and he had to force himself to be patient. "Are you prepared to feel everything that I do, Cannon?" The punk rocker recoiled from his bleak face, but Ulric held him fast in the talons of his mind and opened his heart. It was a cruel thing to do to a being who would not be able to contain his emotions. Because what he felt once his bloodlust was slaked was utter, stark loneliness. Living forever meant that his only companion was an avalanche of boredom that buried him alive.

Cannon screamed and clawed at his own face. Ulric grabbed both of his wrists before he could blind himself and slammed him into the nearest wall. "We all *suffer*," he said through clenched teeth, making a mockery of his own and Cannon's pain. "But you got a second chance. You can choose to be grateful or you can let yourself get trampled to death by horse. I don't care."

Then he was gone, and Cannon could not have said how he left. Was he lucky? He felt like the unluckiest man in Manhattan. Dizzy and sick to his stomach, Cannon curled up in the dark around the baggie of dope and cried himself to sleep. He woke up after a few hours of fevered sleep and realized it wasn't possible to heal on his own from losing that much blood. So he put his clothes on, went down the stairs for the last time, and began a long, slow walk to the hospital. Street by street. A-B-C. First, Second, Third. Relearning the alphabet, how to count, taken back to the barren basics.

Wet
M. Christian

The brush was dry, so he wet it.

The strokes at first were always, for some reason, slow and precise. He knows that nothing will remain of them after it's done, but for some reason it always starts that way: bands, shades of the same color, going vertical, diagonal, horizontal. He guesses, when he does think about the act, that it is a getting-acquainted with the brushes, the canvas—his medium.

Why that should be when he has painted for so long is a mystery Doud never examined.

Dry again—silent, precise strokes now skittering and scratching across the smooth face of the canvas. *Dries so quickly.* He wet the brush again.

Those first strokes were a climb into the work, he supposed (when he does). Painting those stripes, bands of one color—always that one color—are like the rungs of a ladder. Going up, into the act, the glow, of creativity...of making a work.

The next movements of the brush were wild, feverish: All precise control lost in the rising swell of what was fleeting around his mind, just beyond Doud's normal vision. He knew, certainly, absolutely, that he was trying to pin it down now with the brush, the color—to make it stick and stay so he can see it clearly: see if it is pretty or ugly.

Dry again. He dipped it into his seemingly inexhaustible well and continued.

Maybe a man. Yes, perhaps that: like a stroller walking out of a fog, a shape becoming shoulders, a broad chest, legs, and what could be a waist. Then, with more movements of the brush, it grew details like leaves from a tree: The curves of a chest, the tendons in the arms, the contours of muscles and bone, the texture of smooth skin...a face.

Dry again. Doud dipped the brush into his red-filled mouth and tried to capture the man more fully.

~

The street was brilliant with a heaven of shines and reflections from a light rain. The primary neon colors burst from places like JACKSON'S HOLE, THE TEN PIN, THE 87 CLUB, AUNT MARY'S DINER, hit the street, the sidewalk, the faces of the tall buildings like...*like watercolors*, Doud thought, though his own medium was a lot less flowing and fluid.

The Space didn't have neon, and despite the beauty of the rain-shellacked street outside, its owner would never, ever ponder lighting its nondescript doorway with its gaudy attraction. Wellington took extremely cool pride in the austerity of his gallery—going over its rubber-tiled steps, eggshell walls, industrial lighting, stainless steel display stands, and single office countertop with an eye as precise and chilly as a level. Doud easily imagined him thinking the photographs, paintings, and sculptures that paid his rent were a distraction from the purity of an absolutely empty room.

He hoped for a frozen second that the flash had been lightning beyond the window, out among the glimmering night street and its hunched and brisk people.

Doud loved the rain and especially lightning. Like the bands of slow, precise color that started his works, he never examined why the world being lit for a second, frozen and trapped in a blink of pure silver, fascinated him. Maybe it was the raw power of natural electricity—or maybe it was the close comfort of being snug and warm for the evening that he associated with rain outside: Lightning was the tiger prowling outside while he safely warmed inside.

But lightning doesn't come from within (unless you count inspiration). For a second the flash trapped his own face in the window glass: wide, large brown eyes, aquiline nose, brushy brows; curled black hair; deeply tanned and lined skin; large, strong mouth with hidden teeth. Some thought him Italian, others American or East Indian. A few guessed at maybe Eskimo or even Polynesian. Never guessed the truth of New York (son of New Yorkers). Never, ever, guessed his age.

The disappointment over a lightning-free night came quick, a gentle slap (because it was a simple pleasure), and he turned back to the semi-crowded gallery. There he was, a too clean-looking photographer he instantly knew was either the friend of an artist or one of them himself (newspaper shooters were usually a lot more scruffy and exotic). Doud hated to be photographed, hated being frozen in time and having his image in the hands of, and at the mercy, someone else.

"Yours?" the photographer said, his face opaqued by the complex of a flash unit, massive lens, and a matte-black camera body. Dirty blond, almost brown, tall, broad—was all Doud could see.

"Those are," Doud said, nodding to the right-hand wall and the five paintings that were edge on, and so were the colors of their frames. Doud didn't need to see them, an artist's privilege of many hours of work.

The camera came down and he treated Doud with his profile as he scanned the paintings. Pale, hollow cheeks; bones seemingly as thin as a bird's; wet blue eyes that, even across the mostly empty gallery, seemed to see far too much, far too quickly; a mouth that bloomed with lips that Doud found himself instantly wanting to kiss; a nose all but invisible against the beauty of his face (which was fine—having such a profound nose, Doud disliked the same in others); and a fine and elegant body that seemed to be all chest and shoulders, a rack where thin, pale arms and legs dangled with a refined and dignified posture. He was dressed simply elegant in black pants, a tight turtleneck, and an elegant (and probably antique) morning coat—a direct polar extreme from Doud's old sweatshirt, boots, and jeans.

It was a kind of shock to see someone who sported himself so...*dapper* was a word that came out of Doud's memory, along with the smell of horses and raw electricity, the rumble of the "El" trains, and scratchy Al Jolson from a Grammophone. Dapper? Yes, refined and polished. Quite out of character for the Space and for an admirer of Doud's work.

"You probably get asked this a lot—" the man started to say, fixing those darting, smiling eyes on Doud and smiling pure warmth.

"An awful lot," Doud said with a practiced sigh that spoke of a joke rather than true exasperation. "Animals," he finished, answering the question.

"I saw the jar," the photographer said, indicating with a jerk of his camera the large bell jar stuffed with a cow's severed head on the floor in front of Doud's wall, "and thought as much."

"The medium is the message," Doud said with a smile. "People either look at me *real* funny and think about DNA testing, or they think it's a trick of paint and technique."

"It is rather...your studio must stink."

Doud laughed, the sound coming from down deep. "Lots of windows, and I keep my stuff well-covered. Then of course I fix it real good after. Lots of shellac."

The man smiled, shifted his camera, and stuck out a pale, long-boned hand. "Jona. Jona Periliak."

"Charmed," Doud said. Jona's hand was dry and warm, almost hot. "Are you here as well, or taking shots for a friend?"

"I'm in the backroom."

Doud remembered the photographs, on his way in that evening, but since he never supervised his installations he hadn't looked beyond that initial glance. "Would you mind," Doud said, smiling his best smile and hoping he'd remembered to gargle and brush his teeth, "showing me?"

The Space had started to fill up since they'd started talking. The usual wine-and-cheese crowd of artists and their usual mixture of friends. They passed carefully by suits and jeans and piercings and Doc Martens and even a latex bodysuit and a full tux.

The backroom was sky-blue, lit with Wellington's usual baby spots. Maybe a dozen, maybe 14, black-and-white portraits. Jona looking thoughtful with glasses and a book. Jona looking sad with gravestones in the background. Jona looking pained as blood, black as ink (and it could have been), that ran down from a sliced palm. Jona excited, his bare chest slick with sweat and probably oil. Doud scanned them all, lingering long, excited and pained, giving them his examining look— then glanced over at the title of the series: *Portrait of the Artists*.

Doud hated photographs: He saw them as a kind of cheat, a kind of shortcut.

"They're fine—" Doud said, using a word that also came from penny candy and hoop skirts. He didn't like photographs for lots of reasons, but Jona was pretty, even striking, in his pallor and funere-al garb. Being self-portraits made it easy to lie—Jona was fine indeed.

"You don't like them." He didn't seem hurt at all; more like he was calling Doud on his politeness.

"I didn't say that. It's not my medium, is all. Besides, I meant what I said. I like the way these are all parts of you."

"I appreciate that," Jona said, moving the camera behind him so Doud had a nice view of his flat stomach and hard chest—at least what he could see outlined in the black turtleneck.

It had been a long time for Doud. He could barely remember the face, and couldn't, for the life of him, think of the last name of the last person he was attracted to as much as he was attracted to Jona. *You'd think*, he found himself thinking with surprising clarity, *after all this time I'd get better at this*. At least he wasn't hungry—but he did feel that other kind of desperation, the one that wanted to make his gently shaking hands reach up and stroke Jona's soft, pale cheeks and tell him how beautiful he looked. *Go on*, he thought next, *say that you appreciate* him...

"Are you" Doud did say, waving at the row of photographs, "going to be here long?"

"Tonight or the show?" And before Doud could respond either way, Jona quickly added, "Just a few minutes and the end of the month."

The Space had started to fill up and Doud felt himself being pulled by their body heat, their eyes. Going to an opening was rare, staying as late as he had was ever rarer...but Jona, and Jona's beautiful attention, was priceless.

But the people—

"It's kind of getting crowded," the pale beauty said with a smile that made a warm spot on Doud's stomach and his eyes lose focus for a second.

Doud heard himself say, "Let's go outside."

~

Doud liked the ships and the trains. And the rent was cheap. He could understand why others didn't like living next to the yards in front of the bay, especially when one of the big diesel engines revved at 1 A.M. or a tramp steamer blasted its departure at 2.

Despite being jerked awake too damned early in the morning, Doud liked living in the shadow of the simple, huge machines. People made him feel alone and way too unique, outside always looking in and...hungry. The boats and the trains made him feel practically human by comparison.

"You never said why you didn't like my shots," Jona said, sitting on Doud's comfortable burgundy sofa, twirling a glass a quarter full of white wine.

"I guess I think it's a cheat—"

"That it takes a lot less to handle a camera than a brush? Not necessarily—" Jona started to say, leaning forward to look into Doud's eyes.

Doud looked so quickly away it made his head hurt for a moment. "You never asked why I paint the way I do," he said to his spiraling red-and-blue rug.

"I thought it had something to do with the cycle of death—you know; something growing from something dying. Your pictures from dead cows."

Doud found himself frowning; another person who didn't pick up on it. He wondered why he had any kind of following at all, or was it that people liked seeing paintings done in blood on principle? "No," he said, refilling his glass even though he knew he'd had way too much already (he got drunk so damned quickly), "that's not it. I do it to give them something close to immortality."

Jona was rapt. In many ways more rapt than he should be. "But you don't like photographs."

Doud sighed, hated saying these kinds of things but also tired of lying. Yeah, at the time it usually got him company for the night, or even a weekend, but he didn't like how he felt in the morning, on Monday. At least when he told the truth—well, mostly the truth— he liked the company he always ended up keeping: Doud. "Nothing lasts forever," he finally said after a long damned silence (God, Jona was pretty), "except for a photograph. Throw the negative away, then maybe a print will age and fade away naturally. Won't last absolutely forever. I paint because the...animals will last so much longer. Not forever, just a lot longer."

Jona smiled and sipped his own wine. "You don't like forever?"

Doud shook his head, slow and tired: the sound of iron wheels on cobblestones, opium, a harbor full of sails, coal... "Nothing ever is. A long, long time...yes. But not forever. Nothing is ever forever."

Jona thought for a long time, twirling his wine in his glass in what Doud knew instantly could be an annoying habit. Then he put the glass down carefully on Doud's spiraling rug and started to dig in a cotton shoulder bag he had brought from the Space. He came up with a stiff manila envelope and, never once meeting Doud's eyes, undid the clasp and removed a sandwich of gray cardboard. Between them:

A City street in a copy of plate sepia; carriage bus filigreed with advertisements for patent medicines and Clothiers for Fine, Respected Gentlemen; women in hoop skirts, men with top hats and swallow-tail coats; children in sailor suits, pinafores, and button-up shoes; to one side, in a wool coat and a simple bowler, a man with a casual, caught-unawares face: handsome eagle nose, dark features that could be Italian, Mediterranean, East Indian...

I hate photographs, Doud thought hollowly, coldly.

~

Jona sat in a little coffeehouse, the Kona Coast, and kept the words circulating in his mind, trying to keep them fresh, trying not to lose a scrap.

His lips and throat hurt. Getting up that morning, he'd coughed up a fat, dark slug of phlegm and blood into Doud's bathroom sink. By noon his lips were a faded purple and it hurt to smile.

Kona Coast wasn't his first choice, something less loaded would have been much better, but he didn't seem to have any room in his mind to think of someplace new, original: Jeffrey's favorite place would have to do.

It's painful till you get used to it. Let your body acclimate to its new design.

He felt good. Damned good. The world was sharp and clean and crisp. Looking across the tiny coffeehouse, he felt his attention glide like a scalpel across the wooden tables, the stacks of free newspapers, the walls decorated years thick with roommate-wanted, jobs offered, bands playing, films showing fliers, and handbills. Someone walked in and for a second, not even a heartbeat, he thought it was Jeffrey, but with his new focus, his new clean eyes, he saw that the face across the room was not even close. This man had gray at his temples. Jeffrey had been too vain to allow even a single aging hair in his own.

That *almost seeing* irritated Jona. It pissed him off to have Jeffrey come into his thoughts now, when he was trying to hold everything in, to keep it bottled up, commit it to hard memory.

Am I the only one? I guess I might be. I've made...friends like you a few times. You get lonely, and it's hard to get close to your food—at least emotionally. I don't know if they've managed to make...friends like I can. I don't think they can.

I don't know if I'm a myth or a fluke. I was born this way.

Looking down in his coffee, Jona caught and captured the wisps of steam, freezing them with his mind as the words of Doud echoed around the chitchat of the coffeehouse. At first he was too excited, and in too much pain, to hear it clearly. But there, in the Kona Coast, they were there, moving in front of him like the steam from his white and sweet coffee.

Two things. Remember the two things of what you are, now. I give you one but not the other: Murder. Immortality.

Again, Jeffrey intruded on Jona's recollection of Doud: Jeffrey standing in front of him again. Another fight. Another argument. Jona's shock and outrage over something Jona had said or done. That outrage—it made Jona furious. Jeffrey's blank, shocked look, his wet eyes as he tried to understand why Jona had done what he'd done. Didn't matter what he'd done—said something catty, made some remark, flirted with someone's partner, fucked someone's partner, stolen some useless knickknack—there was Jeffrey's smug, shining face whipping Jona with a disappointed look. He hated Jeffrey when he looked at him like that. Hated his boring superiority.

Like I said, I don't know what I am. Many things, labels, work but mostly they don't. Sunlight doesn't hurt, crosses don't do anything, stakes will—but then they'll probably kill anything. I have to eat twice, sometimes only once, if I take it easy, every six months. I can do more but don't.

The photograph. Jona remembered the context with an electric flash. Some friend of Jeffrey's, a smug little queen with an arrogant love, and dedication to, antiques. The little shit was too in love with his partner, an ebony beauty named Tan, to respond to Jona's come-on, so he'd compensated by lifting an album of turn-of-the-century photographs.

Jeffrey had found out, of course, and had shown up at Jona's little Park Circle studio to demand the book back.

Seeing his ex-lover standing in his front room, looking down at him like dirt that had somehow managed to stick to Jeffrey's pristine shoes, Jona had started to softly quake with anger. "Do you see it here?" he'd said, trying not to betray his fury.

"I know you took it, Jo," Jeffrey had said.

"If you can find it then call me a fucking thief. If you don't see it, then get the fuck out."

He never looked, just left saying that he didn't want to know Jona anymore.

After he'd done...whatever it was that Doud had done, he had put him, heaving, panting, and vibrating like a junkie, on his coach, dried and not-dried blood like paste all over his face and chest and mouth. Doud had been crying, almost puking with the tears dribbling from his large eyes: "I'm so sorry. So sorry. I just want some company. It's stupid. I'm so stupid. I don't know you. Don't know you at all—"

In the book, photographs. In one of the photographs, a man he recognized from an upcoming installation at the Space. The medium and the perfect likeness: He didn't think anything about it, didn't put anything together about it aside from another game, another trick. Show Doud the shot, freak the fuck out of him, and pick up the pieces as he'd done so many times before.

With Jeffrey it had been games of fucking anything that moved—especially when Jeffrey liked to "bond" with his lovers. Easy to dick with someone who wants *you*—you fuck someone else.

"You have to, but you don't have to enjoy it. I do it. I do it but I try to atone as best I can. I make it quick, I don't enjoy it. I don't do it for any reason than to survive. And...yes, I try to make it up to them somehow: make them special for their donation to me."

Doud had been standing in front of one of his paintings, running his elegant fingers over the five sharp, clear lines that cut vertically through the otherwise unmarked canvas.

"I promise you a long, long life. I promise you almost immortality. I promise you my company. That's all."

The doors to the little coffeehouse opened again, and Jona's steam, and Doud's words in his mind, vanished in the cool breeze. Glancing up, he saw with his new eyes, crystal-clear, a tall, slender, man with shoulder-length brown curls without a trace of gray.

"Jeffrey," Jona said, motioning him over to his table.

"What do you want, Jona?" Jeffrey said, walking over but standing stiff and straight.

"Have something to tell you—" Jona said.

"Is it about Abbott's book? If you have it you should get it back to him. I don't want to see it, know about it, or have anything to do with you."

"Jeffrey," Jona said, with a spark of playful warmth in his voice, "don't you think you owe me at least a little chance, a tiny one, to end this well? I don't want you to hate me, Jeffrey."

"Is it the book, Jona?" It was rare to see Jeffrey almost angry. Fury crashed through Jona like a metal wave, and he tasted copper in his mouth and on his bruised and swollen lips.

But then Jona firmly recalled Doud, the kiss, the new self in him, the new world he was about to walk into, and so he said, smiling despite his painful lips: "Yes, Jeffrey, it's the book. But much more. Come back to my place and I'll tell you all about it."

~

Jona had slept the night before, his face and mouth wet with blood, in Doud's bed. As the sun started to burn up the city, he had gotten cleaned up and gone straight to the Kona Coast for thought and coffee. Then Jeffrey.

Though Jeffrey was a few inches taller than gaunt and hallow-cheeked Jona, he seemed smaller, somehow, as if the night, Doud, and the blood had added to him. A lot.

Jeffrey tagged along as Jeffrey always did, a few steps behind, scanning the dim and damp streets from the coffeehouse to Jona's place. They didn't talk much: The silence between them was a hard wall of skewed viewpoints. Jeffrey felt betrayed by Jona, deceived and manipulated too many times.

Jona looked back over his shoulder at him. His viewpoint was...simpler: *I like looking down on you, Jeffrey. There is so little to you. So very little. Just like everyone else. So very little.*

"I don't want to come up," Jeffrey said, standing on the slick marble of the foyer as Jona clinked and rattled his keys.

"But you want it, don't you?" Jona said, opening the door and stepping aside.

"I want closure to this, Jo," Jeffrey said, shouldering past and starting up the two flights to Jona's apartment.

"Well, so do I," Jona said, from behind him, as he closed the door.

Another rattle of keys, another door, again Jeffrey stepped in first, scanning the apartment slowly, even though nothing had changed since he'd last been there. Closing the door behind him, Jona smiled wide and broad against the thud of pain from his lips— caught up in a kind of laugh that was coming from deep inside. It had sprung from a kind of giddy relief that he could see Jeffrey clearly for the first time.

So little to you, Jeffrey. So damned little. And to think I envied you, your grace and meticulous gestures. Your subtle humor. Your gliding hands. I loved to make you...all of you...do what I wanted. Cry. Laugh. Get so frustrated. Now I don't need to.

Now I'm much more.

"Can I have a kiss, Jeffrey?" Jona said softly, trying to hide the laughter that wanted to explode out of him, as he put a careful, gentle hand on Jeffrey's high shoulder.

"Jona," Jeffrey started to say, shaking his head against being struck suddenly sad by the tone in Jona's voice.

"I want something to close all this. A kiss would be perfect. Perfect. Then the photograph. I promise."

"Always playing fucking games." Jeffrey's voice was level and smooth, crisp and elegant, as always, but Jona knew that he was furious, that he was shaking with anger beneath his cultivated image. "No more hoops, Jona. You're not in love with me. You never were. You're not anything you pretended to be. I saw you, Jona. I saw you when you dicked us all around and played with my head. When you fucked around. Smiling. Always fucking smiling."

"So I don't even deserve a goodbye kiss ?" Jona said, trying desperately not to smile.

~

The rain was cold and, of course, wet, but his concentration on the one window dimmed it down to the gentle stings of the drops in his eyes. He didn't blink. Didn't need to. Doud stood in a short alley reeking of vomit and urine and watched the shadows moving against a hard light. Didn't need to blink, could now find Jona anywhere in the city: There were other things he could do, but, frankly, he rarely had a need for them.

How many times? Doud thought, looking down at the sparkling streets for a second, listening to the hushing of the passing cars, moving through a night frozen at moments with lightning flashes. He was out and about, walking with the tiger of a storm when he should have been home and warm. It was something he'd done before: *How many times have I stood like this and waited? How many times have I stood here, knowing I'd be alone again in a few hours?*

But there was a little hope in the back of his mind, a little glow, the same little glow that had always accompanied those other thoughts: *maybe just this once.*

~

The heat from Jeffrey was like a open flame in Jona's face. It rolled off him in waves of luxurious warmth. Jona was normally a blackout kisser, letting his eyes squeeze shut with the concentration of a good kiss, rolling in the play of tongue and lips and teeth. But his eyes were wide open now—wide and capturing. Jeffrey was bent down the few inches to kiss him, catching the tiny pores on the end of what he'd always thought of as a perfect nose. He saw the tiny broken blood vessels in his eyes; the silken bags under his eyes that would get worse with age; a hint of wine and garlic on his breath that meant that tall, elegant Jeffrey had been haunting one of his goth friends for company. Jona took him in with a glance and a breath in the moment Jeffrey relaxed to kiss. Jona didn't see, for once, the statue who had deemed Jona good in bed and worthy of his debonair company.

Jona saw bone and sweat and piss and shit and muscle and guts and the raging, boiling inferno of quarts and quarts of blood.

Jona's cock was iron, steel in his pants. He wanted to reach down and stroke it, rub himself to a nice orgasm as he held himself there, high above the simple meat of the man he'd thought of as perfect, idolized. He wanted to orgasm from standing there—the ego rush of realizing what Jeffrey was and what Jona was now. His cock raged full and hard and straining with the pure power of being someone else at last, at being powerful at last.

Kiss me.

The touch was a shock. Jona was so focused, so drawn into his perception of the puppet, the hunk of gristle that was Jeffrey, that he didn't expect the touch to be silken and sparked with tension. He jerked back a tiny amount, breaking the contact as quickly as it had been made. He expected something rough and coarse to match his meaty revelation about his old flame.

Well, he thought, smiling against his painful lips and moving even closer, *rabbits feel nice too.*

The touch was softer this time, and the two old lovers fell into the comfort of each other's bodies. Jeffrey might have wanted something chaste and simple, a gothic rite of departure like a Victorian greeting card ("Nice to have known your acquaintance"), but the jungle fury that was suddenly flickering in and out of Jona washed the practiced distance right out of him. It was like Jeffrey'd been submerged in a powerful electric current and his body was jerking along to it—despite his poised mentality.

It was a good kiss. A fine kiss. It was a lover's kiss at the height of their attraction.

It didn't seem like a kiss goodbye.

As Jona started, Jeffrey's cock went from a strong erection to a painful hardness in his precise pants. It was the first indication that Jona had started it right. He was surprised over how natural, so easy it felt. He'd thought, as he'd asked for the kiss, that it might be hard, that he might even have to resort to another way. But it was like the comfort of...a lover's kiss. Jona followed the way that seemed right and it all flowed along with the simple determination of any biological function. Like kissing, like drinking, like swallowing, like eating.

Like breathing. Jona kissed Jeffrey and started to breathe him in. Gently at first, but then stronger and stronger. Jeffrey liked it, liked the strong suction of Jona's mouth on his, liked the earthy pull of his lungs on his own.

Then he tasted blood and his chest started to hurt.

The kiss climbed up from the edge-hard passion of rough sex, of their cocks pressing—dueling clubs between their frenzied bodies. It went from that flash of painful sex to pure pain to screaming.

But Jeffrey couldn't scream—Jona's mouth was over his and he was pulling Jeffrey inside out through his own throat.

Jona felt Jeffrey's pure, hot blood boil up and out of him and down his throat. He pulled and tugged with his breath and the other of his new self. Jona reached down with his hunger and pulled Jeffrey out of himself. The blood and essence was a scalding wine of life splashing against his lips, teeth, gums, and tongue. He wanted to laugh, to scream his joy and power to the moon, to the sun, but more than that, more than anything, he wanted *more*. He wanted the totality of the meat and blood (oh, yes, the *blood*) of Jeffrey. He wanted to drink him to the last drop, to pull him all the way in, to drink him through their kiss till there was nothing more to hold, to stroke—till Jeffrey's threatening perfection was nothing but a slaughterhouse residue.

Jona's cock was iron, something fundamental and material in the torrent of life that he was pulling out of Jeffrey. He wanted to fuck something, anything. He wanted to drive his spur of metal into a worthy, powerful lover.

He thought of Doud. He thought of the little man in the jeans and the sweater. Doud had stopped, had held back enough of Jona— then had forced the blood, water, tears, come, meat back into him. He'd tasted Jona and put him back into his now changed body.

He could do the same, he guessed, with Jeffrey—but he didn't want to. Didn't want to at all. He was hungry and thirsty, and Jeffrey...tasted too damned good.

In his arms, Jeffrey screamed into his mouth and diminished in stature. Jona pulled the fluids out of him, drew the essence and blood out and down his own throat. Hypnotized, Jona watched Jeffrey's skin darken and lose its shine—replaced by a matte powder; saw blindness glaze over Jeffrey's eyes as the fluid was drawn back into his skull, into his throat, and into Jona. He saw Jeffrey's cheeks concave and his bones start to snap from the pressure, the spreading dryness.

Soon (too soon!) Jona was holding him, the child-size husk of Jeffrey, the dusty bag of whining, chalk-soft bones and papery skin.

Still he pulled and pulled. Jeffrey snapped and tore and crackled like a low fire or a paper being crumpled. The last drop tasted of music: a single high note that passed his teeth and dropped like a bell into Jona's stomach, body.

There was little left of elegant Jeffrey: an ancient doll of hair, scraps of skin, fingernails, and shattered bones like dice in a bag. Not enough to identify—easily buried or flushed down the toilet.

Jona put the dry fragments of Jeffrey down on the floor and stretched, feeling the blood surge and roll in his strong body, feel it start to mix and burn with his own. He felt exhilarated, added to, charged—

Full.

Jeffrey rolled in the back of his throat, a warm wine filling him, draining into him. He caught a steaming reflection in one of the windows and laughed at himself. *Friends sometimes leave an impression on you*, he thought to his normal, slender reflection. *Jeffrey, I guess, didn't on me.*

~

Doud was watching an engine back into the yards when his doorbell rang. He'd known it would, soon enough—but it seemed to have happened faster than he expected.

Going to the door, he absently checked to make sure his hat, coat, and shoes weren't anywhere in sight. His *wet* hat, coat, and shoes.

"Come in," he said to a dripping Jona. Behind him, cars kicked up ripples of inch-deep rainwater as they furrowed through reflections of industrial lighting. "I've missed you."

"I like that," Jona said, entering and shaking his coat off before handing it to Doud. "People don't usually miss me."

"I did. I've missed you for a long time. Longer than today even."

"Been a long time?" Jona said from the front room, looking back at Doud hanging up his coat, the words sinking into him. "I guess it has."

"Very long. It's hard to relate to others. You should find that out quickly. It's the two of us."

"Intimate," Jona said, sitting down on the couch. "I like intimate. Just the two of us against the world."

"The world would win, don't forget. Drink?"

"Sure."

As Doud rattled and banged in the kitchen, Jona called: "How long, Doud?"

"What do you mean?"

"I mean, how long."

"No, I mean how long for what? How long since I was this way? Forever. I told you: born this way. Since I got laid? A month ago this Thursday, in the afternoon. Since I've had real...companionship? Twenty years, give or take two or three years. Since I killed someone for food? Seven months ago."

"Do you like this, Doud?" Jona said from the door to the kitchen. There was something in his voice, in the tones, if not the words. It wasn't a deep pondering or a frightened seeking for answers. Not laughter, not excitement—nothing so obvious. Not even a smile.

Close, though. Close to a smile.

"I don't have a choice. You have a cut cock, Jona—do you miss that inch or two of skin? You miss that much more than I miss the rest of them outside. I've always been this way. Always. I don't know what they are like, all those people out there. I know what I am, and what I have to do to live...for as long as I have."

"But you're not one of them."

"I'm something. Something that needs to suck 'em bone-dry to survive. So I have to keep myself distant from them..." Doud said, handing Jona a simple white wine in a cheap glass. "Can't have cows as friends, you know."

"Is that how you see them?"

"No. I don't. But they're not what I am. I miss someone I can talk to, share my life with. Be with when the 'otherness' is everywhere. I do what I have to do to keep living, but that's all. It's enough, though, to keep them out there and me in here."

"Well," Jona said, knocking back half of his glass with one swallow, "it's not you anymore. It's us."

Gesturing him back to the front room, Doud smiled soft, small, and quick, saying, "I appreciate that. I do."

"I appreciate you, Doud, what you've given me."

"It...almost makes it worthwhile, to be able to see people grow up. Buggies to Neil Armstrong. Typhus and children's bars to Apple and the Web."

Smiling, Jona sat down next to Doud on the couch. "I'm looking forward to it. I'm really—" *smiling* "—looking forward to it."

"I'm glad you are," Doud said. "I'm glad."

Time dragged for a few minutes as they sipped their wine. As it often happens, their heat was a magnet. First, they sat in uncomfortable, hard, silence. Then they were closer, touching cotton pants to jeans. The temperature for both was clearly higher. Doud's hand ended up on Jona's knee. Thinking about it later, Doud thought that he probably (since he usually did) had been talking, maintaining an empty patter of God knew what: stories of elevated trains, "shooting the moon," coonskin coats, outdoor plumbing, "The Yellow Kid," short pants, a woman's "well-turned ankle"—a smoke screen of articulated memories hiding his fear of the temperature between them.

Finally, Jona leaned over and kissed him.

Doud's patter vanished into a low, purring moan—one that made Jona smile a painful smile in the middle of the kiss.

When they broke, Doud was smiling too. He reached out and put a hand on Jona's hard cock, stroking it lightly, ghostly, through Jona's jeans. "No secrets, none at all."

"Wouldn't have it any other way," Jona said, stretching, leaning back till he was a length of crackling joints.

Doud's hands were almost shaking as he undid Jona's fly, pulled his pants away from his waist, revealing softly pale skin—no underwear—and hints of distant, scratchy hairs.

They were in the space between "We're gonna do it" and "We're doing it!" Jona lifted his ass off the couch, and Doud fought and struggled with his jeans till they surrendered and were jerked down to his firm thighs.

Jona's cock was simply average. A pale column of hard meat, head a brilliant pink. Cut. Noticeably fatter at the root than the tip, despite a wide corona. It bobbed, a gentle swaying, with a creamy drop of early excitement gleaming at the tip.

"Beautiful," Doud said, wrapping his lips around Jona's cock.

It was like a pressurized bath to Jona, a silken damp hand strong around the nerves of his cock. A quiet man, a gothic gentleman of the nights, Jona came from a tribe that prided itself on its dour, dark orgasms—he actually made a sound. As Doud kissed the tip, then licked the shaft, then dropped his warm wet mouth over the tip and then the entire shaft of Jona's cock, Jona made a soft, all-but-inaudible mewing sound.

It was hard for him not to instantly come.

Practice, Jona thought, smiling against his graveyard training. *Lots and lots of practice. Years of practice.*

Doud's mouth was more than well-trained. It was magical. It was as if Jona could feel a tongue as nimble as fingers, as strong as an ass, as precise as an eyelash. He was lost to Doud's tongue, teeth, palate, lips, and warm saliva. It was hard for him to focus on anything save the tiny, incredible details of Doud's lips and mouth on him.

Somewhere deep inside the raging sea of Doud's expert cock sucking, a little Jona was smiling and leaning back, sketching the territory of the future in his mind, playing the angles, and seeing where he might take it.

Simple Doud. Very simple Doud. What's yours now...will be mine later with enough time. Now I have lots of time for lots of things...lots of fun things. In there, in his thoughts, he tripped over the corpse of Jeffrey, sticks and stones in a bag of dried, vanishing skin. It was a quiet moment, remembering Jeffrey's eyes crumbling back into their sockets, his last scream vanishing into crackling bones, tearing skin—

Then he came.

It was a screaming come, a deep brass come—all horns and woodwinds. A primal orgasm that pushed, heaved, and kicked its way from the base of his balls, up through his shaft of his cock and out the top, mixing and splashing in Doud's mouth and even foaming his dark lips.

Laughing, Jona leaned forward and mussed Doud's thick curly hair. "That was incredible..."

"Not yet," Doud said, his voice unreadable as he licked the come from Jona's still-hard cock. "Not yet..."

Doud set back to work, working his mouthy magic on Jona's again. And again Jona was on a road to a shaking, squirming come—a fast trip straight down, no bends, pedal all the way to the floor. The persistence of Doud was almost frightening, almost made Jona open his eyes wide. It was so good—too good. It was frightening. It was as if Doud had plugged himself somehow directly into Jona's cock and had thrown a switch to make him come and come and come.

He did and did and did.

It didn't stop. One come after another, each squirt a little less than the one before, each a little less good and a little more...forced. Each one more of a strain.

Then the pain started.

Jona tried to make Doud stop, but the pain was too much. It was all he could do to hang on to the couch and let the hot iron that it felt like was being poured down his cock come out as a deep, echoing scream. His balls felt like they were cracking, breaking apart from the pressure of Doud's suction. His cock was tearing—it was ripping from the inside out from the force of Doud's lips—the strength of his body reaching into Jona and pulling him out through his cock. Again and again he tried to move, to make his spasming, cramping hands let loose of the couch and bring them down on Doud to make him stop, but the cramps were like handcuffs around his wrists, wrapped around his fingers, trapping him there.

Then Doud stopped and said—blood and come dripping down his chin, eyes lit with fire from inside—"I promised you near forever—not a weapon, not a toy for you to enjoy. I gave you years, not murders."

Weak, Jona pushed himself off the coach, trying to speak, trying to get up and get away, but he was old, broken, and drained. Muscles in him, in his stomach, in his chest were wrung tight and locked around broken bones. His cock was stuffed with needles and pins, his balls were crushed and broken—trampled underfoot. Something dripped onto the floor and his cock was wet.

"You have blood on your lips, you know—" Doud said, wiping his mouth on his sleeve. Then he bent down and kissed Jona hard. Very hard.

It started almost soft, almost like a kiss hello, a kiss goodbye, but then became the same special kiss that Doud had given Jona, had blessed him with. But it didn't stop where Doud had stopped before; it didn't change, mix, and reverse. It went on and on and on...a kiss goodbye, like the kiss Jona had given Jeffrey.

Blood boiled up through the bursting, boiling arteries in Jona's throat. He could feel them burst like blisters, feel the blood squirt and run down into his stomach. He could feel his belly pull itself up under the power of Doud's kiss. He wanted to scream, he wanted to cough and puke and cry, but he was a straw, a tube for his own blood boiling out of his rupturing body and into Doud.

He tried to fight, to flail against the horrible pull of Doud, but his strength was laced with agony.

His eyesight was fogged with blood, then with the tearing agony of his eyeballs collapsing into themselves. Distantly, Jona felt his bones break, felt tearings and pullings deep within him and surges of fluids—burning, sweet, sour—come up his throat, into his mouth, and into the vacuum of Doud.

Then all of him—all of him that was wet—did...totally—and he was dead.

~

The brush was dry, so he wet it—again.

Doud never though of changing mediums for his work. Never thought about changing to, say, oils or watercolors. He knew them, had touched them here or there. But always he'd come back to the pure wet.

You have to pay your way. Long life for a long life, he thought as he started. Always the bold, straight streaks: vertical, horizontal, diagonal. The same start. Soon the canvas was a blur of dark and light reds, maybe a form there, maybe not. A foggy world seen by the light of a dying fire.

Scratch...the brush was dry. Calmly he dipped it and fell back into the painting.

Maybe a man. Doud's strokes became bolder, firmer, as he tried to reach into that *maybe*, the potential of the work, and pull it into firmer details. A fuzzy blotch slowly started to become a head. A soft smudge started to become shoulders. Chest. Waist. Legs.

Dry again. Again he dipped the brush into the red well of his mouth and got back to painting.

A face. Maybe someone he remembered. *I promised you a long life, Jona. I promised that you'd be around a long time.*

The brush was dry...

Contributors

Patrick Califia is an avid fan of all things related to sex, biting, death, and blood. His latest book is *Mortal Companion*, a pansexual and deeply kinky vampire romance. When he is not chewing on his slave boy, he is busy searching for new books by Whitley Strieber, Laurell K. Hamilton, Jody Scott, and even Anne Rice. Toothsome messages can be sent to him at patrickcalifia@aol.com.

Paul Crumrine, who teaches composition, mythology, humanities, and literature, loves books, bicycling, and cats. He has traveled in Haiti and researched the mysteries of the "magic island." Weird Tales has purchased his vampire poetry, and Paul, writing as "David Holly," has had stories printed in *Hot Shots*, *Manscape*, *Guys*, and *Travelers' Tales*.

Wes Ferguson has worked as a producer and content editor for AOL and other entertainment sites. He is the author of a popular blog, and his editorials have been featured on several Web 'zines, including OutUK.com.

Jeff Mann's work has appeared in many publications, including *Rebel Yell*, *Rebel Yell 2*, and *Best Gay Erotica 2003* and *2004*. He has published a collection of poetry, *Bones Washed With Wine*; a book of essays, *Edge*; and a vampire novella, "Devoured," in the anthology *Masters of Midnight*.

Max Pierce's writings are influenced by a passion for films and history. His journalism is featured in national magazines, regional newspapers, and online for *The Advocate*. His short stories range from memoir (*Walking Higher*) to erotica, and he has authored two (as yet) unpublished novels. He lives in Los Angeles.

Jordan Castillo Price graced Chicago's mean streets for 15 years before transplanting to rural Wisconsin. A professional artist, Jordan still scrapes together time to write fiction.

Alexander Renault's literary erotica has been published online at Mind Caviar, Ophelia's Muse, Velvet Mafia, and Scarlet Letters. Two of his books can be found at www.renebooks.com, home of Renaissance eBooks: a nonfiction collection of essays, *Queerer Than You Think: Post-Millennial Bodies, Sex, & Porn,* and *Soul Kiss: Confessions of a Homoerotic Vampire*. Renault is the editor for the nonfiction anthology *Walking Higher: Gay Men Write About the Deaths of Their Mothers*, published by Xlibris in 2004. He invites you to visit him at AlexanderRenault.com.

Max Reynolds is the pseudonym of an award-winning queer journalist. His erotica has appeared in several anthologies, including *View to a Thrill, Fratsex, Anything for a Dollar,* and others. Reynolds lives and works on the East Coast as a writer and college professor. His erotic vampire novel *Touches of Evil*, featuring the character of Garcia, is forthcoming.

Daniel Ritter, who lives in the Midwest with an old guitar and a couple of parrots, has written everything from reference work to poetry. His erotica has appeared in various places both online and in print, including *Lovers Who Stay With You* and *Best Gay Love Stories*.

Thomas S. Roche is the editor of the late, great *Noirotica* series of erotic crime-noir anthologies as well as the newly born online version of the series, Noirotica.com. His short fiction has appeared in the *Best American Erotica* series, *Best Gay Erotica* series, *Mammoth Book of New Erotica* series, *Best New Erotica* series, and *Electric: Best Lesbian Erotic Fiction*, in addition to many other anthologies. You can visit his personal Web site at wwwskidroche.org.

Alyn Rosselini is editor in chief and founder of the Web site www.thermoerotic.com, quality stories for the erotica aficionado. Her work has appeared in in various publications. When not writing erotica, she is out exploring the world and trying new things. Sexuality should be embraced, not feared!

Jason Rubis lives in Washington, D.C. His erotic fiction has appeared in the magazines *Leg Show* and *Variations,* plus many anthologies, including *Sacred Exchange*, *Guilty Pleasures*, *Swing!*, *Love Under Foot*, *Blood Surrender* and *Leather, Lace And Lust*. That red stuff he's drinking is tomato juice.

David Salcido is the reigning Chaos Coordinator for the adult e-zine, Blue Food (www.bluefood.cc). His fiction credits include the periodicals *Redsine Ten*, *Yellow Silk*, *Space and Time*, *The Journal of Sister Moon* as well as Suspect Thoughts.com. Living as he does in Phoenix, he is intimately acquainted with the painful torments of hell.

Lukas Scott puts the *man* into *Roman* with his latest queerotica novel *Legion Of Lust*, making *Gladiator* look like *Mary Poppins*. His first novel, *Hot On The Trail*, put the Wild back into the Wild Wild West. You can open his portal at www.ianlucas.org.uk, where he'd love you to probe him further.

Matt Stedmann's erotic fiction appears in the anthologies *Men for All Seasons, Men in Jocks, Out of Control,* and the Lambda Literary Award–nominated *Quickies 3*. His erotica nonfiction appears in the anthologies *Best of Both Worlds* and *ReCreations*, the latter of which was also nominated for the Lambda Literary Award. He is a vegetarian.

Thom Wolf has been writing erotic fiction for more than a decade. He is author of the novels *Words Made Flesh* and *The Chain*. His stories have appeared in numerous Alyson Books anthologies, including the *Friction* series, *Just the Sex, Bearotica,* and *Twink*. He recently collaborated with Kevin Killian on "Too Far" for *Frozen Tear II*, a project cofunded by the Arts Council England. Thom lives with his boyfriend, Liam, in County Durham, England.

Bob Vickery (www.bobvickery.com) is a regular contributor to various Web sites and magazines, particularly *Men, Freshmen,* and *Inches*. He has five collections of stories published: *Skin Deep, Cock Tales, Cocksure, Play Buddies,* and most recently, *Manjack,* an audiobook of some of his hottest stories (QuarterMoon Press). Bob lives in San Francisco and can most often be found in his neighborhood Haight-Ashbury café pounding out smut on his laptop.

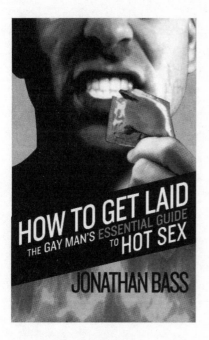